WAYNE STINNETT

FALLEN KING

A JESSE MCDERMITT NOVEL

Caribbean Adventure Series

Volume 6

DOWN ISLAND PRESS, LLC

2015

Published by DOWN ISLAND PRESS, 2015
Travelers Rest, SC

Library of Congress cataloging-in-publication Data
Stinnett, Wayne
Fallen King/Wayne Stinnett
p. cm. - (A Jesse McDermitt novel)
ISBN-13: 978-0692380239 (Down Island Press)
ISBN-10: 069238023X

Graphics by Tim Ebaugh Photography and Design
Edited by Clio Editing Services
Proofreading by Donna Rich
Interior Design by Write.Dream.Repeat. Book Design

FOREWORD

I'd like to take a moment to thank the many people who have helped me to write my sixth novel. As always, my wife Greta, is by far my biggest fan. She helped nurse me through medical problems while writing this book and I gave her complete control of my diet. I lost twenty pounds and feel like a young man again. Guys, listen to your wives.

My youngest daughter, Jordy, became a teenager about the time I started writing this. God help us. She's always the source of a lot of laughs while I'm writing. I wouldn't trade the interruptions for the world.

I drew on my relationship with my older daughter, Laura, in writing parts of this book. She's a strong-willed, independent woman, who is a fantastic mommy to three of my grandkids. My wife's two older kids are always encouraging and advising me, as well. Thank you all.

Tim Ebaugh, of Tim Ebaugh Photography and Design created yet another great cover, the photo was shot on Cape Sable, during a beautiful Florida sunset. A good bit of Fallen King takes place there and I'd love to one day return and show my wife and kids the wild Florida. It's still pretty much untouched there. You can see more of Tim's work at www.timebaughdesigns.com.

Lastly, where would a writer be without a great editorial and proofreading team? The story's mine, but it's Eliza Dee and Clio Editing Services who make it make sense.

After that, Donna Rich has final eyes on all of my books, before they get to you.

Thanks go also to my beta readers, Michael Reisig, Chuck Hofbauer, Marc Lowe, Mike Ramsey, Thomas Crisp, Sergeant Major, USMC (Retired), Alan Fader, Technical Sergeant, USAF (Retired), Debbie Kocol, and Timothy Artus. Your help in cleaning up the story was invaluable.

Much thanks to Tripp Wacker of Ryan Aviation Seaplanes Inc. in Palm Coast, FL, for his knowledgeable assistance with the deHavilland Beaver DHC-2 amphibian.

In the tropics and sub-tropics, when conditions are just right, right as the last of the sun disappears into the ocean, you can sometimes see a green flash. It's been captured a few times on camera. I've only seen it twice myself and made a point out of watching the sunset just about every day, when I lived on the boat.

AUTHOR'S NOTE

Most of the locations herein are fictional, or used fictitiously. However, I took great pains to depict the location and description of the many islands, locales, beaches, reefs, bars, and restaurants in the Keys, and the Caribbean, to the best of my ability. The *Rusty Anchor* is not a real place, but if I were to open a bar in the Florida Keys, it would probably be a lot like depicted here. I've tried my best to convey the island attitude in this work.

Some of this book takes place on the southwest coast of Florida, a wild and desolate frontier. Only accessible by boat for many miles, this area from the tiny town of Flamingo, at the southern tip of the mainland, all the way around to Marco Island, eighty some miles to the north, looks very much like it did a hundred or even a thousand years ago. Cape Sable and the Ten Thousand Islands are in this area on the edge of the great river of grass, the Everglades. I've visited the Cape a number of times and consider it one of the greatest of all of Florida's treasures.

If you'd like to receive my monthly newsletter for specials, book recommendations, and updates on coming books, please sign up on my website:

www.waynestinnett.com

Jesse McDermitt Series

Fallen Out
Fallen Palm
Fallen Hunter
Fallen Pride
Fallen Mangrove
Fallen King
Fallen Honor
Fallen Tide (November, 2015)

Charity Styles Series

Merciless Charity
Ruthless Charity (Winter, 2016)
Heartless Charity (Fall, 2016)

DEDICATION

I'd like to dedicate this book to the many wonderful writers I've met in the Writers' Café forum on KBoards. Joe, Hugh, HM, Rosalind, and dozens of others helped me out with patient answers to newbie questions. Without a doubt, this online group of writers has had more to do with my success than my writing alone. Many of them, I now call my friend.

Thanks, guys.

Mostly, to Michael Reisig, author of the Road to Key West series and the Caribbean Gold series. Michael was the first author that I know of who read one of my books. He helped me polish my writing style and gave me a lot of very valuable tips. Through reading one another's books and emailing, we discovered a lot of similar events and characters in our writing. Having both lived in the Keys about the same time, we likely bumped elbows in a bar, a time or two.

I consider the man my friend and mentor.

"As a child of North Florida, even the whisper of its name would send my imagination reeling. Conjuring fanciful lands of verdant forests teeming with orchids, aviaries, predatory cats, and prehistoric reptiles, the Everglades seemed more like a dreamscape than an actual place in my home state."

\- **Mac Stone**: Photographer
Everglades: America's Wetland

FALLEN KING

MAPS

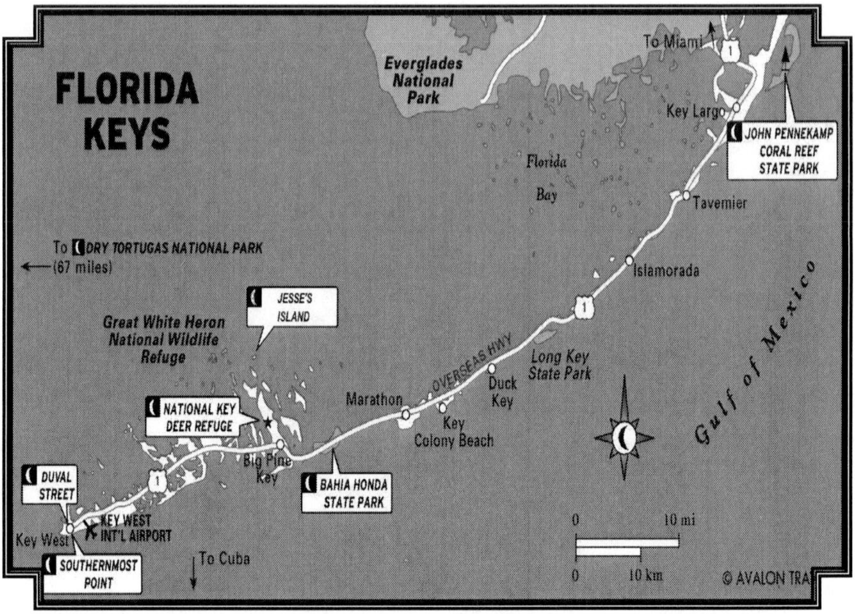

The Florida Keys

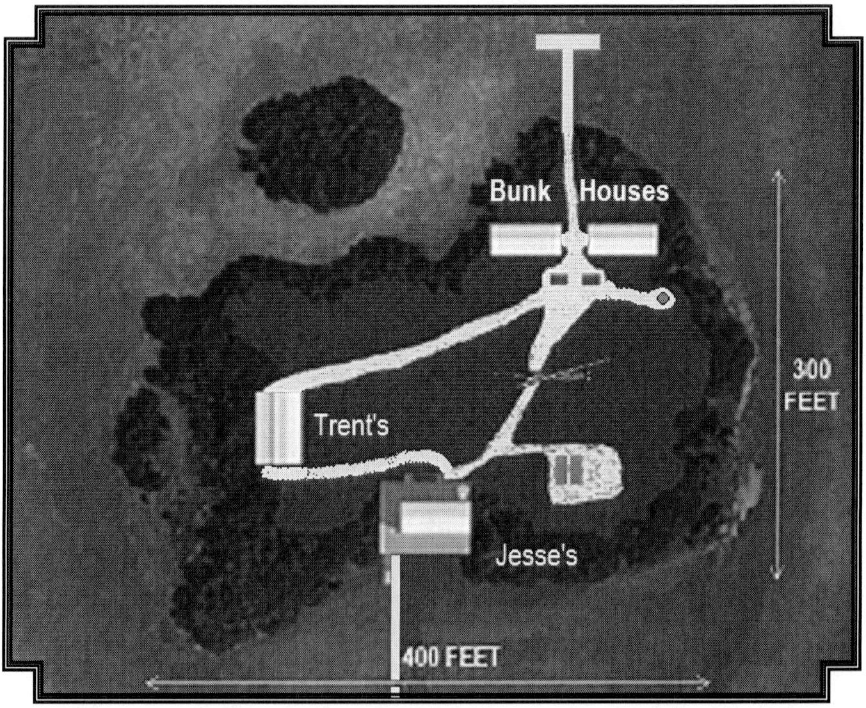

Jesse's Island

CHAPTER ONE

I woke to the gentle sound of a soft rain falling on my tin roof. It's not all that unusual for winter in the Florida Keys, though it is considered the dry season. We really only have three seasons here. Dry from September to June and wet the rest of the time. Somewhere in there, there's supposed to be a tourist season, but since they're here more or less all year round, I've never been real clear on just when that is.

Sometimes a storm will come up in late afternoon during the dry months. Something about a warm air mass colliding with cold air. I try not to watch the TV weather guy unless there's a hurricane. Where I live, you can see a storm coming from a long way off and watch it as it either bears down on you or passes you by. Unless you're out on the blue, it doesn't matter much. The storm will pour down big fat raindrops for thirty minutes, then the sun will come back out and transform it into humidity.

This wasn't that kind of rain, though. It was a light, quiet rain, gently drumming a laid-back rhythm on the tin roof of my little stilt house. I'd caught the NOAA radio broadcast yesterday and knew this was a cold front that had been slowly pushing its way south. The National Oceanic and Atmospheric Administration runs continuous weather updates all along the coast. The front was rolling down the whole Florida peninsula to the long island chain at the southern tip simply called the Keys. This kind of front might take hours, or even days, to slowly pass on through or dissipate.

I live in the Content Keys, a few miles north of Big Pine. I'd built my little stilt house several years ago, mostly out of scrap wood I'd salvaged in several of Miami's smaller, but very busy, shipyards. I have a few friends up there and they used to let me know whenever there was enough of the good stuff that needed to be carted away. Cargo out of South America is usually loaded on pallets made of what to them are local hardwoods. While some of the varieties of wood they use are considered exotic here in the States, they're plentiful south of the equator, which is why they're used for pallets.

The floorboards and beams are made from lignum vitae, or *palo santo*, as it's called around the Caribbean basin where it grows. It's one of the densest woods on the planet. A board cut from this tree will sink in water, even saltwater. The bigger beams were cut from a huge lignum vitae that was blown down in a friend's yard in Islamorada. I had to hire a crane and two tractor trailer rigs to haul it up to a mill in Homestead, then two more to return with the finished beams—it was that heavy. The siding is mahogany, another dense hardwood. Both woods are virtually impervious to the ravages of weather and insects. Really rough on saw blades and drill bits, too. I must have gone through dozens of each in building my home.

Rising from the big king-sized bed in my tiny bedroom, I put on a pair of khaki cargo pants and a faded *Gaspar's Revenge Charter Services* tee shirt and padded barefoot to the head to relieve the pressure in my bladder before going into the combination living room, dining room, and galley.

Gaspar's Revenge is my charter boat. It's actually the second one to carry the name. The first one was six years older, a nearly identical forty-five-foot Rampage convertible. It was destroyed in an explosion a few months ago that was meant to kill me.

After several days of online searching, I found the new one in Galveston, Texas. Aside from its dark blue hull, it's alike in nearly every way. Like the first, it had twin 1015-horsepower engines, but the previous owner of this one had added superchargers, which bumped the power and top speed up just a bit. She could do fifty knots, wide open, in calm seas.

My house is small, only fifty feet by twenty feet, with the bedroom and head taking up the eastern third of it. The front room has a small, little used dining table and chairs in front of a smaller window in the northwest corner. The galley is in the southwest corner, with another small window over the sink. Between them is the hatch going outside to the wraparound deck. Small, simple, and functional.

The rest of the main room is sparsely furnished. A pair of recliners sit against the south bulkhead with a table and lamp between them, in front of a large window that provides a great view of the flats to the south. A small workbench takes up the opposite bulkhead, with another large window above it looking out over the interior of the island. A small fly-tying bench and an old potbellied wood stove fill the bulkhead space between the bedroom hatch and the one to the head. Various parts of outboard motors, storage boxes and other fishing, diving, and boating detritus fill much of the empty space in the room.

As I entered the galley, the aroma from the coffeemaker I'd programmed last night, drew me. It had finished doing its magic and I poured myself a cup of Costa Rican brew. A longtime friend of mine in Marathon by the name of Rusty Thurman found this Costa Rican coffee farm called La Minita and we'd both become hooked on the smell and flavor of their coffee.

Looking through the south window, it was just beginning to turn gray with what little light was able to pierce the low clouds. Light rain was falling on the water out over the flats. *Just another day in paradise*, I thought and stepped through the hatch and out into the rain. It was cool, but not cold. If the front pushed on through, the drier air behind it would be cold, maybe into the low fifties. While people in Montana might think that ridiculous, down here, where even the Walmart doesn't stock jackets, that's cold weather.

I walked over to the north side of the deck by the raised two-thousand-gallon rain cistern that provided our drinking water and looked out over my little island community as the shoulders of my tee shirt slowly dampened from the mist. Rain's never been a problem for me.

I'd learned as a kid growing up in Fort Myers that the human body is pretty much waterproof and you could always dry off in the sun. Later, as a young Marine Lance Corporal, I had a Platoon Sergeant who drilled into us the phrase, "If it ain't rainin', you ain't trainin." He later became a close friend, but was killed a little over a year ago. His killer met justice in a very hard way.

My island is also really small. At high tide, it covers slightly more than two acres. I bought it seven years ago, right after I was retired from the Marine Corps after twenty years of service. At the time, it was a scrub-and-mangrove-covered thicket on a long-dead coral reef and limestone outcropping covered with sand. It took me the better part of two years to clear it by hand and build my little house on stilts. Since then, I'd added two small bunkhouses on the north end of the island to comply with the County zoning requirement that the island be maintained as a fish camp. Then I helped a friend build a tiny home for him, his wife, and their two small kids on the west side. All four structures combined were about the size of an average home up on the mainland.

"Morning, Carl," I called down to my friend and the island's caretaker, who was tending to some winter vegetables in our aquaculture garden. I'd had a crazy idea when I bought the island of growing my own food, but the soil proved to be too sandy and salty. When I met Carl and Charlie Trent, he was up to his neck in smug druglers down in Key Weird, where he ran a shrimp trawler. I helped him out of a bad situation by hiding him and his family here and taking on the drug kingpin with the help of a friend who works for the federal government.

Carl liked it here so much, he put his trawler up for sale and came to work for me.

That's when he told me about growing vegetables in raised beds, supplying them with nutrient-rich water from a fish tank. Or in our case, a crayfish tank. I like Cajun food, so we built it and it worked. We now have two large raised beds and two tanks. The original crayfish tank has supplied several local restaurants with the Cajun delicacy, and a new fish tank would have freshwater catfish ready to harvest in another few weeks.

Carl looked up as I started down the steps to the clearing. "Hey, Jesse. I thought I heard you stirring around up there. I was just checking the nutrient level in the water. You ready to get to work?"

I nodded and together we walked across the clearing to a shed we'd built just a couple of months ago next to the battery shack. The island isn't powered from the mainland. We use a series of wind generators and solar panels with a generator backup to charge a bank of thirty deep-cycle marine batteries. These provide the power for the pumps on the aquaculture system and what little other electricity we use.

"This weather hasn't been very good for curing," he said as we walked into the shed. "But, everything's ready. I checked it out before checking the garden. We can turn her over today."

A small amount of light filtered through the clear acrylic roof panels. It reflected off the newly-finished wood hull before us, which shone with a deep chocolate hue, as if it were wet. Last fall, Carl and I had gotten drunk and talked about designing and building a boat, something we'd both always dreamed of doing. We worked on the plans together, deciding on an antique-looking twenty-four footer.

My grandfather was an architect and I must have picked up his genes, or my subconscious retained enough of what he tried to teach me. My parents died when I was a kid and I was raised by Mam and Pap. They were my dad's parents.

Carl and I soon had a really sharp-looking runabout on paper, complete with cross sections and rib details. Over the last few months, the design in the drawings slowly materialized in front of us in its physical form.

Yesterday we'd hung wide rollers to the ceiling beams in six places, with strap loops threaded through them to create three slings, which we hung up out of the way. Today, we planned to lift the boat hull enough to get the slings under it, then remove the saw horses that it sat on and flip it upright.

A sweaty, grunt-filled hour later, we had the hull swinging free in the slings and slowly pulled on one side, rotating the hull until it was upright. Then we heaved again to remove the slings and lower the hull onto new form-fitted supports. She was actually starting to look like a boat now. She had long, narrow lines, with two rows of seating that were further forward than more modern designs. The forward-sloping transom was gently rounded, with gunwales flaring inboard just aft of the rear seats and a long rear deck covering the engine compartment. Of course, none of that was there yet, but I could see it in my mind's eye.

"She's gonna be a beaut," Carl said once we had her nestled in the four cradles. "What we gonna use for power again?"

We'd hashed over this question for weeks and never could agree. I thought it ought to have a small Perkins diesel, with a three-to-one transmission. Carl thought it should be a big, throaty gas-powered V-8 and a direct-drive transmission. We'd been over it so many times we both knew we'd never agree. Before we could rehash the same argument, Doc walked into the shed.

"Hey, Doc," I said. "Didn't even hear you come up. How you been?"

Doc used to be First Mate for my charter diving and fishing business. He'd served in the Navy as a Corpsman attached to First Battalion, Ninth Marines, not long after I retired. His real name is Bob Talbot, but in the Corps all Corpsmen are called Doc. Before working for me, he was Carl's First Mate on his shrimp trawler, *Miss Charlie*, named after Carl's wife. Doc's a tall, lanky, easygoing guy with sandy-colored hair nearly to his shoulders and sharp green eyes. He had the typical deep tan of people who make their living from the sea, except around his eyes, where he nearly always wore wraparound shades.

Working for me got dangerous at times and when he'd learned a few months ago that his wife Nikki was pregnant, he'd approached Carl about hanging on to his old trawler and letting him skipper it. Carl not only made him the Captain, he helped Doc upgrade his license from Mate to Captain. Doc's wife is the cook on board and de facto First Mate.

"Came in early this week," Doc said. "Maxed out the hold in four days." Carl grinned as Doc handed him a wad of hundred-dollar bills. "Got a good price for 'em, too."

"How's Nikki?" Carl asked, stuffing the roll, uncounted, into the pocket of his trousers. That's how business is done here.

"Really starting to show now. She said to say hi," he replied as he walked along the side of the hull, gently caressing the gunwale. "This looks really nice. What are you gonna use for power?"

"Haven't decided yet," I said, rolling my eyes. "Carl wants a big block Chevy engine and I say we should go with diesel."

"Mind if I make a suggestion?" We both nodded. "How about twin engines?"

I looked at Carl and we both scoffed at the idea. "It's barely beamy enough for a single big block or diesel," Carl replied.

"Yeah," Doc said running a hand along the gunwale again, "but it's plenty wide enough for a couple of Harley engines."

"Motorcycle engines?" I asked. Doc rode an Indian Chief and was always going on about how powerful the engine was.

"Think about it," he went on. "My bike's got an eighty-eight-cubic-inch air-cooled engine. It produces seventy-five horses and only weighs a hundred and fifty pounds. A company called S&S builds a one-hundred-and-twenty-four-cube engine that'll give you a hundred and sixty horses."

"Yeah, but all those chains and sprockets," Carl said. "Plus those motors can't be cheap."

"Belt drive," Doc said. "Connected to a pair of two-to-one marine transmissions. Just think, no water intake strainer to clog, no rusty manifold coolers and over three hundred horses, with a throaty rumble at half the weight."

"That much power on a motorcycle?" I asked. "I had no idea. You just might be on to something. We could put an air intake right behind the rear seats with an electric fan below it to suck in cool air."

Carl and I both looked down into the empty engine bay, visualizing it in our minds. It was definitely feasible. Motorcycle engines were plenty narrow enough and we had yet to cut the through-hulls for the prop shaft. An air-cooled engine would eliminate a lot of the problems usually associated with inboards.

"Did you guys hear about the dynamite fishing going on up in Florida Bay?" Doc asked, peering down into the engine bay. Carl and I both looked up at him.

"Y'all need to get off this rock on occasion," Doc said, standing up straight. "There've been reports of people using explosives to kill fish all up and down the Gulf side. When the Coast Guard or Marine Patrol gets there, the people are long gone and there's dozens of tropical fish and inedible fish floating dead on the surface above big blast holes in the bottom. The last incident wasn't far from here, on Bullard Bank."

"Bullard Bank?" Carl asked. "That's Charlie's favorite grouper spot. She's gonna be pissed."

"Doesn't Vince O'Hare run a trap line there?" I asked.

"Yeah," Doc replied. "He's fuming. What I heard, he took four of his nearly destroyed traps to the Fish and Wildlife office, half full of dead and rotting lobster. Just dumped all four of 'em in the station's lobby and demanded that they do something."

"There's a guy I wouldn't want pissed at me," Carl said.

O'Hare is a rough and ready lobsterman whose roots in the Keys go back to the days of the early wreckers. A big and sometimes mean guy who keeps pretty much to himself. He owns an acre on Grassy Key with a deep-water dock on the Gulf side. He lives in a little tin shack with his lobster boat at the dock and the yard littered with lobster traps, floats, old boats, and cars. Thought to be in his early eighties, though you'd never know it by his demeanor. He lives alone and as far as I knew nobody ever visited his shack.

In this case, I'd go along with whatever he did. Sure, using explosives is a fast and easy way to catch food fish. Using it to pull teeth has the same effect. It gets the job done, but with a lot of unnecessary collateral damage. Explosives kill everything in the water, including the reef.

Most people think of a reef as a pile of rocks, but it's really a colony of tiny animals that filter the water for microscopic food. I'd seen firsthand the results of blasting one. Fallen, crushed, and broken piles of white calcium skeleton that took centuries to grow. It also ruptures the swim bladders of fish, causing them to float to the surface. Not just grouper and snapper, but thousands of brightly colored tropical fish, as well. Even invertebrates like shrimp, crab and lobster are killed by the shock of the underwater blast.

"Does Fish and Wildlife have any leads?" I asked.

"Nothing I heard about," Doc replied. "I gotta get going, promised Nikki we'd go shopping for some baby stuff. I just wanted to drop by and let y'all know that the survey crew on Elbow Cay finished up their work. They should be cutting us a check any day now."

Last fall, Doc and Nikki came across a clue to a lost Spanish treasure while cleaning out her parents' attic. Rusty is a licensed salvor, so a bunch of us headed over to the northern Bahamas after solving the riddle. It took three days, but we located it, along with the skeletal remains of the survivors. What we located turned out to be only a portion of the whole treasure, though. Just what the survivors of the 1566 Spanish wreck were able to recover and bury. We were due a ten percent cut of the value and had been waiting for months for the final tally.

"They give you any idea how much it's going to be?" Carl asked.

"The total worth of the find has been calculated at sixty-four million dollars," Doc replied with a crooked grin. "Between the twelve of us, we'll each get about half a million."

"Twelve of you?" Carl asked. "I thought it was just nine of you that went over there." Then grinning at me, he added, "And ten of ya came back."

He was referring to an undercover Florida Department of Law Enforcement Officer by the name of Linda Rosales. She'd been coming down here on the weekends lately and the two of us would sometimes run or swim. A few times we'd gone fishing, taking my daughter along as chaperone.

"Twelve of us," Doc replied, grinning again. "Nikki and I agreed that Linda should get an equal cut. Then Charlie and Chyrel were just as big a part of finding it as any of us that went over there and they get an equal cut, too."

"You're kidding," Carl said in disbelief.

"No, he's not," I said. "If it hadn't been for Charlie's riddle-solving ability, we'd still be twiddling our thumbs."

"Well," he said, looking down into the engine bay with a wry grin, "if she'll let me, motorcycle engines it is, then."

"Agreed," I said, reaching my hand across the narrow stern to take his. When we shook, I winked and said, "But, Charlie doesn't have to know."

I walked with Doc back to the main house. The sky was a slightly paler gray and off to the north, I could just make out a blue horizon. *Damn*, I thought. *The front's gonna push through and it'll be a cold night.*

"What were you not telling us, Doc?" I asked as we climbed the steps to the deck.

"They're not using dynamite," he replied. "Nikki said I shouldn't even tell you."

"Why? What are they using?"

Doc seemed to think it over, as we walked down the back steps to the pier next to my channel where he'd tied his skiff. "She's worried you'll try to do something about it. Says it's probably teenagers and you could get into trouble with the law. You do have a tendency to piss badges off."

"What are these teenagers using, Doc?"

"What I heard on the coconut telegraph was that they're using grenades."

The coconut telegraph is usually faster and more accurate than the local news. Living on a small chain of islands, anything worth knowing is told by one person to another very quickly.

"Sure. A bunch of kids using frags to kill fish? How do you suppose these kids got their hands on grenades, anyway?"

"See?" he said, untying his skiff and stepping aboard as he pushed it away from the dock. He hit the starter and the big Yamaha outboard sprang to life, burbling quietly with a steady stream from the piss hole. "She was right. You always get too involved in shit that ain't your business."

"Who said I was getting involved?" I shouted as he turned the skiff smartly inside the narrow channel.

"There's been twenty incidents in the last month," he shouted back. "They use chum and several grenades at each spot."

Damn, I thought, *that's a whole lot of grenades.*

I was almost to the top of the steps when the rain stopped and I heard the faint sound of not just Doc's outboard heading south, but another one heading north. Turning on the top step, I could see a familiar twenty-foot Grady-White headed this way. Charlie and Kim were coming back from dropping Carl and Charlie's kids off at school and shopping. My dog, Pescador, was standing in the bow, his shaggy head in the wind.

Kim's been staying with me since September and we've been getting to know one another. Her mother left me seventeen years ago, just before Christmas. Hard to blame her. She was two months pregnant with my older daughter, Eve, when we got married in May of '83. Two weeks later, I reenlisted and two weeks after that, I was deployed for six months to Beirut, Lebanon. Her due date and our date of rotation were only a week apart. Then terrorists blew up our barracks and we rotated out early. I was in a funk for weeks after getting back home. But I was there when Eve was born.

Three and a half years later, I reenlisted for my third tour and was promptly deployed again. This time on a four-month West Pacific float, leaving when Sandy was six months pregnant with Kim. I missed the birth of our second child. Four months after returning from the cruise and without being able to even make a phone call to tell her the Corps was deploying us again, I was in Panama. Sandy packed the kids up and left the next day, right after the CO's wife told her.

Kim was only five months old then. Over the years, Sandy told the girls I was a bad man and finally told them I was dead. My older daughter believed the lies. Kim somehow didn't accept any of it. I'd sent a check every Christmas and on birthdays, but my ex intercepted them and the checks were never cashed. That is, until last July, when Kim picked up the mail one day and found the card and check inside.

She confronted her mother, who insisted she'd told the girls I was dead for their own good. By then, my ex had become an extreme liberal and hated all things military. Kim had skipped her freshman year and had just graduated from high school a year early. She told her mom she wasn't going to go to college right away, so she could be with her own age group when she did. After saving up her money for six more weeks, she found the website for my charter business and came down here to find out for herself if what my ex had said was true.

What she'd told them was only partially true. I can be a very dangerous man. To the enemies of the country I love and its people, or to anyone that threatens a friend. I was chosen early in my career in the Corps to be a Scout/Sniper. When I ended my career, I'd been a Sniper Instructor for over a year, teaching other young Warriors how to be dangerous.

I walked back down to the pier and caught the line Kim deftly tossed as they idled up. She'd really taken to life on the water and was filling in as First Mate whenever I took charters out until I could find a permanent one. She was good with people and the men didn't seem to mind at all having a pretty teenage girl help them land their catches. I made it real clear she was my daughter and my view of the cockpit from the helm was all encompassing. Not that I had to worry, most of our clients were gentlemen. One guy got a little too drunk once and touched her inappropriately. Before I was halfway down the ladder, she had the guy face down on the deck, the offending hand chicken-winged behind his back, while he howled in pain. She'd calmly asked him if there were other activities he liked using the hand for. The man sobered quickly and apologized profusely. Instantly, she released him and resumed her First Mate duties as if nothing had happened. Even wiped the guy's brow with a wet towel an hour later when he'd hooked a really big bull dolphin and was fighting it. He left her a very generous tip.

"Hi, Dad," she said, stepping onto the dock and hugging me. "Was that Doc leaving?"

"Yeah," I replied. "He and Nikki got in early, so he stopped by to give the owner's take of the trawl to Carl."

Kim and Charlie were dressed nearly identically. Lightweight khaki fishing pants and long-sleeved work shirts, the standard garb of watermen all over the Keys. They managed to stay dry behind the Grady's wraparound clear plastic screen, which surrounds the Bimini top and can be rolled all the way down to the deck, just for days like this.

As Charlie handed me the boxes of groceries and I stacked them on the deck, Pescador jumped from the cockpit, shook the water from his coat and sat next to me, waiting for an ear scratch. Since school started, he rode with Charlie and the kids every day to where they caught the bus at Old Wooden Bridge Marina and again to pick them up in the afternoon.

"He also brought news from Elbow Cay," I said to Charlie. "He told Carl that you and Chyrel would receive an equal cut for all your help in solving the riddle."

"I hope Carl told him no," Charlie said, taking my hand as she stepped up to the pier. Charlie's short for Charlotte. Just a wisp of a woman, but big in heart and attitude, like most Conch women.

"Doc wouldn't take no for an answer," I said as the three of us picked up boxes and headed up the steps to the deck.

Charlie's brow furrowed, deep in thought. A quiet woman most of the time, she measured her words carefully. Finally she said, "I don't like it."

"Then put it in the bank," I said. "That way, when Carl Junior and Patty get older, you won't have to worry about college."

After helping put away the weeks' worth of groceries in the large pantry in the Trents' little house, I went up to the deck to make a phone call. Cell service on the island is sketchy at best. The only place where you can get any reception at all is on the southwest corner of the deck, and even there you have to hold your tongue in your cheek just right.

Linda answered on the second ring. "Hi, Jesse. I was going to call you later today. Are we still on for this weekend?"

"Yeah, I was thinking we might do something a little different, though."

"What did you have in mind?" she asked huskily.

"How about we catch some grunts out on Bullard Bank and do some snorkeling?" She didn't say anything for a moment and I thought I'd lost my signal. "Are you still there?"

"Yeah, I'm here. Who have you been talking to?" she asked, all business now.

"Talking to?"

"Come on, Jesse. You're not a very good liar."

"Are you part of the investigation?" I asked.

"Your position with Homeland Security notwithstanding, I really can't talk about it," she said. A friend of mine, Deuce Livingston, heads a counterterrorism team for DHS, based out of Homestead, and I sometimes provide transportation for his operatives.

"You're saying Bullard is off limits?"

"No," she replied. "I don't know how you heard, but I'm assuming you've learned about the illegal fishing practices."

"That's Fish and Wildlife. How's FDLE involved?"

"I said I can't talk about it," she replied.

I thought for a moment, then said, "It's no longer just about taking fish, is it?"

"You didn't hear that from me," she said. "In fact, I think I better hang up now."

"Wait," I said. "I didn't mean to piss you off. I really would like to see you this weekend."

"No talk about the investigation?"

"If that's what you want," I said. "Maybe we can get a few people together and fly up to Cape Sable for a campout and backcountry fly fishing."

"Yeah," she said, her voice taking on its usual cheery tone. "That sounds like it'd be a lot of fun. I really do have to go, though. See you tomorrow night?"

"Pick you up at the *Anchor*?"

"I'll be there by six," she said. "Bye now."

I said goodbye and ended the call.

CHAPTER TWO

Headed south in my skiff the next afternoon, I called Doc. He picked up almost instantly as I threaded my way through the narrow channel east of Big Pine Key. “You hear anything else about that thing we were talking about yesterday?” I asked.

“I knew you wouldn’t let it rest,” he replied, then sighed and added, “Yeah, a girl Nikki works with overheard a couple of local cops talking about it at Hog’s Breath last night. Seems a tourist couple were out in the backcountry two days ago in a rental and came across another boat near Monkey Bank after hearing an explosion. When they came alongside the boat, thinking they might be in trouble, three guys on board pulled guns and robbed them. Cut their fuel line and left them adrift among hundreds of dead fish.”

“So, that’s why Linda’s involved,” I said, thinking out loud.

“She’s investigating it?”

"She didn't come right out and say so," I replied. "I'm picking her up in an hour."

"Let me know if you hear anything," he said.

I told him I would and ended the call. Passing Porpoise Key, I turned east and skimmed the skinny water into Big Spanish Channel and the deeper water east of there and north of the Seven Mile Bridge.

The front had passed on through and left behind a cloudless cobalt-blue sky and cold temperatures. Being built over the water, my house rarely gets uncomfortable in summer or winter. Even if the temperature drops into the fifties like this morning, the water temperature rarely gets below seventy-two.

However, with no insulation, last night was still a cold night by Keys standards. So I'd tossed a few pieces of driftwood in the wood stove and lit it just before going to bed. The coals had still been hot this morning, allowing me to toss on another couple of pieces to take the early morning chill off.

Ten minutes after talking to Doc, I brought my skiff down off plane and idled up the channel to my friend's place, the *Rusty Anchor Bar and Grill*. I first met Rusty on a Greyhound Bus bound for Parris Island. We were in the same platoon in Boot Camp and were stationed together a few times over the next four years. He left the Corps when his wife went into labor early and died giving birth to his daughter, Julie. Raising a daughter alone hadn't been easy for him, but the two had managed. Julie married Deuce last summer and the two were living on their Whitby sailboat at Rusty's dock.

Tying up at the skiff dock I noticed that Deuce and Julie's ketch was gone. The *Rusty Anchor* is an out-of-the-way place, known pretty much only to locals, though it's nearly in the heart of Marathon, on Vaca Key. It's been here in one form or another for generations. Rusty's grandfather made illegal rum during prohibition. The rum shack is now Rufus's living quarters.

Rufus is Rusty's part-time Jamaican cook. Nobody seems to know exactly how old he is, but if I were to guess, he's probably in his seventies. If you made your guess based on his complexion, build or flexibility, you'd guess half that. Only when you look into his dark eyes do you see the wisdom of age. He eats mostly fruits and nuts, grazing pretty much all day long, his lean and muscular frame a testament to his simple diet. Early in the mornings, you sometimes see him standing in the shallows just beyond his shack, practicing some sort of meditation and stretching exercise, contorting his body in ways that would make a Thai hooker jealous.

I crossed the lawn and walked through the door into the dimly lit bar, letting my eyes adjust for a moment. There were already a number of locals sitting at the bar and scattered at the tables. Jimmy Saunders was behind the bar. He used to be my First Mate aboard the *Revenge*, before Doc. His girlfriend, Angie, was waiting tables. Angie is Carl's daughter from his first marriage. It's that kind of community, where everyone knows everyone and many are related.

"Hi, Jesse," Jimmy said. "Get you a beer? Linda's not here yet." Before I could answer, he set a dripping Red Stripe on a coaster at the far end of the bar.

Linda had been coming to visit almost every weekend since we met on Elbow Cay last September. She stays in the guest bunkhouse with Kim and the three of us spend time on the water, fishing, diving, and swimming. Every Sunday, before she has to go back up north, the two of us do a four-mile run down Sombrero Beach Road to the beach and back. We'd become close friends over the last few months, but until Kim left in the summer, I was reluctant to try to carry the relationship any further. Linda, not being the pushy type and in no hurry for a relationship herself, seemed to enjoy the easy way we fell into a friendship, but she still tossed out the occasional sexually-charged innuendo from time to time. The physical attraction was obvious and mutual, we were just in no hurry at all.

"Thanks, Jimmy," I said, taking my usual seat at the far end of the bar. Against the wall. Facing the door. "Yeah, she said she'd be here about eighteen hundred. Figured I'd drop in early and see if I could get caught up on what's going on around the islands."

"Not a whole lot going on, dude," he said as he turned away to wipe down the other end of the bar. Usually Jimmy was one of the best sources for local intel, so his comment surprised me. As I took my first long pull on the beer bottle, Rusty came through the door at the back of the bar.

"Hey, Jesse. Where's Kim?" he asked, looking around and lifting his considerable girth onto a stool behind the bar just across from me. At just five and a half feet tall and over three hundred pounds, he's had more than a few troublemakers make the mistake of assuming he was an easy target. His bald head and thick red beard, just now starting to show some gray, did offset his soft appearance a little, but not much.

"She and Charlie took the Trent kids fishing for the afternoon, over by Raccoon Key," I replied. Leaning forward I asked, "What's the latest you're hearing about the grenade fishing?"

"Grenade fishing?"

I glanced over at Jimmy, who was watching us and quickly turned and started polishing the glasses under the bar even though they were spotless. Looking back at Rusty, he averted his eyes and glanced out the open windows toward the docks.

"Yeah," I said, leaning into his line of vision. "Grenade fishing up in the backcountry."

He looked at me and sighed. "Just leave it to the cops, okay."

"He's not gonna, man," Jimmy said, shaking his head slowly, still looking down at the glass he was polishing.

"Look," Rusty began, "you got your kid to think of now, bro. Lord knows I been hoping the day'd come when you could get to know them. Stay out of it, okay?"

I looked him in the eye, seeing real concern there. Over the years, we'd become the best friends you could imagine. While we were young Marines, I used to hitch a ride in his old pickup to my home in Fort Myers, whenever the two of us would get leave or a four-day pass, what we called a ninety-six. Often, he'd stay over at my grandparents place, before the last leg home. When he left the Corps, I started splitting my liberty and leave time between home and the Keys, staying with him and Julie in the guest room of his little house behind the bar.

"Who said I was getting involved? I just want to be aware of what's going on around my house. Bullard Bank isn't too far from me."

"Okay," he said, leaning in conspiratorially. "Word is that some lowlifes with a Miami gang are down here. Just in the last few weeks, they've blown the hell out of more than twenty patch reefs to collect the dead fish. There's been two incidents of people being strong-armed by these punks and two divers injured who were on a reef nearby."

"A Miami gang?"

"Yeah, a bunch of bloodthirsty Haitians who call themselves Zoe Pound. Been around for a few years, now. They do a lot of importing up there, if you know what I mean. Why they're using grenades to fish, nobody seems to know. Maybe just blowing off steam between drug runs."

"Grenades aren't cheap," I said. "Nor plentiful."

"That's why I'm thinking they're just bored. Cost-benefit thing. Why waste grenades for a few bucks' worth of fish, when you're raking in millions dealing coke and meth?"

"The two injured divers? Locals?"

"No," Rusty replied, with a shake of his head. "A couple out of Indiana, down here to get away from the snow."

"Indiana?"

"Don't appear to be any connection, if that's what you're thinking."

"Just a bunch of teenagers blowing up reefs for fun, huh?"

"You didn't hear that from me," he said, looking over my shoulder as light spilled in from outside the front door.

I turned and saw Linda standing at the doorway, silhouetted by the bright sunlight behind her. The sun seemed to pick out the auburn streaks it had placed in her dark hair over the previous few months, making her look like a phoenix. When she saw us at the bar, she glided our way.

When we met, she was working undercover for a high-end escort service, belying her forty-something age. At five seven and a hundred and twenty-five pounds, you'd have to look very close to find a single flaw in her skin or build that would indicate she was almost my age. I'd looked a few times. Rusty placed a bottle of Dos Equis on a coaster next to my nearly empty Red Stripe as she sat down and leaned over to kiss me on the cheek.

"Thanks, Rusty," she said. "You two look like you both swallowed a canary."

"Just talking about flying up to Cape Sable," I said.

"Yeah," Rusty chimed in. He'd always been able to pick up what I was thinking and carry it. "Supposed to be some great sea trout fishing in Micmac Lagoon and big reds being taken right off the beach."

"I've never been up there," Linda said, smiling. "But I hear it's really beautiful in a prehistoric kind of way."

"Oh yeah," Rusty said, leaning on the bar with his elbows. "It's like going back in time, when you walk along the beach there." Turning to me, he said, "Maybe we can fly out over the Glades and check out Whitewater Bay."

I hadn't even invited the man yet. That's another thing he's good at doing.

"I'm really looking forward to it," Linda said. "When do we leave?"

"First light," I replied, giving Rusty a crooked grin and nodding toward my now empty beer bottle.

"Who else is going?" he asked as he placed another dripping bottle on my coaster.

"The three of us and Kim," I said. "It's just a twenty-minute flight. We can spend the day fishing and exploring, stay the night and fly back here on Sunday."

"Want me to strap the canoes to the floats?" Rusty asked.

"Yeah, that'd make getting around into the lagoon a lot easier."

We chatted a while longer, before the shadows on the wall told me we'd better head up to the island. Even though I knew the channels and reefs like the back of my hand, it's never a good idea running them at night if you don't have to.

We left the *Anchor* and circled the west end of the island. Between there and my island, there's only the house on Sister Rock, a couple of waterfront homes and businesses, and the Seven Mile Bridge to indicate that Marathon is a bustling town of almost ten thousand people. Nearly the whole of Vaca Key has been developed now. I remember coming down here as a kid when there were only a few hundred people on the island. Progress, as ugly as it is at times, can't be stopped. It can be slowed by making a place difficult to get to, like on my island, but anywhere a road goes down here, a bar or tee shirt shop is bound to open.

When Linda and I got to the island and docked the skiff under the house, the sun was already nearing the western horizon. Pescador met us at the dock, so I knew that Charlie and Kim were back from fishing with the kids and would have a seafood feast in the making.

"It's really cold," Linda said as we crossed the deck to the rear steps, the wind blowing from the north around us with nothing to impede it up on the deck, fifteen feet above the water.

"Did you bring warm clothes?" I asked as we descended the steps and started across the clearing. "Tomorrow is supposed to be the same as today."

"I don't suppose there's a hotel with heated rooms up there?"

With a chuckle, I replied, "No phones, no lights, no motor cars."

"Not a single luxury?"

"Like Robinson Crusoe, as primitive as can be."

She laughed, deep and hearty, then leaned into me, holding my arm. "I always loved that show as a kid."

"Yeah, me too. Don't worry, there's plenty of driftwood on the beach up there for a fire and we can pitch our tents around it."

"Tents?" she pouted, tossing out another of her sexually-charged innuendoes.

"Yeah, one for each of us." *But, one of these days*, I thought.

"Hey," Kim called out as we approached the two tables Carl had built in front of the bunkhouses. "You're just in time. We're grilling hogfish and flounder."

"Hogfish?" I asked.

"*Cortesía del señor Pescador*. He jumped in and caught two big ones."

Blackened hogfish is about my favorite seafood. They're extremely elusive for anglers, but plentiful enough around reefs and rock piles that they can be speared fairly easily.

"Charlie is marinating everything now," Kim said.

"Then let's go watch the sun set while we wait," I said.

Sitting on the dock to watch the sun go down is something that Pescador and I have been doing for over a year. I found him stranded on little more than a sandbar just after Hurricane Wilma over a year ago. Not really stranded, because he's a strong enough swimmer that he could easily make it to any nearby island and he was more than capable of fending for himself. Since Kim had come to live with me and with Linda now staying on the weekends, the dock was getting crowded around sunset.

"Give me just a sec," Linda said. "I want to drop my bag and grab a blanket."

"I'll go with you," Kim said. "I want one too."

A minute later, we were sitting on the floating dock off the north part of the island, watching the daily art show provided by Sol and Mother Ocean. It was the kind of evening perfect for a green flash and as I explained the phenomenon, we watched the sun sink lower and lower toward the horizon. I could see Carl and his family watching it from out on the sandbar on the west side of the island. All over the Keys, locals were setting aside their various chores and diversions to watch the sun go down. It's an island thing.

"Watch," I whispered reverently. "As clear as the sky is, it'll look like the sea just reaches up and grabs the sun."

Slowly, the big red orb dropped lower and lower, until the water seemed to just reach right up and snatch it, pulling and elongating it into an oval, pointed at the bottom where the water had it in its grasp. There wasn't a cloud anywhere in sight, just the water and the sun, dancing together as they have since time began.

Kim was sitting to my right, with Pescador just beyond her and Linda on my left. Without asking, Linda reached around my shoulder with her blanket. I pulled it down around me as she leaned against my shoulder. Slowly, the sun flattened out into a horizontal oval shape.

"What's that bright star up above the sun?"

"The light purple one?" I said, pointing about thirty degrees above and to the north of the sun. She nodded. "It's not a star, that's the planet Neptune. King of the Seven Seas."

Linda whispered. "Hey, where'd you learn all this?"

"Rusty taught me. He says the stars and planets are 'timeless and predictable.' He showed me how to figure out where I am using only a sextant and chart, by triangulating the position of the moon, stars, planets and the sun at a certain hour. Ask him to show you tomorrow night. He loves talking about the heavens."

The top of the sun was just about to drop below the horizon, creating a mirage where it looked like a portion of the sun appeared to elongate up away from the main body, like a drop of water in a pond slowly splashing back upwards.

"Watch closely," I whispered to Linda. "As the last of the sun disappears, that little dew-drop-looking part above it might flash green for just a second."

It didn't happen. The green flash is so rare a phenomenon, I've only seen it a few times, and I watch the sun set just about every night. As darkness surrounded us, we left the pier and went back to the others.

Carl was cooking over the large stone grill I'd built. Charlie had the table set, and the Tiki torches that surrounded the table flickered, casting an orange light over everything and giving the appearance of warmth, though it was already down in the sixties.

After eating, Carl and Charlie took the kids to their house, while the three of us cleaned the dishes and started a small fire in the fire pit on the northeast side of the island. We sat around the fire as it grew colder, talking about our trip to Cape Sable in the morning.

CHAPTER THREE

I woke before dawn. It was colder and I immediately stoked the fire in the old potbellied stove, even before pouring my first cup of coffee. Looking out the window to the southeast, the first faint light had yet to purple the sky. Always an early riser, I'd wondered about the need for it anymore. Particularly in winter. It'd be an hour before any work could be done and two hours before it was light enough to head back down to Marathon, where I kept my plane at the *Anchor*.

My plane is a deHavilland Beaver built in 1953 and fitted with a pair of Wipaire floats with wheels that retracted into them. I bought it last September from a friend who was moving back to his home state of Kentucky. With its big Pratt and Whitney radial engine and wide wingspan, it was perfect for the islands, able to land and take off in a very short distance, whether on land or sea.

Filling a thermos, I went down below the house to the dock area, which fills the whole area under both the house and the wraparound deck. Although it's a tight squeeze, we keep six boats down here, including the *Revenge*. There's a narrow walkway all the way around three sides, and two sets of doors facing south. Down the middle is another narrow dock, connecting the rear dock to the piling between the two sets of huge double doors. Stepping down into the cockpit of the *Revenge*, I unlocked the hatch and turned off the alarm.

Sitting down on the settee in the salon, I powered up my laptop computer. Jimmy had set up a satellite-based Internet account for me and installed a wireless modem in the cabinet next to the flat panel TV in my old boat.

Deuce had upgraded my system on the new boat so it could be used whenever I was transporting his team to or from a mission and had switched the satellite feed over to a government satellite. It was much faster and more reliable than the company Jimmy had used and provided access to a few other things the old service couldn't.

I ran a couple of Google searches to see if there was any public news about the people blowing up reefs, but didn't find anything I didn't already know. In fact, I already knew more than I was able to find on the Internet.

Knowing that whatever Deuce's team was doing, Chyrel would be in her comm shack up in Homestead, I clicked the Soft Jazz icon on the computer's desktop, which opened a direct video feed to wherever she was. After a couple of seconds the window expanded and her face appeared, a completely blank white wall behind her. I recognized by the starkness of the background that she was in her little office. The other walls are decorated, but not the one facing the camera.

"Hey, Jesse," she said. Then giggling, she asked, "How's it hanging?" The joke was getting old. When we were on Elbow Cay last September a woman had drugged me with some kind of homemade aphrodisiac that left me with an eighteen-hour erection.

"Hardy-har," I said. "Hey, we're flying up to Cape Sable in a little while. Just wanted to check in and see if you guys needed anything." Deuce and his entire team were in training with a newly-formed second team that would operate out of Key Largo in pretty much the same fashion as the original team did here.

"I can check with Deuce," she said. "But I think we have everything covered. Why'd you really call?"

"What? A guy can't touch base with his friends?"

"You're a real crappy liar, you know that?"

"So I've been told. Look, have you heard anything about a Miami gang called Zoe Pound that's expanding down here? Anything to link them to blowing up reefs with grenades?"

Her face turned serious for a second and her eyes glanced down and to the left. "Zoe Pound? Never heard of them."

I bent toward the screen, raising my left eyebrow. "And you call me a bad liar?"

She leaned a little closer to the screen. "Deuce said since Kim was down there, we shouldn't pass on anything about it. Julie told Rusty and told him to tell everyone else down there."

"Why?" I asked, realizing now why Rusty and Jimmy had been attempting to be vague.

"You have a reputation for getting involved in things you shouldn't, Jesse. We just don't want anything to happen between you and Kim."

"I'll find out what I want to know one way or another. So far, all I know is that two people were robbed and set adrift and another couple were injured while diving."

Chyrel should never play poker. I could read the surprise in her face as easy as a card shark can read a rookie who just got dealt an inside straight.

Realizing her face had given her away, she tried to become official. "Where'd you hear that, Jesse? It hasn't been released to the media."

"Heard it on the Coconut Telegraph," I said, which made her laugh.

"Are you sure you're not a Parrot Head?" she asked.

"What is it with you and parrots?" I asked, confused. Talking to Chyrel almost always left me confused. She has a mind like a steel trap and could run circles around the best computer hackers, but at times goes off on some weird tangent, often involving parrots for some reason. A pretty girl in her late twenties, she has short blonde hair and bright blue eyes. Before she came to work for Deuce, she was a computer analyst and programmer with the CIA. Apparently, her skills were the stuff of legend. Lately, she'd been staying on the island and even bought her own skiff.

"Look," I said, "if things are happening around me, I want to know. One of these incidents was only a few miles from my house."

She stared blankly at the screen for a moment, then seemed to come to a decision. "They came up on the DHS radar when message traffic indicated they were bringing arms in from Haiti. Up to then, it was strictly a DEA thing. We haven't gotten enough actionable intel yet, but we're working on it. The leader of the gang, Jean-Claude Lavolier, disappeared for over a week earlier this month. When he reappeared, he gave the news to his seconds that the gang was going to move in a different direction. The word on the street is that he's personally responsible for sending gang members out into Florida Bay and the Gulf to drop grenades on the reefs and collect fish. When one of his men challenged the wisdom of that, Lavolier beheaded him. Put his head on a spike in the backyard of his house in the Grove, pulled the tongue down from the severed throat and nailed it to the post. At least that's what we're hearing up here."

"Damn, that's a harsh way to make a point," I said. "But it probably works to keep others from wagging their tongues." I rubbed my face. "It makes no sense at all, though. From what I hear, they move a lot of drugs. Fish just aren't profitable. Not like drugs, anyway."

"You're right. No sense whatsoever. Which is why we haven't gotten a handle on it. When Lavolier reappeared, all telephone, Internet, and text chatter within the gang ceased within a day of the beheading. We're not getting anything. Only what the cops are hearing on the streets and they're reluctant to share, so I just take it from their computers. Apparently, all communication within the gang is done in person now. Deuce thinks something big is coming up pretty soon."

"Okay, thanks. If I hear anything down here, I'll let you know. Like I said, we'll be up on Cape Sable, so only the sat-phone or laptop will work."

"Just don't tell Deuce I told you, okay?"

"Mum's the word, kid. Bye."

I thought about what I'd learned. This Lavolier had to have some motivation for doing something as stupid as blowing up coral reefs for the food fish. But what was it? A single pound of coke meant way more profit than a ton of fish, no matter how quickly they were caught.

I found the idea of fragging a reef for fish not only ludicrous, but unconscionable. The damage done to the reef would take dozens or even hundreds of years to recover. If it ever did at all. Grenades are totally indiscriminate. On land, a grenade can kill nearly everyone within a twenty-foot circle with shrapnel, tiny shards of the metal casing. Underwater, the shrapnel is rendered harmless except for a couple of feet near the point of the explosion, but the concussion wave is compounded through the density of the water. Man's ability to create things really knows no bounds and is second only to his ability to destroy.

I Googled Lavolier and found a few news stories and some pictures, but nothing that steered me even remotely toward a possible motivation. A friend told me once that it was hard for law-abiding people to understand the criminal mind and nearly as hard for the criminal to understand a law-abiding person's motivation. After twenty minutes I gave up, powered down the laptop, then went back topside.

CHAPTER FOUR

An hour later, with the sun still below the southeastern horizon but casting enough gray light to see by, I started the outboard on the skiff. Pressing the button on the key fob, I released the latch, and the big doors in front of the east half of the docks slowly began to open on spring-loaded hinges. Linda stepped aboard and put her bag in the port-side fish box up in the bow, then sat down beside me at the helm. Kim cast off the lines and stepped aboard with Pescador. After stowing her bag, she took a seat on the bench in front of the center console, with a blanket wrapped around her, her long-billed fishing hat pulled low. Pescador took his usual spot, standing in the bow.

Once clear of the doors, I clicked the other button on the fob, and the twelve-volt-powered electric motors pulled the doors closed as we idled down the short channel to Harbor Channel.

We were dressed for the weather, in jeans and long-sleeved shirts, Kim and I in denim and Linda wearing a blue flannel shirt that brought out colors in her hair. Even dressed against the cold air, it was a chilly ride once we got up on plane. I cut the distance and time shorter by taking the narrow, winding channel through Cutoe Banks. At high tide, it had just enough water for my skiff, with maybe six inches to spare. Coming out into Big Spanish Channel, I followed it south-southeast for a few minutes, then turned due east into another "smugglers cut" and then southeast again until we were clear of Johnson Keys.

Making a beeline for the eastern side of the Seven Mile Bridge from there, I pushed the throttle to the stop and we crossed the skinny water south of Teakettle Key into deeper water. Linda leaned closer behind the windscreen, shivering slightly. I couldn't help but turn my nose toward her to breathe in the smell of her hair. It was a clean, fresh scent that reminded me of the night-blooming jasmine up on the island in summer. The wind and waves were calm and we made it to the *Anchor* just ten minutes later.

Idling up the canal, I saw that Rusty had indeed strapped his two twelve-foot canoes to the pontoon braces on the *Island Hopper* and there were two small stacks of camping gear next to the plane.

Being a Saturday, the Trents had slept in, so I was looking forward to Rufus's Caribbean breakfast buffet. We tied off the skiff and grabbed our gear before heading across the lawn to the bar.

While eating breakfast in a bar might seem strange on the mainland, down here certain bars are more than just drinking establishments. Some are a gathering place for locals at all hours. A place to eat, share stories, news, and gossip, or make deals. The *Anchor* is just such a bar, where locals gather and everyone knows everyone else. There just aren't many places like this left in the Keys, most proprietors preferring to target the tourist dollars.

Rufus's breakfast didn't disappoint. After catching up with a couple of the liveaboards, we ate quickly and were in the air less than an hour later. Jimmy and Angie would run the bar while Rusty was gone.

Setting a course just a couple of points west of due north, I let Kim take over the controls at one thousand feet.

"Shouldn't we be higher?" Kim asked over the headphones we all were wearing to be able to hear one another over the roar of the big radial engine.

"It's only thirty miles," I replied. "We're almost halfway there already. Think you're ready for your first water landing?"

"I don't know, Dad. I've only made a few on land so far."

"The shallows at the Cape extend out for miles," Rusty said from the back seat, next to Linda. "With the water as calm down in Marathon as it was, there won't even be a ripple at the Cape. It'll be like a mile-long runway that's ten miles wide."

Kim looked at me and I nodded.

"Okay, take me through it," Kim said.

"It's no different than landing on a runway," I said. "Except that we'll slow down a little faster, due to the friction on the water, and you don't have to lower the landing gear. Go ahead and start your descent. When you get to a hundred feet, add twenty degrees of flaps and cut your speed down to ninety miles an hour."

She eased the yoke forward and we began to descend. When we were still three miles off the beach, I said, "See that smoke curling up off to starboard near the point?" She nodded. "That's someone's campfire on East Cape Sable. Turn a little more north and we'll set down a few miles from them, between East Cape and Middle Cape."

At a hundred feet, she added flaps and reduced power. The plane slowed to a hundred, then ninety miles an hour after another slight throttle adjustment.

"You're doing fine," I said. "See that cluster of tall palm trees straight ahead about halfway between the two points of land?" She nodded again. "Line up just to the left of them and once we're down, you can turn directly toward them. That's where we'll pitch camp."

Kim gently turned the wheel, changing course slightly away from our campsite. The tide was low and we'd have to anchor in shallow water a hundred yards from shore.

"Add another ten degrees of flaps and bring her down to just above stall speed."

She did as I instructed and we were now just barely flying at seventy miles an hour, descending at about a foot every second. With its broad wingspan, the Beaver has a stall speed of sixty.

"Nice and easy," I said, looking ahead to see if anything was in the water. A sudden collision with a floating log could spell disaster in really shallow water. "Keep looking straight ahead for anything in the water and I'll watch your altimeter."

At thirty feet, I started giving her five foot readings, until we were just ten feet off the water. At five feet, I said, "Ease back gently and reduce power."

Kim flared the plane perfectly, the middle and rear of the pontoons making smooth contact with the water simultaneously.

"Come up on the throttle a little as the water slows us down," I said calmly. Truth is, the girl's a natural flyer and needed no reassurance at all. But she was still a young girl. Wise beyond her years, maybe, but still young.

"No more wheel steering," I said as we slowed to just above planing speed. "Use your pedals to steer us gently straight toward shore. When we're a couple hundred yards out, bring her down to an idle and wait for the feel of the pontoons on the bottom."

A few minutes later, after we'd all congratulated Kim on a picture-perfect water landing, she shut down the engine and started a quick post flight check. Rusty and I climbed out over the canoes and splashed down into the knee-deep water. We each carried two small Danforth anchors and tied the lines fore and aft on the pontoons before walking them out fifty feet and burying them in the soft sand. The *Island Hopper* was as secure as we could make her. Unstrapping the canoes, we floated them on either side of the plane while the girls handed all the gear down to us. Pescador leaped into the water and was already bounding his way toward the beach to explore.

"How cold's the water?" Linda asked.

"Much warmer than the air," I replied.

"Feels downright balmy," Rusty said. "We'll have to wade ashore and pull the canoes."

After Kim and Linda stepped down into the water, I locked up the plane and the four of us sloshed ashore, pulling the heavily laden canoes behind us.

We quickly unloaded the supplies and pitched our tents in a circle above the high tide line, facing a fire pit. It only took a few minutes to gather enough dry driftwood and deadfalls to keep a fire going all night.

"So what's on the menu for lunch?" Rusty asked.

"I saw a small school of redfish," Kim said.

"Sounds good to me," I added. "We have steaks in the cooler for supper."

"I don't suppose you have a good red wine to go with it," Linda asked as she put her fly rod together.

"Yeah, as a matter of fact, I do."

"Do we need to leave someone here to watch over the camp?"

"No, we can see for miles up and down the coast," I replied to Linda. "Let's split up into twos. Remember, over eighteen inches but less than twenty-seven and only one per person."

"Come on with me, Kim," Rusty said. "I'm not real good with a fly rod. Maybe you can give me some pointers."

Linda and I started down the beach to the south with Pescador running ahead of us, while Rusty and Kim went north. It didn't take long at all before we came up to Pescador standing in the water at the shoreline, looking out at a small school of reds. They were scouring the sandy bottom less than fifty feet from shore. The tide was rising and the water was warm as we moved slowly toward the school in the calf-deep water, approaching from different angles. Pescador walked through the shallow water around to the other side of the school, taking cues from me, but watching the schooling fish carefully.

"Let me and Linda catch one, boy," I whispered. He seemed to understand and held back a few feet behind me. "You can get your turn once we catch ours."

When Linda was in casting range, she waited until I was in position on the school's flank. We both started stripping line, our casts snaking out at about the same time. Each of us knew that once one of us hooked up, the rest of the fish would scatter. They were in a loose school, and it was easy to pick out the ones that were legal size. I'd improved my casting ability over the years and Linda picked it up even faster. My late wife said once that most men lacked grace, an essential element of fly casting.

At nearly the same time, our flies touched the water and were instantly attacked by the two reds we'd chosen. The fight was exciting, but all too short as we began working them towards shore. Both were legal size, Linda's just a bit larger than mine, and we had them landed in just a few minutes. Pescador went quickly after a really big redfish that darted the wrong way, trying to go around me toward open water. I could see at a glance the fish wasn't just over the legal size, but way over. I called Pescador off.

He splashed his way over to me as I lifted my catch from the water. "Sorry, bud. He was way too big."

"That didn't take long," Linda said as she walked toward me carrying her own catch.

"We're probably the first humans they'd ever seen."

Looking around the flats and the beach, and over the dune to Micmac Lagoon, she said, "Probably the first dog they've ever seen as well. Rusty was right, this is probably what most of south Florida looked like five hundred years ago. How far away did you say the nearest town is?"

I pointed east, across the dunes. "Flamingo's about fifteen miles that way. Nice little drinking village with a fishing problem. We should visit there some time." I could see Rusty and Kim in the distance as we neared the camp. Kim was carrying a nice-sized redfish, but Rusty's hand was empty.

"You shoulda seen the one that got away," Rusty said as they approached the camp.

"Fisherman's rule," I said, with a grin. "Whoever gets skunked cleans the fish." I knew that Rusty would insist on it anyway. He was an artist with a filet knife.

While Rusty prepared the fish on the other side of the dune, I got the fire going and opened the kitchen crate, unloading what we'd need. Rufus had given Rusty a couple of his recipes and a small box with assorted herbs and spices. An hour later we were enjoying Rufus's blackened redfish sandwiches and fire-roasted corn on the cob. Rufus had included a rub for the corn, telling Rusty, "Pull di husks down and rub it in good, mon. Den pull up di husks and put dem neah di fiah." It was delicious, whatever he put in it, as was the fish.

The sky was as crisp and clear as I'd ever seen. It wasn't quite as cold as the day before, when the front first pushed through, but it was still pretty cool. As we were cleaning up, Pescador got up from where he'd been lying next to a fallen palm tree, looked south and barked once. I followed his gaze and saw a man and woman approaching from the south. They were walking hand in hand and the man appeared to be carrying something. As they got closer, I saw that it was a bottle.

"Ahoy, the camp!" the man shouted at a fair distance away. In the backcountry, it was customary to announce your approach so as not to surprise others.

I stood up and watched as they approached. "Welcome!" I shouted back. "Come on in!"

The man looked to be a few years older than me, maybe in his early to mid-fifties with dark hair, graying at the temples in a very distinguished fashion. Tall, fit and tan, he had the look of success.

The woman at first appeared to be much younger. As they got closer, I could tell she was about the same age, though. She had blond hair to her shoulders, without a hint of gray, and the tiniest of lines at the corners of her green eyes. Shorter than the man by almost a foot, she too was tan and healthy looking. Both were wearing jeans and crewneck sweaters over tee shirts.

"Name's Toliver," the man said. "Eugene and Nancy."

I stepped toward him and offered my hand. "Jesse McDermitt." Nodding to the others, I added, "Rusty Thurman, Linda Rosales and my daughter, Kim."

He took my hand in a firm, dry grip. "Pleased to meet you."

"Gene said he had to see your plane close up," Nancy said. "He's a pilot as well. I hope we're not intruding."

The man looked out to where the *Hopper* sat at anchor and said, "I used to fly a Beaver up in Canada. A long time ago. Paid my way through college as a bush pilot during the summer." Holding out the bottle, he added, "Thought you might like a welcome gift. We've been here two days and you're the first people we've seen in four."

I thanked him and accepted the bottle, handing it to Linda. He went on to explain how they'd been kayaking the backcountry all the way down from Chokoloskee and decided to stay on the Cape a few days.

"You paddled here from Chokoloskee, Eugene?" I asked. "That's gotta be fifty miles. How long did it take?"

"My friends call me Gene," he replied. "We weren't in any big hurry. We stayed in chikees along the way for a day or two whenever we got tired. It's been the trip of a lifetime starting about a week ago. We're meeting friends in Flamingo on Tuesday and go back up to Chokoloskee with them on Thursday."

"What's a chikee?" Linda asked.

"The ones built by Native Americans are sort of a thatch-covered hut on stilts," Nancy replied. "The ones built by the Parks Service are on a dock out in the middle of the water. One end of the dock is covered with a tin roof to shade your tent, but open all the way around. They're built right over the water and are set up all along the water trail. Very romantic. Well, except for the big blue Port-A-Johns at the other side of the short dock."

"Y'all have a seat," Rusty said. "We just finished lunch, but there's some leftover redfish, if you're hungry."

"No, thanks," Gene said as he and his wife sat down next to Kim on a palm log. "We ate before we came up here."

"Guess that means it's yours," Rusty said to Pescador and placed the fry pan in front of him. Pescador looked up at me, waiting.

"Go ahead," I told him and he started inhaling the two leftover fillets. Linda had put one uncooked fillet in a bag in the cooler for breakfast.

"That's a well-trained dog," Nancy remarked. "How long did it take you to teach him not to accept food from others?"

"I didn't. He won't eat even when I put food in front of him, unless I tell him to. He adopted me about a year ago after Hurricane Wilma. We never could find his owner."

Nancy insisted Linda open the wine and we sat around the fire sipping it from paper cups and talking about their trip, fishing, flying Beavers, boating, and the remote beauty all around us. I even permitted Kim to have a small cup of the wine.

The Tolivers were originally from Chicago, but moved to Tampa when he sold his very successful advertising firm to his vice president a year ago. Kids through college and retired at fifty-five, they bought a house in the suburbs near Pinellas Park, across the Bay from Tampa.

"Sounds like you're living the dream," Linda said.

"We're happy," Nancy said. "Two years ago, we visited Sanibel. One day on a whim, we drove down to Flamingo and rented kayaks and camping gear. We spent the night right here and loved it. Originally we'd wanted to build somewhere near Port Charlotte, but friends talked us into the Tampa area. We already knew a few couples that retired there. What do you do?"

"I'm in law enforcement," Linda replied. "Jesse owns a charter business, Rusty owns a restaurant and bar and Kim starts college in the fall. She's taking a year off to help her dad." Kim smiled at the compliment.

The truth is she's a lot of help. She'd taken over the scheduling and created a calendar on the laptop that prompted me to take care of certain preparations for an upcoming charter early enough that it didn't get to be a last-minute thing. I insisted that she keep it to one charter a week, two at the absolute most. The calendar was filled with one charter a week for the next five months. Certain regular clients filled in a second day in several of those weeks. I'd given her my handwritten notebook of clients with notes as to how much they'd be willing to pay and how good they tipped the crew. The crew being her for the time being.

"Do you charter your plane, Jesse?" Gene asked.

"Not yet. I own a sports fisherman for offshore charters and a couple of smaller boats for clients who want to fish or dive the backcountry."

"You could make a killing with that plane," he said. "There are isolated lakes and springs all over the Glades that fishermen would pay dearly to be dropped into for the weekend."

The conversation continued and I found that I liked Gene and Nancy. They had a deep, abiding love for south Florida and for being outdoors. They also had the time to enjoy both. It was obvious they weren't hurting for money, but didn't act like a lot of wealthy people I'd known.

As the sun slowly neared the horizon out on the Gulf it began to paint the high clouds above the Glades a burnt orange. Gene said they should be getting back to their camp. We all said our goodbyes and agreed to stop by their camp before leaving tomorrow.

"Nice folks," Rusty said, as the couple walked hand in hand back to their camp and we prepared the steaks for dinner.

That evening, after watching a spectacular sunset, we feasted on choice rib eyes, baked potatoes, and coconut swamp cabbage. Afterward, we walked along the beach to the north, getting away from the light of the campfire, so the stars were more visible.

Aside from our fire and that of the Tolivers, the nearest artificial light was in Flamingo and as small a town as it is, there was no spillover from that direction. Just a hundred yards from our camp, the vastness of the stars filled the night sky as our eyes adjusted to the darkness. Rusty pointed out and named many of the prominent stars, planets, and constellations to Kim, who soaked it all in like the proverbial sponge. He explained that if you knew the time and date and could measure the angle of certain stars above the horizon, you could determine pretty accurately where you were.

"If we're only thirty miles from the Keys, why doesn't anyone ever come here?" she asked. "I've never seen a place that was half as beautiful."

"Ever hear of the English writer, Gilbert Chesterton?" Rusty asked her.

"I remember reading a book by G. K. Chesterton in English Lit."

"Same guy," Rusty said as he stopped and looked up at the Milky Way, stretching from horizon to horizon. "I remember a line from one of his works. Don't remember which one. But it's always stuck with me. 'The traveler sees what he sees, the tourist sees what he has come to see.' Tourists don't flock to the Keys to be isolationists. They're not interested in seeing the natural beauty all around us. They come down Highway One for the fun and booze. Folks like the Tolivers? They're travelers."

"Pretty deep for a redhead," I said, quoting one of my favorite childhood heroes, Matt Dillon.

Rusty must have liked the show as well. He responded with Miss Kitty's line, "Well, I'm a pretty deep redhead."

Kim pointed to the west, near where the sun had disappeared two and a half hours earlier. "That's Neptune just about to set, right?"

"Sure is," Rusty replied, impressed. "The king has fallen."

Strolling along the beach of Cape Sable with my daughter and friends, it was easy to let my mind drift back, remembering the first time I was here. It was 1967, and my dad was home on leave for Christmas. Pap had let Mom and Dad borrow the thirty-four-foot cat-rigged shallow-draft sailboat that he had just finished building the previous summer. I'd spent weekends at Mam and Pap's house, helping him work on it. That two weeks on it spent here with my parents was a very special time for me.

At the formative age of seven, most of the kids I knew were tucked into nice warm beds on Christmas Eve, anxious to see what Santa would bring. Sailing south out of Fort Myers four days before Christmas, it took us two whole days to get here. We stayed close to the coastline, less than a mile offshore most of the way and sailing straight through the night. Mom and Dad were both great sailors and took turns all night long. I remember passing miles and miles of desolate coastline once we cleared Marco Island. Arriving here just before sunset on the second day, seeing nothing but white sand beach stretching out in both directions and the vast emptiness of the Glades just beyond it, I was certain there was no way Santa and his reindeer could find this place and I began to worry. We spent the following day just walking on the beach and splashing in the warm water. Occasionally Dad would pull a deadfall out of the higher part of the dune and drag it down to the sand, well above the high tide mark.

"Wood'll rot in the vegetation, son," I remember him telling me. "Even if we don't need it, someone else might come along later and want a fire. You should always leave a place better than you found it for the next guy." Kneeling on the sand so as to be eye to eye with me, he said, "We'll be here for two weeks, son. Then I have to go away for a while."

Dad was a Staff Sergeant in the Marine Corps and in my child's mind, he was the King of the World. He was deployed a lot, so Mom and I didn't see him all that often. On one deployment, he was gone for over a year.

That two weeks here would be the first and only Christmas I remember spending with him. Sometimes, we'd pack our clothes up in the summer and go to where he was stationed, if he was able to get family quarters. But he always insisted we maintain a home in Fort Myers, so I could go to the same school.

"Two weeks?" I'd asked him.

"Don't worry," Mom had said, smiling at me and tousling my hair. "The jolly, fat man can find you, no matter where you go."

I wasn't so sure. But the following morning, the three things that I'd written to Santa about, the three things that I wanted more than anything in the world, were right there in the tiny salon of the boat. My mom and dad sipping coffee and laughing together on Christmas morning, my very own coffee mug with my name on it, and a brand new rod and reel.

Just two months after that trip, Dad was killed in the recapture of Hue City, in Vietnam. Days later, my grief-stricken mother overdosed on sleeping pills. My whole life was shattered just weeks before my eighth birthday.

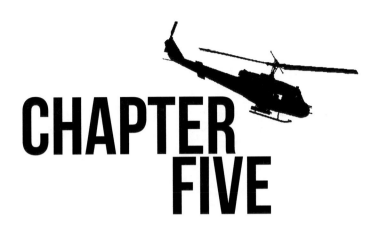

CHAPTER FIVE

The night had been only slightly warmer than the previous. This cold front was taking forever. We each had a small dome tent, set up so they encircled the fire pit at the center. When I woke up, it was still dark outside, but the moon had risen, and coupled with the millions of stars, there was plenty enough light to see. I dressed quickly, stumbling out of my tent, still fixing my trousers and nearly bumping into Linda as she was dragging a large piece of driftwood over to the fire with three forks like a trident.

She glanced down as I struggled with a stuck zipper and grinned. “Are those jeans coming off or going on?”

Finally, the zipper pulled free and I adjusted my heavy denim work shirt while looking at her. In the moonlight, she was even more beautiful, the soft light caressing away the tiny lines of her face and accentuating the shadowy curves of her body even in the red flannel shirt she was wearing.

I took the driftwood from her hand and tossed it nearer the fire. Then, taking both her hands in mine, I slowly pulled her toward me, until we were standing toe to toe, her breasts pressing against my chest and the now faint smell of jasmine filling my nostrils.

Moving my hands to her waist, I pulled her into my embrace as her arms wrapped around my shoulders. Burying my face in her hair, the scent was stronger. It was a good, clean, fresh smell, with just a touch of the salt and iodine from the sea. I liked it.

I leaned back a little and looked into her eyes. They smoldered with an intensity I'd not seen before as she pressed her hips tighter to my groin.

"The waters you're steering toward could get rough, Jesse."

"I'm a pretty fair sailor. If it gets too scary, either of us can drop anchor at any time."

"One day at a time? No promises or plans?"

"Yeah, I think that'd be a safe tack."

"Me too," she sighed and tilted her head up. I lowered my lips to hers and we kissed for the first time on a beautiful stretch of moonlit beach that held so many great memories for me. It wasn't a deep, passionate, all-or-nothing kind of kiss. Just two good friends, taking one tiny step.

She stepped back, smiling. "We better get some coffee on. I'm told you're real grumpy without it."

She turned and walked toward the fire, my eyes following her. I'm pretty sure she put a little more sway in her hips than usual just for my benefit. Or maybe it was just the fine, powdery sand. Bending at the waist to pick up the driftwood I'd thrown, she tossed her hair over her shoulder, looked back and caught me staring. She smiled, laying the driftwood on the fire. *No*, I thought, *that was all just for me.*

Kim nearly sprang out of her tent, wearing gray sweatpants and a red hoodie sweatshirt. Holding a roll of toilet paper in one hand, she saw me, then looked all around.

"Across the dune," I said. "Rusty thought to bring a portable. Just toss a little sand in the hole when you're done."

Kim raced across the dune as Rusty crawled out of his tent and stood up, stretching, with a big grin on his face. "Someone say something about coffee?"

"Be ready in just a minute," Linda replied, surmising from his grin that he'd heard everything we said in front of his tent and approved.

"Good, we're burnin' daylight. I gotta hit the head, be back in a minute."

"Me too," I said, walking along with him toward a cluster of sea grapes a little way down the beach that had become our urinal.

Once out of earshot, Rusty said, "I like her."

"Who?"

"Linda, ya dumb Grunt! I think y'all would be pretty good for each other."

"We're just friends, bro."

"Yeah, right. Ya know, that's what I always said about Juliet, too." Juliet was Rusty's late wife and Julie was named for her. As far as I know, Rusty's never even looked at another woman since her death.

As we walked back toward camp, he said, "Seriously, though. She's the only one that's come along since Alex that's even close to being your match. It's been a year, man."

"A year, two months, and twenty-one days," I said.

I was married three times and divorced twice. I'd met Alex four years ago. We were just friends, too. We went out a couple of times, nothing serious. We ran, swam, and worked out together nearly every day and became very good friends. She left a year after that when her kid brother was diagnosed with cancer. Two years later, she reappeared without warning and things moved a lot faster. A week after her return, we were married and looked forward to a life together. She was murdered that night. I still see her face in my dreams from time to time, hear her laugh in the rustling of a coconut palm, and catch her scent on the morning breeze.

"We're just going to take it one day at a time," I finally said, quietly ending the conversation as we walked into the camp.

The coffee was ready and Kim was frying the last fillet for use in omelets, while Linda was stir frying peppers, onions, corn, and swamp cabbage in another skillet.

Thirty minutes later, we washed down the last of the omelets with the last of the coffee and started getting the fishing gear loaded into the canoes.

Some of the most challenging fishing in south Florida is for sea trout along the mangrove fringed inland estuaries of the Glades. While trout aren't all that difficult to catch, coaxing them out of the millions of mangrove roots is difficult, and they can dart between them, either tangling your line or cutting it on the oysters and barnacles that are also found there.

We'd be taking the canoes around East Cape Sable into Micmac Lagoon then on up into Lake Ingraham, a total of about eight miles round trip. From our camp, it would only be a few hundred yards portage straight over to the Lake, but the trip is more a part of the adventure than arriving at the destination.

We shoved off, leaving Pescador to watch the camp. I knew he'd wander around, dig in the sand, swim, and chase fish and crabs, but he wouldn't stray far from the camp and I'd be able to hear him bark if anyone came near. Besides, six hours in a canoe wasn't his style. Too much pent-up energy in the morning. Just as the sun began to peek above East Cape Sable in the distance, Kim jumped into the canoe Rusty was pulling into knee-deep water. Smiling over at me, she said, "Bring me the far horizon, Uncle Rusty." I smiled back at my daughter and helped Linda aboard my canoe.

Moments later, we were paddling toward the rising sun, just a hundred feet from shore. The tide change was an hour earlier and the rising water created a current along the flats, helping push us south so that just forty minutes later we were passing the Tolivers' camp. They were on the tip of East Cape, sitting in folding chairs, sipping coffee and watching the sunrise. They waved as we passed and Gene called out to us, reminding us to stop by on our way back.

Rounding the tip of the sand spit a hundred feet to the south, I tapped Linda on the shoulder. When she turned, I nodded back to where the Tolivers sat watching the daily spectacle of a new day dawning and said, "Where they're sitting is the southernmost part of mainland Florida. They seem to fit in with it pretty nicely."

She nodded and looked over at the couple. For a moment I saw something in Linda's face, a sad, almost longing expression, as if she'd lost something and knew she might never have it again. I felt that way at times, also. Just as quickly the frown faded, she looked at me and smiled. "I thought Key West was the southernmost point."

"It's an island. Doesn't count. That's the mainland."

She smiled again. "You really love it here, don't you? You seem more relaxed and at ease than any time since I met you."

"Yeah, this is one of my favorite places in the whole world. My parents brought me here when I was a kid and later, my grandparents brought me many times. Later still, I came here by myself or with friends. I grew up just a hundred miles north of here and spent a lot of weekends down here in my teen years."

We passed the first small creek that goes back into the interior of the island. It's an interesting creek, better left to kayaks even at high tide. Twisting and turning, it runs for more than five miles, but eventually gets to the lake. We turned into the larger second creek a hundred yards past it. Just a little further east is a manmade canal that allows larger boats access to the lake, but bypasses the lagoon. By larger, I mean flats skiffs, or maybe a small center console.

The current in the narrow creek was reversed by the flooding tide, bringing clean seawater into the lagoon. It was so clear, you could make out the details of the sandy bottom four feet below us. We drifted silently upstream with it, twenty feet apart, paddling only to adjust course. This was the Florida I remembered as a youth, wild and natural. No cars or roads, no planes overhead, nothing but time to enjoy the things you could see and hear and the company you were with. I was eager to see if this canoe trip would have the same effect on Kim and Linda as it did on me all those years ago.

Kim rode silently in Rusty's canoe, sitting tall on the front bench, looking all around and watching the bottom glide by. They were ahead of us as we rounded a bend in the creek and I heard her sharp intake of breath. Rusty slowly and quietly back paddled the canoe until we caught up. Rounding the bend and coming alongside, Linda had the same reaction.

The predominant color on Cape Sable is green, with many variations from bright to dark, set against the white sand that covers all the dry land and a smattering of brown and tan bark. There before us, wading in the shallows of the lagoon, was a large flock of flamingos, nearly a hundred of them. The sudden appearance of the vibrant pink and red birds foraging in the yellow-and-cream-colored shallow water was startling against the customary green background.

"I've never seen anything so beautiful," Kim sighed.

Linda turned toward me, her face full of wonder, smiling. "You knew this would be here?" she barely whispered. I nodded and she mouthed, *Thank you.*

We drifted silently on, slowing as the current decreased in the broad expanse of the lagoon, making no sound to intrude on the birds feeding in the shallows. If they hadn't been here, we could have fished along the edge of the lagoon for the elusive sea trout. Instead, we floated slowly past the flock, drifting toward the short creek mouth that would pass us on through to Lake Ingraham.

Once in the much larger lake, we separated by a few hundred feet and fished the mangrove-covered banks.

Kim was first to catch a trout, using the same rod and reel I'd received as a kid only a few hundred yards from this very spot and what seemed like a lifetime ago. I'd given it to her on Christmas just a few weeks earlier.

We drifted and fished the morning away, talking little and enjoying the warm sun, light breeze, and beautiful scenery. Again there wasn't a cloud to be seen except way to the east, over the heart of the Everglades. I pulled off my work shirt and felt the sun warming my arms and shoulders through my light tee shirt.

Well before noon, we'd all caught our limit of four fish, keeping them in two coolers we'd brought just for that purpose, filled with seawater from the lake. Sixteen trout would make for a great dinner back at the island tonight.

As we were getting ready to take advantage of the outgoing tide, I heard Pescador bark once. A moment later, I could just make out the high-pitched whine of an outboard engine getting closer. We were on the north side of the lake, away from the narrow isthmus that is Cape Sable. Beyond that was our camp and Florida Bay. Standing up in the canoe, I could just see the wings of the plane over the far dune.

"We better paddle across and check it out," Rusty said.

The pitch of the outboard increased as we started across the lake to the far shore. Pescador started barking more when suddenly the sound of the engine raced and then died completely. The fool had run aground, which meant it probably wasn't a skiff. I paddled harder as Pescador continued barking even more nervously.

We made it to knee-deep water and I jumped from the canoe, splashing ashore as fast as I could, distancing myself from the canoes. By the time I made it to shore, Pescador's barking was mixed with viscous snarls. He was pissed. I ran headlong into the tangle of sawgrass, young mangroves, casuarinas and sea grapes, crashing through them with reckless abandon. Somehow I sensed that this wasn't good.

When I got to the top of the dune, I heard the first gunshot. I quickly pulled my Sig 9mm from the holster in the back of my pants. The center console was aground fifty feet beyond my plane, and two black men were wading toward it. Pescador was in the water, swimming toward them and still barking. One of the men took aim at him and fired again, missing by ten feet. I was two hundred feet away, well beyond anything remotely considered accurate range for a handgun. I stopped, planted my feet and aimed. I squeezed off two quick shots, then ran down the slope toward our camp.

The two shots were both wide. I knew I didn't have a chance of hitting anything from that range. I just wanted these guys to know they were in for a gun battle if they decided to continue. I called Pescador off and he turned immediately and started swimming toward me. The two men had reached my plane at the same time that I reached our camp and sprinted past our tents to the water. Two more shots rang out and kicked up twin geysers to my left.

The men had made it to my plane and one had climbed up on the starboard float, but the door was locked. I started walking toward them, gun raised and aiming at the guy still in the water. Suddenly Kim was at my left side, her own Sig Sauer P229 raised and taking aim. Hers is a smaller version of my P226, but the same caliber.

"What are you doing here?" I said. "Get back up to the camp and take cover!"

"He's my dog, too," was her only response. I was only seventy feet from them now. Still a long distance for a handgun.

"Drop your weapons!" I shouted, stepping between Kim and the two men by my plane.

The guy in the water took aim and fired again. I started quickly forward, firing with each footfall in the shallow water. I hit him high in the shoulder with my third shot, barely noticing that Kim was also firing. From the corner of my eye, I glimpsed a splinter of gelcoat fly off their boat. *Good girl*, I thought, *keep firing at their boat*. The man I shot spun and nearly went down. His friend jumped down from the pontoon and grabbed him as they both splashed their way back toward their boat. I changed my aim and joined Kim in firing at their boat, a steady barrage that I know hit it quite a few times. Maybe we damaged it, no way to tell. The two men struggled on through the water and a moment later one man helped his injured friend into it and began pushing on the bow, trying to get it into deeper water. Finally, it broke free and the injured man started the engine. He helped pull his buddy aboard and reversed the engine, throwing too much throttle to it.

Hit a rock, I thought, *or a shallow spot, or a log, anything*.

Willing it to happen was unsuccessful and the boat was soon in water deep enough to put the engine in forward and turn away from us, just as Linda and then Rusty came splashing up beside us, guns also drawn. The guy hit the throttle too hard, and the prop churned up the sandy bottom as the stern sank lower. It didn't stop them and they were soon up on plane, rocketing away to the south, heading out into Florida Bay.

I turned and took Kim in my arms for a second, then held her out at arm's length. "Are you hurt?"

"No, I'm okay."

"What the hell were you thinking? You could have been killed!"

I could see the sting in her eyes. "My bad, bro," Rusty interjected. "She jumped out before I could stop her."

"She's not your responsibility!" I shouted. Then it dawned on me. *She's my responsibility.* My first instinct was to advance toward the sound of trouble. It's what I was trained to do. What I should have done was protect my kid.

"What did they want?" Kim asked.

Rusty looked from me to Kim and said, "To rob the plane or maybe even steal it." Turning and still breathing hard, he trudged back toward camp.

"Don't ever do anything like that again!" I said to Kim.

"None of us were in range, Dad. And I can outshoot a couple of thugs."

I hugged her to me, again realizing that it was my actions that had put her in danger. "All it takes is one lucky shot. I'm just glad you're alright."

"They're turning!" Linda shouted.

I looked where she was pointing and saw that the boat had turned and was heading straight for East Cape Sable.

The men in the boat reached East Cape before we could reach the plane and untie the anchor lines from the pontoons. A couple of minutes later, we heard a single gunshot as we were climbing aboard. I skipped the preflight, and a few precious minutes later we were skimming the glassy surface as Rusty called the Coast Guard on the emergency channel. I could see the boat's wake as it headed due south, away from the Tolivers' camp. A part of me wanted to give chase, but we had to stop and check on the Tolivers. The flight lasted only a few minutes and I brought the *Hopper* down smoothly on the water, then turned toward shore.

"Coasties are putting a bird up out of Boca Chica," Rusty shouted. "They'll be here in thirty minutes. They said to stay put."

I came in a little too fast and was still at planing speed when I felt the port pontoon skip off the bottom. As I quickly cut the throttle to idle, the plane jerked to the left and the other pontoon grounded.

Great, I thought, *run aground in shallow water with an outgoing tide*.

I climbed out of the pilot's seat and splashed into the water, yelling back over my shoulder, "Stay in the plane, Kim!"

Linda was already halfway to the Tolivers' camp as I splashed through the water behind her. She had her own handgun out, held straight out with both hands as she moved toward the camp. She came up short at the water's edge and I was beside her a moment later. Gene Toliver lay face down in the sand fifty feet beyond their camp, a pool of brown sand around his head.

CHAPTER SIX

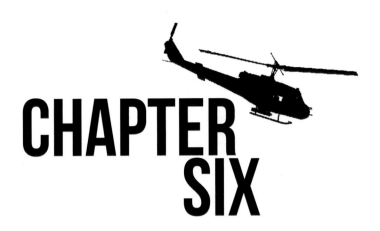

Linda had grabbed a blanket from the Tolivers' tent and covered Gene's body after first checking his pulse. Both were futile gestures. She told us to be careful and not disturb the crime scene. Rusty took Kim down the beach, away from the carnage, but she'd already seen him lying there in a pool of his own blood.

I followed Linda's lead. After covering the body, we walked wide around the camp back to the water, following the shoreline until we found the footprints coming out of the water. From there, it was easy to see what had happened.

There were two sets of tracks that came out of the water, where the two shooters had probably beached their boat. Following the tracks, Linda pointed out where they went from a walk to a dead run around the curve of the cape.

Passing the Tolivers' tent, she pointed again. "There's where Gene and Nancy tried to make a run for it. Running inland might have been a better idea. Maybe he was trying to get to the creek."

It was obvious the Tolivers had run from their camp as the two men approached. Knowing there was strength in numbers and we would be coming back out on the tide, maybe they were trying to get to us, not knowing it was me doing most of the shooting. Having heard the gunshots and being unarmed themselves, it was hide or seek help. Gene chose wrong.

"If they'd bolted into the brush, they might have been able to hide long enough for us to get here."

Linda looked at me for a moment. "It happens most of the time," she said. "Victims in a panic rarely make good choices."

Same with trained Marines, I thought.

We arrived to where Gene's body lay about halfway between their camp and the first creek. We kept to the water, reading the tracks. I was good at following tracks. In the Corps it wasn't "what is the quarry doing and thinking?" as much as "where is he?"

Linda pointed to a patch of sand just past the body that was churned up with many prints. "This is where they split up. Gene stopped to face his attackers. Nancy realized it and stopped as well. He must have told her to keep running and hide in the mangroves around the creek mouth, before walking toward the shooters."

Where he took his stand was where his body was lying. Even I could tell that they'd forced him to his knees and shot him in the back of the head, while barely breaking stride.

Following Nancy was easy for them. Hers were the only tracks in the sand. They found her in the first, narrow creek mouth. The tracks returned closer to the waterline, occasionally washed away by the small waves.

"Here, they were dragging her," Linda said as we followed the footprints back toward the camp. "One on either side. She struggled to get free right there."

Linda stepped closer to the tracks, where only two sets continued back to the boat, one much deeper than the other.

"She got free for a second," I said, pointing to where a scuffle had occurred. "One of the men probably knocked her out and carried her. See how one set of tracks is deeper?"

Linda nodded and looked all around at the southern horizon.

Nancy was gone.

We heard the heavy whump-whump of an approaching helicopter and looked southwest. The unmistakable orange and white markings identified the Sikorsky MH-60 Jayhawk as being a Coast Guard bird.

The chopper landed on the beach, just to the north of the Tolivers' camp and two men jumped out. Both were armed. Linda approached them, holding up her badge to identify herself as an FDLE Agent, and explained what had happened. There was nothing they could do for Gene. The two Coasties stayed with us, asking more questions as the chopper lifted off and headed south, looking for the boat.

Within an hour, more choppers had joined in the search and two small boats had arrived, one a launch from a Coast Guard Cutter lying offshore and another from the Monroe County Sheriff's Office. Rusty knew one of the sheriff's investigators and went over everything that had happened with him. The investigator said the sheriff's office also had a chopper in the air and they were doing everything they could to find the missing woman.

They found her another hour later. She was floating in Florida Bay near Sand Key, ten miles southeast of Cape Sable. She was wearing only a tee shirt, a hole in the back of her head.

After making the plane secure and setting the big Danforth up near the beach, we walked back to our camp. The next high tide wouldn't be until an hour before sunset and there was no chance of getting the *Hopper* off the bottom until the tide floated her.

We portaged the canoes across from the lake and began taking down the camp, loading everything into them. It took a while, but we found the four smaller Danforths we'd anchored the plane with yesterday. We'd untied them from the plane in a hurry to get to the Tolivers' camp.

What the two men did made no sense at all. I know I shot one of them and he was injured. The smart thing would have been to get far away as fast as possible. Why had they taken the time to kill Gene, then kidnap and rape his wife, before killing her?

We were in knee-deep water, pulling the canoes toward the plane two miles away. Rusty and Kim following along behind us. I'd so wanted this trip to be special for Kim. A trip full of the wonder and beauty that is south Florida. Instead, it turned into something a teenager might experience in Miami, or Chicago.

"It's not logical," Linda said, as if reading my mind. "They should have hightailed it right back to where they came from." Then thinking out loud, she muttered "Why stop and kill the Tolivers?"

"I was thinking the same thing," I replied as we trudged along, doing the stingray shuffle. "It's almost like they were targeted for some reason."

"I'll dig into his background when I get back to my office. Remember, he said he was a pilot, too. Whoever those men were, they might have thought your plane was his."

Except they escaped southeast, I thought. Instead of saying that, I said, "If they came hunting the Tolivers, they probably would have started in the Tampa area."

Linda looked over at me, her face conveying the serious cop look. Still beautiful in the late afternoon sun, but with a totally different purpose now. She came to the same conclusion I did.

"You're right. They went south. I'll check into his business dealings anyway. Maybe he has something going on in Miami."

When we got to the plane, I asked Linda to go up and check with the investigators to see if they'd learned anything else and the three of us started loading the plane. Linda returned as we were strapping the last canoe in place on the struts.

"They found a shell casing," she said. "A forty-five ACP, with one good print on it. The lead investigator thinks it was a retribution murder, but now I'm just not buying it."

"What's your cop instinct tell you?" Rusty asked.

She looked back up to where the body still lay, covered with the blanket. "It's a statement."

Then she turned to me. "They said we can take off any time we want."

I checked my watch. It was still an hour before high tide. I leaned against the starboard pontoon and tried to shove it with my knee. It didn't budge. "We're here for another hour."

We walked up the beach a little way so Gene's body was out of Kim's sight. She'd been quiet since we landed, hardly saying anything. I blamed myself. I'd have gladly given up the plane and everything in it, if I could only turn back time to spare her the trauma she'd experienced seeing him lying on the beach like that.

Sitting in the sand, we waited for the tide to float the *Island Hopper* so we could go home again. I thought about a book I'd read once by Thomas Wolfe. Published after his death, it was called *You Can't Go Home Again*. A single passage in that book haunted me for years. "I have to see a thing a thousand times before I see it once." I'd seen death many times and experienced the pain of losing people who I was very close to. This was my daughter's first experience with death and I was finally seeing it for the first time.

I hung my head. "I'm sorry I brought you here," I whispered.

Kim leaned on my shoulder. "Don't be, Dad. It's a beautiful place that can only be marred by evil."

I looked into my daughter's eyes and wondered how a child could become so wise in only seventeen years. I put my arm around her and pulled her close as a small wave reached up and touched our toes. The tide was full. It was time to go home.

Rusty pulled the heavy anchor out of the sand and all four of us pushed on the pontoons and struts, until the sand finally released its grasp and the *Hopper* floated free. As Rusty and I continued pushing her to deeper water, Linda and Kim climbed aboard. We slowly turned her toward deeper water and continued pushing until the water was up to Rusty's waist.

I ran through a quick preflight and started the big radial engine. Idling further out, I turned her into the light west wind and a moment later we were in the air, banking south toward Marathon as the sun neared the horizon. We arrived a half hour before sunset, talking very little during the thirty-minute flight.

CHAPTER SEVEN

I woke late on Monday morning. Sleep didn't come easily. Linda had to leave right after we got the plane tied down at the *Anchor* last night. Kim and I got back to the island well after dark, though I don't like being out on the water at night in the skiff.

It's not so much local boaters I worry about. It's just that even in winter we always seem to have a healthy mixture of alcohol, tourists, and rental watercraft. A bad combination anywhere, but throw in shallow water and coral outcroppings and it's a recipe for disaster. We have dozens of incidents with tourists wrecking rental boats in shoal waters and colliding with one another when neither has running lights on after dark. Hell, most of those jet skis don't even have lights.

Fortunately, we didn't have any trouble getting back to the island. I was worried how Kim would process the events on Cape Sable and suggested we sleep on the *Revenge*, where we'd be closer together. Kim insisted she was okay and went to the west side of the western bunkhouse. Carl had converted the one-room bunkhouse, creating two rooms. The west side of it was Chyrel's office and sleeping quarters for up to four women, while the other half remained the way it was, with bunks for eight men. I'd originally built them identical, but mirrored, with six sets of bunk beds inboard, a small open area outboard and doors at either end.

When sleep did finally come, it was filled with bad dreams. Dreams I hadn't had in years. Sometime after midnight I got up and went into the east bunkhouse. I keep a few bottles of good rum in a cupboard for whenever the team comes down and there's something to celebrate. I poured two fingers of Pusser's in a highball glass and went back out to the fire.

Tossing a few more pieces of driftwood on, I sat on part of the old coconut palm that once stood in the middle of the island and stared into the multihued flames. At least it was warmer than the last few nights. *Spring's just around the corner*, I thought and downed about half the rum.

Being a full-time dad wasn't something I was ready for. Hell, I wasn't ready for it when Eve was born and then Kim, just a few years later. The concern I was feeling for her wellbeing was akin to the way I'd once felt about the men under my command, but way more intense. Though she'd been with me for over four months and I knew she was a capable young woman, I still felt the need to "hold her hand while crossing the street."

The rum was taking effect and my senses were slightly dulled. Not enough to slow my reaction, but hopefully enough to let me get some sleep. There was something about the actions of the two guys in the boat this morning that I couldn't put a finger on.

Foregoing my warm bed in the house, I slept in my hammock by the fire pit. Close to the bunkhouses. I'd lost everyone I'd loved and because of my rash actions, I'd nearly lost Kim. *That's not gonna happen again*, I thought as I stretched out in the hammock.

Rising stiffly the next morning and looking around, I saw Carl working on the garden across the yard and realized that Charlie had already left to take the kids to the bus stop down on Big Pine Key. I looked over at the west bunkhouse and saw no movement. Had Kim gone with Charlie like she always does?

Noticing a carafe on the table with steam rising from it, I walked over and poured a cup from the stack on the tray. We never knew who or how many people might be here suddenly, so Charlie had taken to always having coffee and plenty of mugs on hand. I walked to the far side of the yard, where Carl was working.

"I'm disappointed, Jesse," Carl said as I approached. "Kim was all excited this morning, telling us what happened yesterday."

"I screwed the pooch, man."

"Ya think?" he said irritably, setting aside a water test kit and turning toward me. "You're a dad now, Jesse. A full-time dad. Ya gotta get your warrior instinct under control, man. What were you thinking charging through the brush like some kinda Rambo to confront men with guns and your little girl right behind you?"

He was a hundred percent right and I knew it. "I wasn't thinking, Carl. It was just like you said, instinct. And it might have gotten Kim hurt."

"Well, that's my 'Dad Lecture' for the day, old son. Want to start installing the foredeck beams and braces today?"

"You have them already?"

"Got 'em back yesterday."

"Let's get on it, then," I said, anxious to get my mind off of the events of the previous day.

The beams for the foredeck of the boat we were building had had to be made by a friend of Carl's, a professional carpenter on Big Pine. He also made their matching ribs several weeks earlier. The beams were made from single pieces of solid maple, with mortise-and-tenon joints to attach them to the ribs. Joinery was something we couldn't do here. Each rib was notched on the top of the inboard side to the depth of the mortise. The tenons on the beams would slide into the top of the mortise and then a cap rail, fitting the rib notches, would hold them in place, completing the mortise.

Before gluing anything, we test-fit each beam. If even one of them was too long, it would spread the ribs slightly and create a small gap in the next joint. Each one fit perfectly, no gaps anywhere. We used a strong marine-grade wood glue and, working quickly, we soon had each beam in place. In just an hour, we had all four beams in place and the cap rails glued to the tops of the ribs, with twenty clamps holding them until the glue set. We'd wait twenty-four hours, then remove the clamps and sand the joints smooth before laying the teak, mahogany, and maple deck planks. With any luck, we'd have the foredeck complete in a few more days.

Charlie and Kim returned while we were taking a break and Kim and I walked out onto the north pier with

Pescador. Sitting there, I asked her how she felt about what happened up on Cape Sable the previous day.

"I was scared," she said. "More scared for you than me, I guess. It was stupid for me to run after you."

"It was stupid of me to go running off," I said. "I'm sorry I put you in that situation."

"Why'd you do it? Pescador was just barking at a passing boat for all we knew. How'd you know it was bad people?"

"Tough question. I don't know, really. I've just always had sort of a sixth sense for trouble, I guess."

"When they started shooting, I was halfway up the bank and you were at the top. I dove behind a dead palm tree and when I looked up, you were standing at the top of the dune, shooting back. Then you went charging down the dune. Most people would have done what I did, but not you."

"Running away from danger is the most elemental, natural act of self-preservation. But I was trained for many years to move toward it. That's not natural and I should have thought ahead. I'm sorry."

She looked at me. "You couldn't foresee what happened."

"Look, everything that I've taught you these last several months—shooting, fighting, surviving on your own—those are all for your own self-defense. You've learned a lot, but you're a defensive asset, not offensive."

"Asset?"

"You know what I mean. I'm new at this whole 'dad' thing. I know fighting, strategy, and tactics. My actions could have gotten you killed."

"Everything turned out okay," she said. Then her face dropped and she added, "For us anyway."

"Want to talk about that?"

"Not much to talk about. I liked Mister and Missus Toliver and could tell that you liked them, too. I hate that it happened, but I don't think it would have been any different if we weren't there."

"Yeah, I liked them. They were easy people to like."

We talked some more, sitting there on the pier. She asked more questions about my past. Things I was reluctant to share with someone so young. Things that apparently still woke me in a cold sweat at night. Up to now, her questions about my past had been about my recent past. My social life, my late wife, my charters. I gave it some thought. She was more mature than her years and knew there was evil in the world. Wherever there's evil, there has to be good to fight it. It was like she said yesterday—evil can mar the most beautiful places in the world. I remember a stretch of beach in Somalia that looks a lot like Cape Sable, wild, natural, and untamed. Just across that particular dune, you run smack into the reality of war, famine, greed, and poverty. The cause of all that was evil and no good there to stop its spread.

I answered her questions. I wanted her to know about me, how my past had shaped me into the man I am today. It was noon before we finally left the pier.

Charlie was making fish sandwiches and I suddenly realized I was famished. The four of us ate quickly, then Kim and I washed the plates and glasses in seawater, rinsing them at the freshwater shower at the end of the pier. As we were walking back, the sat-phone in my pocket chirped. It was Linda.

"Go ahead," I told Kim and walked out to the end of the pier.

When I answered, Linda said, "They found the boat. It was stolen out of a marina on Long Key. The owner's happy he'll get it back, but pissed about all the bullet holes in it."

"Any clues about who the guys were?" She was quiet for a moment. "Linda, I'm involved in this, like it or not. I screwed up yesterday at the lake and put my daughter in danger. I know that. I don't want it to happen again."

"They found more prints," she said. "One matched the one on the shell casing they found on Cape Sable. Several prints also matched those found at half a dozen petty crime scenes in Miami. All gang related and unsolved. No match through IAFIS."

The FBI's Integrated Automated Fingerprint Identification System held digital records of the fingerprints of every criminal that had been charged with pretty much any crime. The computers could scan them in hours, something that used to take weeks to do by hand. Not getting a match only meant that the two guys had never been arrested before, at least not in the States. Matching them with other gang crimes in Miami was a step in the right direction, though. Petty crimes and drug dealing were one thing, but murder and rape would bring in the heavy hitters of law enforcement and investigation.

"What gang?" There was silence for a moment. "Linda, what gang?" I asked again.

"Zoe Pound," she finally replied. "DHS is taking lead in the investigation."

"Really?"

"One of the guys' prints came back connected to a suspected arms smuggling deal in Miami. One of Deuce's team is flying down to interview you. He didn't tell you?"

Just then, my phone chirped, telling me I had another call. When I saw that it was Deuce, I told Linda I'd call her back and ended the call, picking up Deuce.

When I answered, he said, "Is it possible for you to stay away from even the slightest bit of trouble?"

"I'm doing fine, Deuce," I said, ignoring him. "How's things in Homestead?"

"I'm sending Charity down there to do composites. You got the best look at the guys. She and another agent should arrive at the island in ten minutes."

"Ever stop to think I might not be on the island?" I said. "I do take shore leave now and then."

"Your phone is there and I'm talking to you on it."

Damned technology, I thought, looking at my phone.

"I'll try to give her the best description I can, but at two hundred feet, it won't be much. Who's coming with her?"

"Talk to you later, Jesse," he said and the connection ended.

As I started back to the foot of the pier, I heard the sound of a chopper coming in low over the water. Scanning the sky, I finally picked it out, approaching from the northeast. The pilot must have been here before, as the chopper was no more than twenty feet over the water. Noting the wind direction from the flags flying on their pole east of the two tables, the pilot soared out over the water beyond the pier and performed a steep climbing turn to bleed off speed, sure to put any passenger's stomachs in their throats. He came back in from downwind and landed without my help.

As the rotors slowed, Charity jumped from the pilot's seat, removing her flight helmet. She was letting her hair grow longer, I noticed. She'd always preferred a short hairstyle, but now her dark blond hair was nearly to her shoulders. She was tall, attractive, and in her late twenties. I should have known it was her by the maneuver. I'd seen her do it a few times over the last few months, training to board a moving boat from a chopper.

Charity Styles is a former Olympic swimmer and served as a medevac helicopter pilot in Afghanistan. She'd been captured by the Taliban and sexually assaulted for days before she was able to escape. She channeled the experience into her martial arts training and had been a Krav Maga instructor with Miami-Dade Police when Deuce recruited her into the DHS. She's also a gifted sketch artist.

Striding across the yard toward me, her long legs covered the distance quickly as the copilot's door opened and a man climbed down, carrying a small duffle bag around the front of the bird. It was Paul Bender. Deuce had mentioned a few months back that Bender was joining the team. He's a former Secret Service Agent, the head of the Presidential Protection Detail when President Bush visited the Keys many months ago. Close-cropped brown hair, graying at the temples, he was a stout, blocky sort of man, quick witted and a consummate professional.

"Good to see you again, Jesse," Charity said, then as always got straight to the point. "We can use Chyrel's office."

"You want to take me back up?" Bender asked Charity. "I think I left my stomach out over the water somewhere." Then looking around, he said, "So this is the famous island? I thought it'd be bigger, McDermitt."

"How are ya, Bender?" I asked, taking the hand he offered.

We started towards the bunkhouse as Kim came out of the Trents' house, angling toward us. "Doing well," Bender replied. "Nice to finally get to see this place. The guys talk about it like it's some kind of tropical nirvana."

We stopped as Kim reached us and I said, "Kim, you remember Charity Styles?"

"Nice to see you again, Kim," Charity said, shaking my daughter's hand. They'd met briefly before we went to the Bahamas in September.

"And this is Paul Bender. Paul, meet my daughter, Kim."

She shook hands with Bender, saying, "Nice to meet you, Mister Bender."

"We need to use the office for a little while," I explained.

"Sure, Dad. Let me grab a few things."

As she trotted toward the bunkhouse, Bender asked, "You have a daughter?"

"Two daughters. Kim's the youngest." We reached the bunkhouse as Kim was coming out with her rod and reel.

"Okay if I go fishing with Charlie?" she asked.

"Where are you going?"

"Raccoon Flats, for grunts." I never met a kid who didn't like catching grunts and Kim was no different. They actually make a grunting noise when you get them out of the water.

"Sure," I said. "Just keep an eye on the sky and don't be gone too long."

"We won't," she said and dashed off toward the main house and the boats.

The three of us entered the bunkhouse and Charity produced a sketch pad from her briefcase. Within half an hour, she had pretty good likenesses of the two men who killed the Tolivers. At least as good as I could provide.

Bender asked, "Any idea what kind of guns they had?"

"Only one of them was shooting. He had a Colt forty-five semiauto."

"You didn't get much of a look at the shooter, but you're sure about what kind of gun he had?"

"Yeah," I replied. "Investigators on the scene found a forty-five ACP casing, which confirmed what I already knew it was. I have one just like it."

"Doesn't surprise me," Bender said. When the President visited, Bender had been concerned about my having guns aboard the *Revenge*, but the Secretary of Homeland Security had smoothed things over.

"I gotta get back," Charity said, putting her sketch pad back in the briefcase after making a few copies on Chyrel's machine.

"You sure you can't stay for supper? Grunts and grits."

"No, I have to get these sketches to Deuce right away. Enjoy yourselves."

"Wait, what?"

"I'm staying here for the time being," Bender said.

"What the hell for?" I asked, as the three of us walked back out into the yard.

"Deuce thinks you might need extra security here," Charity said.

"Well, I don't. Nothing personal, Bender."

"Not an option," she said, cracking a rare smile. "His words."

A few minutes later, Charity lifted off and once clear of the low trees, dropped back down close to the water as she headed northeast.

"What exactly are grunts and grits?" Bender asked, as the sound of the chopper faded away. "Sounds painful."

"It's a southern thing."

"Okay, so where do I sleep?"

I jerked my thumb toward the other bunkhouse. "The east bunkhouse. There's a wood stove if it gets too cold. Supper's at sunset."

I walked over to the shed where Carl had disappeared earlier, leaving Bender on his own. What the hell was Deuce doing, anyway, sending a nursemaid down here? Did he know something I didn't? And why Bender? He's the new guy on the team and they're all up in Homestead training. These and many more questions ran through my mind as I walked into the shed.

"Who's the new guy?" Carl asked as he fitted the king plank down the center of the foredeck.

"Name's Bender. He used to be with the Secret Service and is part of Deuce's team now."

"Secret Service? Like the guys that protect the President?" He removed the king plank and worked the pointed end with a hand planer.

"Yeah, he was the head of the President's security detail last fall, when we took him fishing."

Carl handed me the idiot end of the plank and we fit it in place again. I held my end dead center on the deck beams, which were already scribed for the plank, while he eyeballed the fit at the forward end. Pulling it up and sliding it forward, he hit it a few times with a hand sander and pushed it back again.

"There," he said. "Perfect fit. Tomorrow, we'll start planking. I just wanted to get the king plank ready. The others will be a lot easier."

I examined the fit at the bow. "Nice work, Carl."

"If he's the new guy on Deuce's team, how come he's not up there with them?"

"Because they're on the pistol range for two days," Bender said, standing in the doorway.

I turned to face him. "What gives you an out on the range?"

"I'm a lousy instructor. Never could explain to someone how to shoot. I don't have the patience for it, I guess."

"Some of those guys are really good shooters, Bender."

He shrugged. "Not my call. I just do what I'm told."

"Did he give you any idea why he wanted you down here?"

"Not really," Bender replied. "But I pick things up. Those two guys you described to Charity? They're definitely with Zoe Pound, that Haitian gang in Miami. Deuce figures if you got a look at them, then they got a look at you. Something about the murder of that couple, though. It just doesn't sit right with me."

"You investigated a lot of murders with the Secret Service?" I asked him.

"Not a one," he replied. "I was with Chicago PD before being tapped for the Service ten years ago."

I appraised him with new eyes. "You were a detective in Chicago?"

"Homicide Division. Fifteen years."

I studied his eyes, noting for the first time the narrow lines at the corners. "You're older than you look," I remarked.

"I get that a lot. Twenty years as a Chicago cop and ten with the Service. I'm fifty-one. A little long in the tooth for the job in DC."

I would have guessed ten years younger. "So what about the murder doesn't sit right with you?"

"The fact that they committed it," Bender simply replied.

The same thing Linda and I had surmised. "I'm no investigator," I said as we walked back out into the yard. "Just an old warrior, but I understand human nature. They should have just hauled ass."

"But they didn't," Bender said as if punctuating the fact as we walked across the yard to the main house. "What's that?" he asked, pointing to the aquaculture system. "A vegetable garden?"

"Yeah, something like that. Why do you think those guys attacked the Tolivers?"

"You got any coffee up there?" he asked, nodding toward the house.

"Come on up," I replied, turning toward the rear steps leading up to the deck.

I gave him the nickel tour of the house and poured a thermos from the fresh pot on the burner. "Mugs are down on the boat."

"What boat?" he asked as we walked back out onto the deck. "I didn't see any boat when we flew over."

At the bottom of the front steps, I opened the door to the dockage area and let him step through ahead of me. The overhead light clicked on automatically with a motion detector and Bender let out a low whistle as he walked along the dock toward the stern of the *Revenge*. "I wondered where you kept this." Pointing to the far side of the dockage he asked, "Is that the other boat we took out fishing?"

I stepped over the transom into the cockpit of the *Revenge* and opened the hatch, switching on the interior lights. "Yeah, that's *El Cazador*. Come aboard."

"You painted this one? It used to be all white."

"New boat," I replied. "The first *Revenge* was blown out of the water last fall."

Glancing across the cockpit as he stepped down, he asked, "And the Cigarette?"

"Deuce confiscated it in a drug bust," I replied, getting two mugs from the overhead cabinet. "You were saying about the murder?"

"Criminals usually try to run when they're caught in the act," he said, taking a drink of the coffee. "Mmm, that's good java. Anyway, I don't recall ever encountering a witness to a crime who said that the bad guys ran and then stopped to commit an even worse crime. Never. Not once. Like you said, they should have hauled ass once you discovered them trying to break into your plane. Hey, where is your plane, anyway?"

"Down in Marathon, at Rusty's place."

"Deuce's father-in-law? The big guy? You guys are tight?"

"I met Julie just a few days after she was born. Rusty and I were best man at each other's weddings."

Bender looked into his coffee for a moment as he sat down at the settee. When he looked up, he said, "Both you and Agent Rosales said they headed straight away from the beach for almost a mile, before suddenly turning and making a beeline for the victims' camp. That strike you as odd? I mean, aside from stopping to commit another crime, the suddenness of the change in direction."

"Yeah, now that you mention it."

"Almost like they reported to someone that they'd failed at one thing and were told to do something else. Something worse."

"Linda thinks the Tolivers were targeted and we were mistaken for them."

"Linda? Oh, Agent Rosales." He seemed to mull that over, looking for answers in his coffee mug. "Or maybe you were the target from the get-go and they were told to show you what might happen to you."

"Me? I don't have many connections with Miami and none to any gang activity."

"You've never popped up on Zoe Pound's radar?"

"Never even heard of them until the other day."

"Like I said, I hear things. A word here, a word there. Little connections are made in this old cop's brain," he said, tapping a finger to his temple. "You're connected somehow and killing that couple was a statement."

A statement? Directed at who? Me? I had zero connections with any kind of gang or drug activity. How was this connected to Zoe Pound's recent blowing up of the patch reefs in the backcountry? What did Bender suspect, if anything? A lot of questions. He was a hard one to read, probably a pretty good poker player.

"Want to go for a boat ride?" I asked Bender suddenly.

He grinned. "I think Deuce knows you'll go poking around and that's why he sent me down here. Will your kid be alright here?"

I thought about that a moment. If this gang was trying to get my attention, to draw me out for some reason, they didn't know where I lived. The trees on the sides of the house and all around the whole island shielded the house from view, except from the south, and then you had to be pretty close to see it from that direction. It was real skinny water down there. Anyone not familiar with the cuts and channels was sure to run aground before they got close enough to see the house.

"Yeah, she's safe here," I decided.

"Where we going?"

"To see a lobsterman."

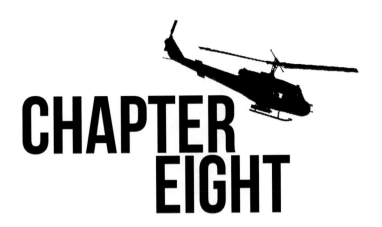

CHAPTER EIGHT

I called Kim's cell, even though I knew she wouldn't have a signal over on Raccoon Flats. The *Cazador* drew too much water to get out there, so I left her a message telling her I'd be back by supper, knowing she'd get it when she got in range of a cell tower when they returned.

While Bender might have been a hotshot detective in the Windy City and would step in front of a bullet for the President if he had to, he wasn't much of a waterman. I had to tell him which end of the mooring lines to untie while I started the boat's big diesel engine.

Clicking the button on the fob, I released the catch and the door slowly swung open. As we idled out from under the house, I clicked the other button to pull the door closed again.

Turning into Harbor Channel, I pushed the throttle and the big five-hundred-and-seventy-five-horse Cat engine lifted the thirty-foot boat up on plane with ease.

I kept close to Turtlecrawl Bank, then turned south into East Bahia Honda Channel toward Marathon. Approaching John Sawyer Bank, I turned east, following the coastline of Vaca Key.

I'd never been to Vince O'Hare's house, but I knew his boat and figured it'd be easy enough to find on Grassy Key. Angling closer to shore, I scanned the few structures along the bay side and finally spotted the antenna mast of his boat above the mangroves. He flew a tattered Jolly Roger on the mast, thumbing his nose at society.

As I idled up to his dock, it was obvious this was the place. I'd heard others describe it as a cross between a junkyard and a slum. The dock didn't look all that promising, leaning slightly toward the east, with a number of planks missing in the deck. The rusted hulks of a half dozen old cars, trucks and boats, along with broken lobster traps, floats, and other detritus, littered the yard. The house just beyond the dock didn't even look habitable. It too was leaning a little, but the other way from the dock. The whole scene looked like a painting by Salvador Dali. The roof was corrugated metal, but looked to be almost completely covered with surface rust. A window in the middle was open, with tattered and yellowing drapes hanging out of it.

As I shut down the engine and started to tie up to the dock, I heard a screen door slam. "What the hell you think you're doing, boy?" a loud baritone voice shouted with menace.

Before I could answer, O'Hare was striding down the dock. The shotgun in his hands had my full attention. Seeing it, Bender started to reach for the pistol I'd noticed earlier was holstered at the small of his back.

"Stand down," I whispered, as I continued to tie off.

"I asked you a question, boy!"

Snubbing the line to the rotting piling, I leaped quickly up to the dock. O'Hare leveled the deck sweeper at my midsection.

"Name's McDermitt," I said. "Come to talk to you about what happened on Bullard Bank."

He studied me a second then glanced at Bender. "You a cop?"

"No," I replied, before Bender could say anything. "I run a charter business."

"Wasn't talking to you, McDermitt," the old man spat. "I know who the hell you are."

"This is Paul Bender," I said, my eyes never leaving his. "He's a friend of mine. We just wanted to talk to you about what happened to your traps."

He looked back at me and finally lowered the shotgun. "Step over," he said as he dropped easily to the deck of his lobster boat and opened a cooler. Taking three cans of Budweiser out, he tossed one to me and another to Bender, who now stood on the dock with me. I dropped down to the deck of the boat and cracked open the cold beer, drinking down half of it, as Bender clumsily stepped down into the boat beside me.

"What you wanna know?" O'Hare asked as he leaned the shotgun against the starboard rail.

"How close to the bank do you run your traps?" I asked.

"Not close. Five to eight feet of water on the west side. Why?"

I'd fished Bullard Bank quite a few times. The bottom on the west side was mostly turtle grass, with a few small patch reefs on the east side.

"How many traps were destroyed?"

"Six," O'Hare replied. "Spaced out ten or twelve feet and every one blown the fuck apart."

A line of traps sixty to seventy feet long on a grassy bottom?

"You see many greens when you pull?" I had an idea.

"Sometimes," he replied. "Them turtles mostly eat grass. Lobsters like the grass for the turtle shit. What the hell's all this about? Why's a charter man interested in some busted-up lobster pots?"

I ignored his questions. "Ever see anyone around there?"

"All the time. Good grouper spot."

"I mean people that look out of place."

O'Hare leaned on the gunwale and scratched at his beard. I'd only met the man a couple times. His face was tanned and wrinkled like old leather, his wild and scraggly shoulder-length hair almost all white, as was the quarter-inch stubble of beard on his face.

He was at least in his seventies, probably older. But his pale blue eyes were bright and clear, moving quickly, seeing everything. Probably a powerful man in his youth, he still had a look of menace. Nearly six feet tall, broad shouldered and lean. He hadn't survived all these years by being soft.

"Seen some colored boys cruising by there not long ago," he said thoughtfully. "Not that it's strange seeing colored folks, but they weren't dressed like most you see around here."

"How do you mean?" Bender asked.

O'Hare looked at him, as if seeing him for the first time. "You're a cop, ain't you boy?"

Bender once more started to say something, but I interrupted him again. "He used to be. Way up in Chicago a long time ago."

"Folks round here, if they got any sense, keep their skin covered in the sun. Even colored folks. These boys weren't from round here. They wore city clothes."

"City clothes?" Bender asked once we were heading away from O'Hare's dock. "Colored boys? What's he, some kind of inbred hillbilly transplanted to the tropics?"

"You're wearing city clothes," I said, pointing out his running shoes and polo shirt.

He looked down at what he was wearing and what I was wearing, which was my usual khaki cargo pants, denim work shirt, and bare feet, now that it had warmed up.

"So what was all that racist crap about? Don't tell me you condone that?"

"Colored? Have you ever left the States, Bender? I mean aside from protecting the President?"

"What's your point?"

"Black people are only called African-American here in the States. In most of the Caribbean, people are mixed ancestry. He wasn't talking about black men. In the Basin, the accepted term for mixed race is colored. And he called both you and me a boy. The guy's probably in his eighties—everyone's a boy to him."

"You're saying that guy's not racist?"

"His late wife was a Creole woman from the Antilles. Very beautiful, I heard. Ebony skin and bright green eyes. It was after she died that he started hitting the bottle. That was twenty some years ago as the story goes. By all accounts, he stays pretty sober these days. It's just that without her, he's rudderless, nothing to work for. Just an old guy marking his days."

I thought about my little island as we made our way through Vaca Cut and into the Atlantic. Would that be me sometime in the future? A wrinkled, drunk hermit, sitting on a trash-covered island and counting the days? I turned into the channel to the *Rusty Anchor* and we were soon tied off in Deuce and Julie's slip.

"You talked to Vince O'Hare?" Rusty asked over a beer after I told him about our visit to Grassy Key.

"He's not so bad," I said.

"Tell that to the three tourists he put in Fisherman's Hospital a month ago. Yeah, they had a beat down coming, but O'Hare damned near killed 'em."

"What's the latest you heard locally?" I asked.

"Heard from a guy I know up on Matecumbe," Rusty said. "There was two more reefs hit just yesterday. Arsenic and Pontoon Banks. He said the explosions could be heard from his dock at Caloosa Cove and another boater, who was untying his dink when he heard it, took off to see what was going on and got shot at for his trouble."

"How'd you hear about that?" Bender asked. "That information hasn't been released to the press."

"We have our own press down here," Rusty said, glancing sideways at the former cop.

"You mean the media does know?"

"A different kind of press, Bender," I said. "Neighbors talking to one another. I guess you never lived in a small town, either."

"Anyway," Rusty began, "Folks are starting to wise up and arm themselves while on the water. The guy in the dink started shooting back and suddenly a half dozen boats took off outta the marina, guns blazing. The bad guys hauled ass." Then as he picked up a glass and started polishing it, he added, "One of 'em's arm was in a sling." Rusty looked up from his polishing and grinned.

I showed him copies of the sketches Charity had done. "Think you can get one of these up there and see if the guy in the dinghy recognizes these guys?"

"Sure, I can scan 'em and email 'em to the marina right now. Won't take but a sec." Rusty took the two printouts and stepped into his office behind the bar.

"You can?" I asked through the open door.

"You ever visited a place called the twenty-first century?" Bender asked me with a cockeyed grin, jabbing me back for my comments on his lack of experience down here. "Almost all business is done online."

The machine in Rusty's office continued to make a whirring sound for a few minutes then Rusty came back out. "Emailed those to every marina, boat ramp, bar, and dock from Key West to Key Largo." Handing me a stack of about twenty copies, he added, "Thought you might want a few yourself."

After leaving the *Anchor*, Bender and I looped around the west end of Boot Key, under the Seven Mile Bridge, and continued north. *Civilians shooting back with handguns at thugs with automatic weapons?* I thought. *This is only going to get worse and end bad.*

"How long you lived down here, McDermitt?" Bender asked, yanking me from my train of thought.

I glanced sideways at him and raised an eyebrow.

"Okay, so, yeah, I know the answer. Just making conversation."

Having been fully vetted by the Secret Service while Bender had been the head of the Presidential Protection Detail, I knew that he knew everything there was to know about me. I also knew that cops don't usually make detective and get tapped by the Secret Service without having a pretty good memory.

"Your type doesn't make idle conversation," I said. "Ask your question."

"These guys have an agenda," he began. "There's always an agenda. It festers out of motivation and finally ends in action. Well, with the exception of psychopaths, but they aren't joiners, and this is a group agenda, controlled by one or more people. Find the agenda and we find them."

"Cop one oh one?" I asked. "That's just plain old common sense."

"So what's the agenda? We can rule out money. They could drop all the grenades at Hawthorne on every reef up and down the Keys and not make more money from the fish than from a single day of drug sales."

He was talking about Hawthorne Army Depot in western Nevada, the largest ammunition storage facility in the world. And he was right, money wouldn't be on the agenda for what this gang of ecoterrorists was doing.

"Ruling out money," I said, "what's the second biggest motivator for criminals?" He stared straight ahead for a moment as we powered north in East Bahia Honda Channel.

"Who said they're criminals? It could be terrorism."

I glanced over at him. "I read up on this gang. Their motivation is greed and they're ruthless, but I don't think they're terrorists."

"Me either," he conceded, with a downward shake of his head, as if pushing a file to the side and down out of the way. "Besides greed, there are dozens of other reasons people commit crimes. Politics, love, hate, pleasure, hunger, curiosity, significance, and self-preservation, just to name some of the top few."

"Politics?"

"Not the same as terrorists, more of a revenge angle, maybe. More likely than terrorism and we have to consider it a possibility, being that Zoe Pound is a Haitian gang. I just don't see the connection to blowing up fish. Love, hate, and pleasure could be lumped together as an emotional motivation. What kind of response is all this creating?"

"Fear," I replied. "And people fighting back. The people who live here and pull their livelihood from the sea every day are tough people. They don't take being pushed around for very long. There was serious consideration a few years back about secession. The Keys are considered by many that live here as the Conch Republic. Fighting back's not gonna end well, if you ask me."

"I agree," Bender said as we made a wide, sweeping turn to the west between Sideboard and Bullfrog Banks, straightening out with the Harbor Key light dead ahead and the entrance to Harbor Channel before it. "Civilians fighting back is a side reaction, I think. They might not even have considered the possibility. My guess is that this gang has a more specific reaction in mind."

"You're jumping around. I thought we were talking about an agenda."

"An agenda resulting from motivation," he corrected me. "Motivation resulting in specific actions that causes a specific reaction. If we're talking an emotional motivation, like love or hate, which can be interchangeable at times, then the agenda would be designed to get a specific reaction, usually from one certain individual. Like when a father raises his voice and the child stops instantly."

"Who?" I asked.

"If whoever is pulling the strings wanted to find someone down here, it wouldn't be that hard, would it?" Bender asked, as I slowly brought the *Cazador* down off plane in Harbor Channel.

"Island people are tight," I replied. "But with the right resources and connections, I guess anything's possible."

"What if they don't have those resources and connections? What if they are comfortable with a more predatory means of finding someone?"

"Like a hunter?" I asked.

"Or a trapper," he replied. "Set a trap and wait."

"Ah, you think what they're doing is meant to draw someone out? Seriously, there are easier ways to find someone down here."

"There is one person down here that would be a little harder to find. One that's known for his love of the sea and the environment."

My southern dock came into view, jutting out from the mangroves ahead of us. It's a low dock built on the spoils from dredging my little channel, so really only the posts were visible from more than a hundred yards away and only when approaching from this direction. We came to the southerly curve in Harbor Channel and I made the tighter turn to the north into my narrow channel. That's when my deck railing and the upper part of my house came into view above the trees, to starboard. Only the big doors to the dock area were partly visible through a tunnel of mangroves.

As we idled up the short channel along the dock, I pressed the fob on the key chain, and the eastern door below the house started to slowly swing open. One of the giant spring-loaded hinges squeaked in protest and I made a mental note to spray it with some WD-40.

"Me?" I asked with a laugh, reversing the engine. "There's harder people to find down here. Besides, who would want to find me?"

I brought the *Cazador* to a stop alongside the turning basin and toggled the bow thruster to spin her around, before backing under the house to the docks.

Bender stepped up to the dock with the bowline in his hand and looked down at me while tying it off. "Sonny Beech."

CHAPTER NINE

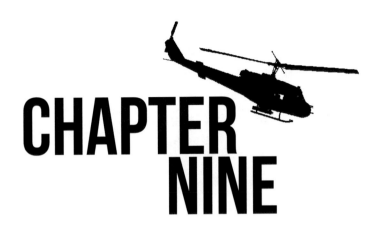

"What do you mean he escaped?" I asked Deuce over the satellite video connection on my laptop. "Nobody's ever escaped from Gitmo."

"He had help from the outside," Deuce replied. "A diversionary attack by a group of radicals on the west side, near the detainee barracks. He was being moved, along with another American detainee. One Marine killed and another injured."

Damn, I thought.

"Radicals? Can you be a little less vague?"

"We think it was Haitian nationals."

"You gotta be kidding," I said. "Zoe Pound?"

"It doesn't sound like it," Deuce replied. "These people were trained militants. It was a coordinated attack carried out with precision. They were in and out in a matter of minutes. Cuban forces turned a blind eye and Beech disappeared into the jungle with the militants. Witnesses said he didn't appear to be going voluntarily."

"Haitian militants kidnapped a Gitmo detainee," I mumbled. "Story at eleven."

"There won't be a story," Deuce said flatly.

"Well, at least there's that."

"I gotta go," Deuce said. "If I learn any more, I'll let you know."

The screen went blank and I closed the laptop. Stepping down into the cockpit and up to the dock, I heard the sound of an outboard approaching. The noise was muffled somewhat by the big doors, but I recognized it as the Grady-White. Charlie and Kim returning from their fishing excursion.

I went down to the dock to meet them. As Charlie idled the twenty-foot center console up toward the dock, Kim stood in the bow, ready to toss me a line. My daughter had melded naturally to the island lifestyle. Her hair was lighter, streaked by the salt and sun. Her skin was darker even though she took great care to not overdo the exposure, like what she was wearing now, a long-sleeved lightweight denim shirt and long-billed fishing cap. She was a natural boat handler, preferring the skiff and fishing the backcountry, but could handle the *Revenge* almost as well as me.

"How'd it go?" I asked as Kim tossed me the line and I tied it off to a dock cleat.

"Half filled the cooler," Kim replied.

"She caught most of them," Charlie chimed in, opening the cooler.

Carl came up behind me and peered down. "Now that's a good day's catch. Hand it up, honey. I'll clean 'em."

Carl Junior and Patty scampered past us with Pescador bounding after them, barking. Charlie followed behind them, all headed to the other dock on the far side of the island to swim and clean up before supper.

"Do we have time for a swim, Dad?" Kim asked.

I glanced toward the sky, raising my head so that the sun shone fully on my face from the southwest. "Yeah, a short one. Half a mile?"

"Would you like to go, Mister Bender?" she asked over my shoulder. *I must be losing it*, I thought, having not heard him approach.

Bender declined, so Carl drafted him to help clean what looked to be about fifty grunts and a few red snapper.

"I talked to Eve yesterday," Kim said after an invigorating swim. When we got back to the pier the sun was near the horizon, so we quickly bathed in seawater, rinsed in the cold-water dock shower and sat huddled under two big heavy towels, watching the sunset.

"That's good. How are they doing?" Eve was married to a lawyer in Miami and gave birth to my first grandchild just a few weeks ago. Last September, her husband and his father had become involved with some activities that were over the line, legally speaking. He had his chain yanked hard and both he and his father were now following a much better path. And doing better for it I gathered, based on what Kim told me, after the two of them talked.

"She wants to bring the baby to meet his grandfather."

What the hell! I'm not old enough to be a grandfather.

"Here?" I asked.

"Yeah, here on the island."

"When?"

"She asked if next weekend would be alright. She sounds anxious to meet you too."

I'd been blindsided meeting Kim for the first time after not being a part of their lives for so long. I'd received a phone call at the *Anchor* one evening and met her five minutes later. Now I had five days to prepare myself. I wasn't real sure which was better—slowly peeling the bandage off, or just yanking it.

"This weekend, huh," I said.

"You're nervous?"

I shivered a little, wrapped inside the heavy towel. Whether it was just the cold air or something else, I couldn't be sure.

"Have you thought about what you want him to call you?" Kim asked.

"Who?"

"Your grandson, Dad," she replied, nudging my shoulder with hers. "It's the only time in your life that you get to choose what someone else will call you for the rest of your life."

"Granddad, I guess. I never really thought about it."

"You don't look like a 'Granddad.' And that's, like, plain. Maybe Pops?"

I looked over at her and arched an eyebrow.

"What, then?"

"Pappy," I said without thinking. Gregory Boyington was a WWII Marine ace in the South Pacific. He'd received the Medal of Honor for his actions and his men had called him Gramps. Though he was only in his early thirties at the time, he was ten years older than the most senior pilot under his command. Later, he was popularized by the nickname Pappy in a song, and much later in a TV series starring Robert Conrad. Gramps didn't suit me, but Pappy did. He was a man I looked up to.

"I like that," Kim said. "I told her I'd pick them up at Old Wooden Bridge Marina at noon on Saturday."

CHAPTER TEN

After breakfast the next morning, Kim went with Charlie as she always does, to take the kids down to Big Pine to catch their school bus. From there, they were going shopping.

I told Bender we'd be making a run up to Miami—I had some things to pick up. A friend up there by the name of Anthony Schultz has an old-school style cabinet shop and he'd called last night to tell me my storage compartments were ready to pick up.

My old boat, the one blown out of the water on the Bahama Banks, had two secret compartments built into the engine room. They were actually false bottoms under the couch and settee with a hidden panel in the overhead of the engine room. Inside one of the compartments was a specially-built stand that fit into the fighting chair mount in the cockpit. The other held the M-2 .50 caliber machine gun that mounted on the stand, along with a spare barrel. We'd recovered them while diving the wreck and now Anthony had finished the precision-fitted storage lockers based on drawings I'd given him two months ago.

Going down the steps to the dock area after Kim and Charlie had left, I said to Bender, "While we're up there I want to stop in and see Linda. Maybe you can catch a cab and visit Deuce to see what else he's turned up."

"What's the address where she works? I'll arrange a car."

"Arrange a car?" I asked as I opened the door to the dock area.

"Yeah," he replied. "You're not the only one with contacts in Miami."

He started around to the far side of the docks, where the smaller boats were tied up, and I turned up the middle dock, stepping down into the cockpit of the Cigarette boat and placing the cooler I'd brought on the deck behind the right seat.

"We're taking this one," I said, clicking the fob to release the big door on the west side.

"Just to the *Rusty Anchor*, right? You're not planning to fly up there in that old airplane, are you?"

"We're taking this all the way to Miami," I replied with a grin. "No speed limits out on the blue."

While I started the two powerful engines, Bender untied the lines fore and aft and stepped down into the boat, mumbling, "Do you even have a car?" I engaged both gear selectors in forward as he sat down in the contoured custom passenger seat.

"Yeah, I have a car," I replied. Then, pointing to the eight-gauge cluster in front of him, I said, "Keep an eye on the gauges while we're underway. The top four are manifold temperature and ammeter for both engines. Below that are oil pressure and oil temperature for both. Those are also displayed on my side."

He glanced at all the gauges on both his side and my side and nodded, seeing that all eight gauges on his side were also on mine, along with the tach, knot meter, and trim indicators.

"Four eyes are better than two?"

"Yeah," I replied, idling out into Harbor Channel and turning toward Upper Harbor Key. "These boats are built for racing. Once we get offshore we'll be running about eighty knots and I'll be busy watching the water and working the throttles and trim. Both engines should have the same readings on all four sets of gauges. If one is just a little different, you'll notice it easily and can warn me."

Nudging the throttles, the stern dropped and the long, narrow bow lifted as the boat slowly came up onto the step. I kept the speed below thirty knots until we were out of Harbor Channel and headed south. Now in deeper water, I shoved the throttles further, bringing the speed up to sixty knots.

The wind and water were calm, barely a ripple on the surface, and the go-fast boat seemed to be running perfectly, her bow sniffing out the open water and a steady, low roar from her powerful engines drifting off astern. A thin line of disturbed water ahead and just to starboard meant another boat had passed through East Bahia Honda Channel in the last twenty or thirty minutes.

"You're going fishing," Bender shouted over the wind. It was a statement of fact, not a question.

"This ain't exactly a fishing boat," I said, feigning ignorance.

"No, it's the boat DHS impounded from Sonny Beech."

I glanced over at him out of the corner of my eye. He was pushed back in the seat, his knees slightly bent and his feet braced against the bulkhead under the gauge console. Every few seconds, he glanced down at the gauges. I shoved the throttles to the stops and the engines responded, shrieking to an ear-splitting roar as the boat surged forward, pinning us both into the seats.

Minutes later, I saw Bender lean over to see the knotmeter as we shot through the gap in the old bridge at ninety knots. A second later, we went under the high arch of the new Seven Mile Bridge and out into the open Atlantic. I throttled back a little. Ninety knots was insane on flat water, but with the low rollers coming in from the east, we'd be taking them on the port bow until we turned east into them.

Bender leaned toward me and said, "This boat's highly recognizable."

"Yep."

"If Beech is in Miami, he'll find out through the grapevine that his old boat is at the downtown marina?"

"We call it the Coconut Telegraph. Actually, the boat'll be at the dock right next door to his old warehouse on the Miami River."

What I didn't say, but he'd probably already surmised, was that it would be at the same warehouse where I, along with Deuce and his door kickers, had found my wife after she'd been raped and beaten. And where I'd nearly been stabbed to death.

"What are you not telling me?" Bender asked, sensing more to the story. *Maybe he didn't know everything*, I thought.

"Just going with your hunch, Bender. If someone's looking for you, the easiest way to find out who it is would be to get found. If the Haitians are looking for me, and Beech was kidnapped out of Gitmo by Haitians, then finding him should tell us why they're looking for me."

I began the turn when we reached the ten-fathom line, well outside the reef. Headed due east into the low, well-spaced rollers, I bumped the speed up to just over eighty-five knots and adjusted the trim so we didn't get too much air under the hull, coming off the tops of the waves.

He took out his cellphone and asked for the name of the place we were going to dock. I gave it to him and he typed it into an email, sent it, and put his phone back in his shirt pocket. Less than two minutes later, he took it out again and, after looking at the screen for a few seconds, put it away once more.

"Where you go, I go," he said. "A car will be waiting at Trans Global for both of us."

I glanced over at him and asked, "Who's supplying the car?"

"Not who you think," Bender replied. "A private contractor I know."

I handed him my phone and told him to text Linda with the message, "Meet me for lunch at Area 31?" He sent it and a few minutes later handed it back and said, "She said 'okay.'"

We rode in silence for the next hour and were soon entering the mouth of the Miami River, downtown Miami's skyline soaring up from the edge of the water. The river isn't so much a river anymore, not in the truest sense of the word. Oh, it still has its source, deep in the Everglades, and the mouth of the river is still in the same place, where it was once settled by the Tequesta, but it's now the home of the bustling Port of Miami. Today, once you pass through the heart of the city and Little Havana, which grew up around it, it's been dredged, diked, and straightened for most of its six-mile course, following a perfectly straight line northwest alongside US-27.

Go-fast boats aren't an uncommon sight in Miami, and most are custom painted just like this one and easy to tell one from another. I'd removed the name from the transom a year ago, changing it from *Beech's Knot Cream* to *Fire in the Hull*, but the distinctive paint scheme was just like it had been when Beech owned it, canary yellow, cerulean blue, and lime green over a fire-engine-red hull. A gaudier boat in Miami would be hard to find.

Arriving at the Trans Global docks, I reversed the engines and backed into a canal on the south side of the river, tying off at their little-used small boat dock under an overhanging bald cypress, one of the few still standing in Miami.

Anthony's woodworking shop was just a few blocks from here, so after checking in with a friend at Trans Global, we walked out front, where a black Escalade sat idling in the parking lot.

Both front doors opened and two tall black men got out. The driver stayed by the door and the passenger came around the hood and extended his hand to Bender. Bender shook hands and pulled the man into a shoulder bump.

Turning to me, Bender said, "Jesse, I'd like you to meet David Norton, former Chicago narco detective. David, this is Jesse McDermitt."

At first glance, the man had appeared younger than he did now that he was closer. *And vaguely familiar*, I thought as he removed his dark wraparound sunglasses and turned toward me. Both he and the driver were tall and fit looking. Both with shaved heads, wearing dark slacks and jackets over button-down shirts. Norton, the taller of the two, was just under my six foot three.

"Pleasure to meet you again, Gunny," he said, showing a perfect set of white teeth. "You don't remember me, do you?"

"You two know each other?" Bender asked.

I shook Norton's hand and said, "I remember an armorer named David Norton. Three Six?"

He nodded and turned to Bender. "I worked in the armory at Lejeune. Third Battalion, Sixth Marines, must be eleven or twelve years ago. During a weapons inspection, the Gunny here chewed my ass over a speck of dirt on a weapon we rarely employed anymore."

"So, being an asshole has been a lifetime occupation for you?" Bender asked me.

"Yeah, pretty much," I replied. "Bet you never got a gig on an inspection after that, did you, Norton?"

"Absolutely not," he replied, with a wide grin. "You guys have us for as long as you need. Where to?"

Walking to the car, I said, "First stop is just a few blocks away, Northwest Fourteenth Street and Thirty-First Avenue."

I climbed in the back with Bender, who explained that Norton had helped him out on a case just before he'd left Chicago to join the Secret Service in Washington.

"I didn't help him out," Norton corrected. "I was a flat-foot on the south side who just happened to be in the right place at the right time. Bender was about to leave and didn't want to be wrapped up in all the paperwork and testimony. He dumped the whole case on me and made out like I'd solved it all on my own."

"You had all the answers," Bender said. "You just didn't know the questions yet."

As we backed out of the parking lot and crossed the short bridge where River Drive becomes Delaware Parkway, Norton turned in his seat, placing a beefy arm on the console and said, "So, what's the case you guys are on?"

Before Bender could say anything, I said, "Case? We're just picking up a couple of boxes a friend made in his cabinet shop."

Norton looked at me, then Bender, his mouth widening into a big, toothy grin. "Uh-huh."

I looked at Bender and got an almost imperceptible nod. Truth is, I know Bender's a good judge of people. So am I. Which is why I took his nod to mean he trusted Norton.

"What do you know about anything Zoe Pound is involved in lately? Do you know Sonny Beech?"

"Beech?" Norton responded, his curiosity piqued. "He disappeared without a trace about a year ago. Word on the street at the time said there was a shooting. Right back there at what used to be his warehouse. Nobody I know has spoken his name since summer. Zoe Pound has gone to ground lately. About two weeks now, no headlines, no shootings, no heads on pikes. They're still running drugs and a little prostitution on the side, but for the most part they've been really quiet since the beheading thing."

Just then, the driver, who had yet to say a word, pulled into a small crushed-shell parking lot and said, "Schultz Cabinets?"

"This is the place," I said, opening the door. "Open the back, would ya?"

Bender and Norton climbed out of the Escalade as well. I made a quick survey of the area. Two empty lots, overgrown and fenced, and a shuttered business on the opposite corner. Though I could hear activity two blocks away on the riverfront, it was quiet here, no cars on the streets or people walking around.

A neighborhood in decline, I thought. I noticed the other two men made the same quick survey. We walked toward the front door of the business, while the driver opened the back doors of the big SUV and stood by them, also looking around the area. It becomes habit in some occupations, I guess.

"Hey, Jesse," Anthony said from behind the worn countertop as I stepped in and removed my sunglasses.

The front room was small, with a large window facing the lot that was covered with heavy steel bars. Inside were a few displays of handmade wooden cabinets. Anthony specialized in making odd-size and shape cabinets which couldn't be found at the big box stores. He had a lot of customers who were amateur boat builders and restorers, as well as the usual kitchen remodelers and builders.

Standing up to his full six-foot-six height, he came around the counter. He always reminded me of an old buzzard, his head cocked forward on narrow shoulders, with a long, hooked nose being the most prominent feature after his height. Though he was three inches taller than me, I probably had sixty pounds on the man. He still wore his hair in a crew cut, the remnants of a past in the Army. He was mostly gray, except for a little around his collar.

"Hi, Anthony," I said, taking the hand he offered. "Good to see you again. How's Anne?"

"Mean as a cottonmouth and twice as deadly," he said, glancing at Bender and Norton.

"These are a couple of friends, Paul and David. Guys, meet Anthony Schultz, the best boat cabinetmaker in all of Miami."

They shook hands all around and Anthony invited us back to the shop. Walking through a heavy door, the dim sound of work being performed that could barely be heard in the lobby now grew louder.

We passed through another door at the end of the hall into the workshop, where Anthony's crew of four young men were busy cutting, milling, and sanding, the sound of power tools filling my ears. The noise and smell of the wood dust reminded me of my childhood, helping Pap build boats.

"Yours are over here," Anthony said, leading us to a corner where two narrow cabinets stood on end, each having a full-length door, which was coated in white fiberglass, like a boat's hull. I touched the spot where I knew a hidden latch in the back would release the door. It opened smoothly, with the quiet hiss of hydraulically dampened spring-loaded hinges. The interior revealed a cloth-lined recess that would fit the titanium stand now stored in the rafters of one of the bunkhouses. I inspected it closely, using a micrometer and yardstick that Anthony handed me. It was perfect.

I opened the other one in the same manner and caught Norton's eyes widening just a fraction of an inch. Bender didn't seem to notice anything unusual. That, or he was very good at hiding it. I inspected the clearances on this one even closer and found it to be as flawless as the first.

"Great work, man," I said as I closed the second cabinet's door.

"Easy when I get such detailed drawings," Anthony replied. "If you ever get tired of fishing, you could make a decent wage in the design field."

I looked out over the work area. His workers were all young men, one black, two Hispanic, and one white. All were busy performing various tasks, learning the basics from a master carpenter. It was a good trade to learn. A skill that might get them out of the neighborhood. One day, one of them might be Anthony's competition, but he never let that stop him from sharing his talents and secrets.

"Nobody touched these but me," Anthony said, drawing my attention away from the workshop.

"Thanks, I appreciate that." I handed him a small roll of hundred-dollar bills, which disappeared into the front pocket of his coveralls without being counted.

The four of us each took an end of the two cabinets and carried them out to the waiting Escalade. Loading them and closing the doors, I turned to Anthony. "Y'all come down sometime. Rusty has a cook that performs magic with some Jamaican spices and herbs."

"I heard about him," Anthony said, bobbing his head on a long skinny neck. "Even up here in the big city. We'll have to do that."

"It's all true, brother," I said, shaking his hand. "Thanks again."

We climbed in the car and Norton immediately turned in his seat and looked at me. "I recognized what that's for, you know."

"Well, now I'll just have to kill you," I said with a grin.

"What?" Bender asked.

"Need to know," I told him. "And right now, you don't."

"Where to?" Norton said, through his big toothy grin.

I glanced at my watch and said, "The Epic. How about you join me for lunch, Norton. Bender here has to go see someone down in Homestead."

Ten minutes after unloading the cabinets onto the boat, the driver dropped me and Norton at the luxurious Epic Hotel on the corner of Biscayne and Brickell, then pulled back out onto US-1 with Bender in the front seat, headed south.

"Who are we meeting?" Norton asked.

"An FDLE agent by the name of Linda Rosales. Know her?"

"Heard about her," he replied, as we walked across the expansive patio area to the front doors. "Good cop. You always meet cops in such high-priced places?"

"Only when I'm in Miami," I replied. In the lobby, we boarded the elevator and I pressed the button for the sixteenth floor. We rode up in silence with two couples.

We got out at the terrace bar of Area 31 Restaurant and I looked around and found Linda sitting at a table off to the side. Not the best view of the waterfront, but a commanding view of the rest of the terrace. She had her hair pulled back in a loose ponytail and was wearing a light grey skirt and jacket, with a pale red, almost pink blouse beneath it. *And a Glock*, I thought.

I introduced Norton to her as we sat down. A waiter was ready to take our drink orders, leaving a menu for each of us. I set mine aside as Linda leaned over and gave me a kiss.

"So what brings the Old Man of the Sea to the big city?"

Norton grinned at the public display.

I just smiled and said, "A boat."

She laughed at my joke. A hearty laugh. "Good one," she said.

The waiter arrived and we placed our orders. Linda ordered crudo, a local Cuban dish of grouper ceviche. Norton went for a hamburger and I got my usual blackened mahi sandwich.

After the waiter left, I said, "I thought you two ought to meet. David here is a private contractor and has a close ear to the ground, I think." Linda looked at me, then at Norton.

"Actually, Agent Rosales, I do mostly security work."

"Just Linda," she said with a disarming smile. "What kind of security?"

"Some alarm and surveillance work and the occasional private tactical training, but mostly my team is contracted to provide protection for high-value clients. Usually privately, but sometimes the city offers up a contract."

"Tell me what you've learned about Zoe Pound," I said.

"I have to use the restroom," she said, standing up. "Give me just a minute."

As Norton and I sat back down, we both watched her walk across the terrace. "She'll have my complete background on her Blackberry in two minutes, won't she?" Norton said.

"Anything you want kept secret?" I asked. My offering up Norton to Linda as an informant in the way I did got the desired results. She'd let me know anything she learned about the man.

He grinned and replied, "I'm an open book, Gunny."

CHAPTER ELEVEN

You served together?" Linda asked after we'd finished lunch and come down to the parking lot, where she'd left her gray Ford sedan. "That's how you know each other?"

"Yes and no," I replied. "We'd known each other briefly in the Corps a dozen years ago. He knows Bender from when they were both Chicago cops. Bender's the new guy I told you about on Deuce's team. Former Secret Service."

"Well, Norton checked out clean," she said, glancing at him waiting for me by the idling Escalade. "Real clean, in fact. His company was hired by the State several times and he worked alongside one of my counterparts a few years ago." Then she leaned in close enough that I could smell the scent of her hair. *Frangipani*, I thought, while she whispered seductively, "Do you have to go back today?"

Do I? The invitation was more than a little tempting.

"Yeah," I finally stammered. "Kim's alone on the island."

She smiled and said, "This weekend, then?"

This weekend, I thought. *Shit, Eve's bringing her husband and my grandson.*

"My other daughter and her family are coming down," I blurted out. Then recovering and not wanting her to think I didn't want her to come, I added, "We'll be a bit crowded on the island."

"They can have the house and we'll sleep in that luxurious stateroom of yours."

We both wanted it, that I was sure of. I gazed into her smoky, dark eyes and said, "Yeah, I think that's a good idea."

It must have surprised her a bit. "Really?"

"Why not?" I said. "But we promise each other that no matter what happens, we stay friends."

Getting in the back seat of the Escalade with Bender, he started to fill me in on what he'd learned from Deuce. Like a hound on a scent trail, he began baying in short sentences before we even backed out of the parking spot. "A go-fast boat was used. They took Beech to Haiti. Deuce doesn't think there's any connection. Not to Zoe Pound, anyway."

"There might not be," I said thoughtfully, trying to slow his roll just a little. "All we have is conjecture and even that's pretty thin. The only connection is if your hunch is right, and I'm not convinced they're trying to draw me out."

"Then why did you choose to come here in Beech's Cigarette?"

Norton suddenly turned around in his seat. "You have Beech's boat?"

I glared at Bender and then glanced to Norton. "It's not his anymore." Turning back to Bender, I added, "Fishing, remember?"

I shrugged it off after that. No sense in bucking the wind. Norton was good, I felt comfortable in trusting him, more based on my gut instinct than Linda's summary in the parking lot. It was obvious that Bender did. I just don't like a lot of people knowing about my private life.

"What'd you learn from Rosales?" Bender asked.

"FDLE has a lead on one of the guys that killed the Tolivers," I said after a moment.

"How come we don't have that lead?"

"This is sounding more and more interesting," Norton said from the front seat, climbing higher on the seat back. "Where to now?"

"Back to Trans Global," I replied. I reached into my pocket and got a card from a little metal case I always carry and handed it to Norton. "You hear anything at all about Beech, or Zoe Pound, call me, okay?"

"You got it, Gunny. And thanks for the intro to Agent Rosales."

When we crossed over the little bridge just before Trans Global's parking lot, I glanced down to where the boat was tied up. There was a black woman standing beside it, as if waiting.

We got out of the SUV and said our goodbyes, promising to stay in touch. I still hadn't learned the driver's name. When they pulled out of the lot, Bender and I walked around the side of the building to the gate and took the path down to the dock.

The woman still stood there as we walked out onto the dock. She was wearing a blue skirt that hung loosely to her ankles and a flower print blouse in hues of bright orange, yellow, and blue, with a long beige coat hanging open.

Smiling at us as we approached, I saw that she was an older woman, probably in her sixties, with a broad, flat nose and high cheekbones. Her skin was the color of ebony and only slightly lined, and her hair was a wild mane of long braids. Not dreads like some island men wear, but each braid carefully crafted and hanging below her shoulders. She was probably very beautiful in her youth. It was her eyes that got my attention, though. She had clear, pale blue eyes that darted around. When she fixed those eyes on me, a charge of electricity seemed to course through my body.

"Dis is yer boat," she said, in that singsong accent of the people of the Caribbean. But it wasn't a question.

I nodded and she continued, "I am Margaret, from Trinidad."

She said it as though it was meant to explain something more, but I'm sure I'd never met her before. Her smile never wavered.

"I feel a sense of honor and order in yer presence," she said. "It comforts me." Then, her smile fading somewhat, she continued, "I know dat dis boat has come in search of someone. But, you are both di seeker and di sought?"

I looked at Bender, who'd already untied the stern line and come to stand beside me, holding the boat against the dock with the line.

"I'm Jesse, from Marathon."

Her eyes sparkled at the reply and her smile widened again. Her eyes never left mine and in them I saw a quiet honesty, a life spent helping others. Visions seemed to dance into and out of my consciousness, like memories.

"Di mon you seek is not here, but will be soon. Di woman you seek is here now."

An island mystic, I thought. Most would dismiss these people as frauds and con artists, but I'd been around the islands some and had seen a lot that couldn't be explained rationally.

"I'm not looking for a woman," I responded.

"Ya are, ya just don know it yet, mon. Move with caution, Jesse from Marathon. Der is danger here for you. Di woman is a dark one. Not on di outside like me, but dark on di inside. She di one dat will control di mon you seek."

"A dark woman?"

"Light on di outside, but a dark heart on di inside. Ya turned yer back on her once and her heart is darker for you now because a dat. Do not make dat mistake again." Then she turned and started toward the back of the warehouse. "Have a good day, Mistah Jesse and Mistah Polease-mon." The cackling laughter followed her around the corner of the building.

I dropped into the cockpit and started the engines as Bender untied the bow line and shoved the boat away from the dock before stepping aboard.

"What the hell was that all about?" Bender asked as we turned out of the canal into the river. An island freighter about a hundred feet long was just ahead of us, its big diesel chugging and belching gray smoke. "And what made her think I'm a cop?"

"No idea about the first," I replied. "A fortune-teller of some kind, I'd guess. As to her knowing you're a cop? You are a cop. You look like a cop, you act like a cop, and you talk like a cop. Nothing mystical about that deduction."

"Don't tell me you believe in that shit."

I turned and looked at him. "I've seen a lot more unbelievable things than that, Bender."

It took twenty minutes to reach Biscayne Bay, due to the small freighter's very slow speed. I had to shift to neutral and drift, then idle forward for a minute before doing it again, as we slowly followed the freighter downstream. While we drifted along, Bender asked questions about living in the Keys and daily life on the island.

Since he probably knew anyway, I told him about the inheritance I'd received from Pap after he died. He'd worked hard all his life, building his own architectural firm. On weekends, he worked equally hard, building boats and selling them. Being his only heir, I inherited everything.

Mam passed away in her sleep a few years before I retired from the Corps and Pap had her cremated. I was overseas at the time, and he waited until I could get home to spread her ashes on the Peace River. He died not long after that and I added his ashes to hers.

A little more than a year later, I retired from the Corps after twenty years of service. With the inheritance and having saved a good bit during my years in the Corps, I could have pretty much done anything I wanted. With no family to speak of and no plans, I ended up in Marathon, where I wound up buying and living on a boat, then buying my island.

Though I'm sure he already knew these things, he nodded appropriately as I told him. Passing under the Metrorail Bridge, Bender said under his breath, "Don't be obvious, but check the pier at two o'clock."

I rose up in the seat slightly, looking over the port bow at the water, as if checking for obstacles, and then did the same to starboard with my head, but my eyes scoured the docks and piers on that side, shielded behind dark wraparound sunglasses.

Three dark-skinned young black men stood by the seawall in a mostly vacant parking lot. All three wore variations of the same gang-style clothes, sagging pants or shorts and caps turned crooked, and one had on a tee shirt emblazoned with the Zoe Pound logo in bright yellow, red, green, and blue. The parking lot they occupied was where the river widens slightly before curving to the left.

"Got 'em," I said. "See any guns?"

"No, but they're armed."

"Don't get jumpy," I said. "Liberty City is their turf, several blocks north of here. They're in Little Havana and won't start anything if they know what's good for them."

I took the engines out of gear and drifted in the wake of the freighter as it slowed to make the last two turns before the river's waters flowed into Biscayne Bay.

We both dropped any pretense of watching covertly and stood up, looking directly at the three young men. I engaged the engines and we slowly idled past the parking lot, looking straight at them all the way. They stared straight back at us as well. Only when we'd put the stern toward them did one of the thugs say something to his cohorts, and all three turned around and left the seawall.

We cleared the mouth of the river a few minutes later, with the freighter chugging due east in Fisherman's Channel, toward Government Cut and the open Atlantic. I turned south and brought the boat up on plane, heading to the fuel dock at Rickenbacker Marina.

While I was fueling up, Bender paced the dock. Finally, he stopped and said, "Scouting us out, or making a statement?"

"I'm starting to lean a little more in favor of your hunch," I said. "We got a bite while the boat sat there at the dock."

"Maybe that voodoo lady tipped them?"

"I don't think so," I said, climbing up to the dock. I went over to the Dockmaster and handed him my bank card for the fuel.

Back at the boat, I started the engines as Bender untied the lines. Minutes later, we passed under the bridge at the north end of Key Biscayne into open water. I turned south and kept the speed down to sixty knots with the quartering sea.

"Let's assume for a minute," Bender began, "that what Zoe Pound is doing in the backcountry really is connected to Beech in some way other than drawing you out of hiding."

"I'm not in hiding," I said. *I just don't like hanging around people I don't know and have no need to impress*, I thought.

"Intentional or not, you'd be difficult to find on any given day, but let's put that aside. What possible connection could there be between a group of Haitians springing Beech from Gitmo and a Haitian gang in Miami blowing up reefs?"

I thought about it as we bounced over the wave tops off Elliot Key, following the long, sweeping curve of islands, bays, and sandbars to the southwest.

Beech was a loan shark, primarily. He ran a few drugs on the sides, some gambling and prostitution, and he also owned a junkyard for some reason. Nothing Deuce had dug up about the man pointed to any environmental concern, and when it comes to the environment, that's not real high on any kind of gang's agenda.

"The lack of either having an environmental connection seems like the only connection."

"Exactly," Bender said. "So the activity can't possibly be about a bunch of inner city gangbangers suddenly turning tree hugger."

"I pretty much ruled that out from the start," I chortled.

"The activity, but not the motivation. If there isn't a connection to you, then how could the gang and Beech be connected?"

"I can't think of any," I said.

"Then that only leaves two things. It's just a coincidence or they are, in fact, trying to lure you out."

I've never subscribed to the idea of a series of coincidental random events being the causation of something. A butterfly flapping its wings on the Ivory Coast doesn't create a hurricane that destroys a city in Texas. In my mind, coincidence is ruled out. *He's right*, I thought. *Zoe Pound wants to find me. But why?*

"An outside influence," I finally said. "A wild card that we don't know anything about."

We glanced at each other and Bender said, "Now you're starting to think like a cop. Somebody pulling strings to make both happen? How many enemies do you have?"

"We'd both have to retire and sit in a couple of rockers for the rest of our lives to cover that. But the vast majority of them never knew my name and are thousands of miles away."

He laughed. "Why don't I find that hard to believe? What about the recent past?"

"Not so long a list," I replied. "Since I left the Corps, I've tried to lead a normal, quiet life."

"Until your wife was killed. What about before that?"

I turned slightly south to avoid a fishing boat trawling the deeper waters. "A few dust-ups, mostly slight altercations in bars, nothing important." *Nothing that would have a gang of Miami thugs come looking for me*, I thought.

Off northern Key Largo, I pushed the throttles forward, increasing speed to eighty-five knots now that we had a more following sea. I wanted to get back to the island and my mind was already plotting the fastest route.

A few minutes later, I turned toward the western tip of Long Key and the low bridge over Channel Two. We had plenty of clearance, but I slowed as we neared it anyway. Fishermen used the old bridge, which was closed to vehicles, and divers dove the pilings.

Once clear of the bridge, I pushed the throttles to the stops and roared across the placid waters of Florida Bay at over ninety knots, with a twenty-foot-high rooster tail trailing behind us. The shortcut across Florida Bay cut half an hour, and running flat out cut another half hour.

Less than two hours after fueling up in Miami, we idled into the channel toward my house. I was relieved to see Pescador laying on the pier and breathed a sigh of relief when he stood up, stretched his forelegs and began wagging his big tail. Everything was just as I'd left it.

"You were worried," Bender said as I backed the boat up to the center dock, next to the *Revenge*. "If my hunch is right, it's warranted."

"I'm still not a hundred percent on that," I said. "But barring another plausible explanation, that's the way I'm going to play it."

Later, as Kim and I sat on the north pier with Pescador, watching the sun set once again over a perfectly clear horizon, I explained Bender's theory to her.

"Want me to call Eve and see if Nick knows anything about this gang?" she asked.

"No," I replied a bit too quickly. "I mean, I doubt he'd know anything that Deuce wouldn't be able to dig up."

"You're probably right. Can I ask you something?" I nodded and she continued. "Why do you do it?"

"Why do I do what?"

"Going back to when you first joined the Marines. Then after that, getting involved in other people's fights against bad people. It's caused you so much pain. Why do you do it?"

I thought about that a moment. Taking on the bullies of the world ever since I was little, I'd never questioned myself as to why. In grade school, I'd stepped between the playground bullies and whoever they were picking on.

As a Marine, I found it natural to fight against those who did harm to others. Since leaving the Corps almost eight years ago, I'd tried to maintain my privacy here on my little piece of paradise, but there was always some schoolyard bully that needed to have his chain yanked.

Though it had cost me a lot, personally, I knew I was good at yanking chains.

"Ever hear of an Irishman named Edmund Burke?" I asked.

"I've heard the name before."

"You're Irish, lass," I said in my best brogue accent. "You should learn more about your clan. He was a politician in old Britain before and during the Revolutionary War. I don't remember much about him, can't recall what his position in government was, but he was for peace above everything else. Not peace by force or capitulation, but true peace where all people lived in harmony. I remember that much from a lesson in grade school. Knowing that true peace was only possible in a world full of good people, he said something along the lines of the only thing needed for evil to win is for good men to do nothing."

"But why you?"

"What? You don't think I'm a good man?"

"No, not that. Why does it have to be a certain good man?"

"Not sure if I can answer that, kiddo. When a man sees evil things being done to good people he has two choices. Intercede or ignore. Ignoring evil only makes evil stronger. I guess it just goes against my nature to see good people get walked over."

We watched as the sun slipped its bond with the sky and sank into the shallows beyond Raccoon Key, leaving Neptune to watch over its retreat.

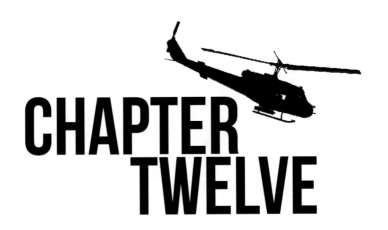

CHAPTER TWELVE

Waking the next morning, my first thought was that in just three days, I'd be meeting my grandson for the first time. And my oldest daughter. And her husband, who had once tried to have me killed. Not directly, but the men he sent would have done it without a second thought.

Late last summer, Doc and his wife found a clue to a long-buried treasure and we decided to try to locate it. What we didn't know was that the agent who represented Florida in an earlier and much smaller treasure find, a guy named Chase Conner, had planted a bug on my boat during the sale of some gold bars to the Florida Historical Society. Conner wanted the new treasure find, but didn't know where to look. He brought in some muscle in the form of a Croatian mobster who was represented by my son-in-law's father's law firm. The father and son attorneys, Alfredo and Nick Maggio, sent four people, two men and two women, to try to take the treasure from us. One of the two women was Linda, working undercover. Their plans failed and Deuce's boss showed the two attorneys the error of their ways, in deference to the younger Maggio being married to my daughter. A few weeks after it happened, I asked Stockwell why he went out on a limb like that. He shrugged it off with a comment about maybe one day needing a legal asset.

Neither Kim nor Eve knew about any of this and I preferred it stay that way. *But how will I deal with someone who wanted me dead being here on my island?* I wondered.

Pouring a cup of coffee and heading toward the door, I heard a muffled boom to the east. I dashed out the door, leaving the mug on the counter in the galley. Racing around the deck toward the south side of the house, I heard heavy footfalls on the rear steps. I stopped and looked back as Bender bounded up the last few steps, gun drawn.

"It came from the east," I said and continued around the front of the house, to the east end of the deck. The same trees that blocked the view of the house partially blocked the view of Harbor Channel angling away to the northeast. It did nothing to stop the sound of the voices and the outboard motor. They were close. Too close.

"Where are they?" Bender whispered.

"Out near the end of Harbor Channel. We can catch them, if you're game." I started back to the door to get my Sig.

"No," Bender said forcefully. "A defensive perimeter only."

I stopped in my tracks and turned around, furious. "Defense? Are you outta your fucking mind?"

"You have innocent people here!"

Kim, I thought, calming and thinking rationally in an instant. "You're right, Bender. What the hell was I thinking?"

"You weren't. You were reacting."

"Come on," I said. "We need more firepower than that Beretta and my Sig."

As we rounded the corner of the house, Kim was coming up the steps, with Carl not far behind.

"Kim, get in the house," I ordered. "Carl, go get Charlie and the kids and join her."

Carl raced back down the steps and Kim joined me at the front steps leading down to the dock area. "What's going on, Dad?"

"Get inside. My Sig's on the nightstand by my bed. Bad people are close."

"You're not going to—"

"No," I interrupted her. "We're going to go down where we can see them better and just watch. With luck, they won't come up the channel and see the house."

"And if they do?"

"We'll heed Mister Burke's advice," I replied. "But only as a last resort."

With that, Bender and I went down the steps and I leaped aboard the *Revenge*, making my way forward, with Bender right behind me.

"You any good with a rifle?" I asked him.

"Better with a pistol, but okay."

I punched in the code on the digital lock below the end of the bunk in my stateroom and it raised up with a hiss from the hydraulic arms. I grabbed two long fly rod cases and lowered the bunk back down. Stepping around the bunk, I opened the small dresser beside it and took out

Pap's old Colt 1911, checked the magazine and racked the slide, chambering the first of eight .45 caliber rounds.

Flipping open the first case, I took out one of my M-40 sniper rifles and inserted a fully loaded magazine. Handing it to Bender, I said, "The scope's zeroed at two hundred yards. At that distance, a man's body will fill it." I opened the second case and slapped a loaded magazine in its twin and said, "Head through the mangroves beside the vegetable tanks. There's a trail that leads to a dead palm tree near the water that you can use for cover. I'll be at the south side of the house, down by the turning basin."

We met Kim and Carl and his family at the top of the steps. I handed Pap's Colt to Carl and said, "There's only one way into the bedroom. Defend your family if you have to."

Carl took the gun and pulled the slide back a little, ensuring that a round was already chambered. He did this with practiced ease, but I'd never known him to carry a gun.

"Be careful, Dad," Kim said.

"Open the window above the headboard. You won't be able to see much from there, but you can hear and the deck doesn't go around to that side."

When they were inside and the door was locked, Bender and I went down the rear steps and split up. I worked my way through the tangled undergrowth along the east side of the house, my bedroom window directly above and Pescador at my heels. Reaching the water, we slogged as quietly as possible through the shallows at the edge of the small turning basin toward a spit that stuck out into the water just east of it.

Reaching the narrow spit, I crouched low and made my way up to a few ancient coral rocks that I'd piled there while digging the basin. Peering over the crack between two rocks, I could see not one, but two boats. The nearest was an eighteen-foot bowrider that was adrift on the south side of Harbor Channel with two men on board. It was the other boat that caught my attention, though. A shrimp trawler just coming into the channel at full speed, Vince O'Hare's unmistakable skull and bones flying from the antenna mast.

Flipping open the covers on the Unertl scope, I rested my left arm on the top of the rocks and looked through the scope, just as one of the men on the bowrider threw something overboard. A second later, a geyser of water shot up from where he'd thrown it, followed by the same muffled boom a second after that.

I looked beyond them at the trawler. O'Hare was at the helm inside the small wheelhouse, his shotgun protruding from the open windscreen. *You idiot*, I thought as I watched his ancient trawler charging like a decrepit elephant toward the two men on the boat, who hadn't yet seen him.

The two men looked out of place on the water. Their boat was in danger of grounding on the shallows and they seemed oblivious to the fact. Both were young black men, dressed like they were from the city. Gang clothes. They didn't look like the same two who'd murdered the Tolivers, though.

They suddenly looked up toward the trawler as the boom of O'Hare's shotgun got their attention. I chambered a round.

O'Hare's trawler was bearing down on them at its top speed of about twelve knots. The men could easily have started their engine and outrun the old trawler, but instead they both pulled out handguns and started shooting toward it.

They were within easy range and I'd have no problem putting both of them down. *Not my circus, not my monkeys*, I thought. In the Corps, I taught my snipers that there would be times when they'd be tempted to take a shot to stop something from happening. It had happened to me. Once. Sure, it stopped the immediate action that my spotter and I were witnessing, a young boy being beaten by a Somali warlord, but it gave away our approximate location and drew the attention of the dead warlord's men. The boy's body was found an hour later, mutilated and discarded by the new warlord. Another one always steps up. I taught my Marines that unless it had a direct impact on the mission, it was usually better to let it play out than risk giving away their position.

This wasn't Mogadishu, and this was my circus. I ignored my own advice. As I sighted in carefully, my mind picked up on subtle variances and changes in the air. I looked through the scope with my right eye, and my left, having noted wind direction and speed on the water, slowly closed. I took another breath and slowly released it as my right index fingertip found the trigger and slowly squeezed, reaching the three pounds of pressure required to release the firing pin. The resulting explosion inside the casing of the round created over sixty thousand pounds per square inch of pressure in a microsecond, forcing the steel-jacketed projectile from the barrel.

Spiraling as it flew through the air, the bullet was affected all along its path by both air and temperature, all of which my mind took into account in an instant, before pulling the trigger. Covering the two hundred yards to the target in a quarter of a second, the steel jacketed projectile penetrated and destroyed everything in its path upon impact.

My first shot hit the engine on the bowrider about where I expected the aluminum block to be. I quickly chambered a second round and sighted in again. The heavy boom of my rifle's first shot got the attention of the two men on the bowrider, who both turned away from the immediate threat of the approaching trawler. I watched as they scanned the water between them and me, not knowing where the shot had come from.

I fired again, giving away my position. Their handguns were useless at this range, yet they started shooting at me anyway, their rounds falling well short and hitting the water a hundred feet in front of me. My second shot shattered the casing of the shifter and throttle handles, mounted on the gunwale. If the first round hadn't disabled the engine, there'd be no way they could control it now. I chambered a third round.

Just then, O'Hare's trawler rode up onto the shallows on its own bow wave and crashed into the starboard bow of the much smaller boat. The impact and the wall of water the trawler pushed ahead of it rolled the small boat, sending the two occupants flying into the shallows and swamping the bowrider. O'Hare's boat stumbled and lurched forward, grounding on the shallow sandbar, its prop churning up a foamy froth at the stern.

I watched as O'Hare shut down the engines and came out of the wheelhouse with his shotgun, moving faster than a man of his age ought to be able. He ran out onto the pulpit and shouldered the shotgun. I was sure he'd shoot both men if given the chance.

My third shot impacted the leading edge of the pulpit, sending shards of wood into O'Hare's lower legs. He looked up and scanned the horizon in my direction.

"Don't shoot them!" I heard Bender yell from his position just a few yards to my north.

The two men slowly stood up in the shallow water as O'Hare covered them. I could see him saying something, but the distance was too great for the words to carry. He motioned them to the port rail of his trawler, now hard aground and listing to that side.

With the two men moving toward the far side of O'Hare's boat and him covering them with his shotgun, I quickly made my way back to the house.

I met Bender there and we went up the rear steps two at a time, Pescador bounding ahead of us. I banged on the door and hollered, "All clear!"

A second later, Carl cracked the door a little, Pap's old Colt clearly visible. He breathed a sigh of relief and said, "What's happening?"

"Looks like a couple of Zoe Pound thugs had a run in with O'Hare. He's got them aboard his trawler." I turned to Bender and said, "Let's go see what we can do."

Kim took the rifle from Bender, but I kept mine with me. I told Pescador to stay with Kim and a few minutes later, we were idling out from under the house aboard the *Cazador*, headed to where the big trawler was stuck on the sand. The tide was rising, so if her back wasn't broken from the impact or her hull wasn't holed, we should be able to get her off in just a few hours. If she was holed, the tide would fill the hull almost to the decks, flooding the engine room. If that happened, recovery and repair would cost more than the old tub was worth. *Hope he's got insurance*, I thought, bringing *Cazador* up on plane.

A few minutes later, I eased the *Cazador* up onto the sandbar next to the trawler and tossed an anchor as far as I could. Leaving a good twenty feet of line dangling from the bow, I tied it off and jumped from the bow into the knee-deep water. Pulling the line tight, I jammed the flukes into the sand before retrieving my rifle from the bow.

O'Hare had thrown a rope ladder off the starboard side and when I climbed up I found him sitting on a lobster trap on the trawler's work deck. The two thugs, hands tied behind them, sat uncomfortably on the deck, their backs against the rough planks of the gunwale.

"You fuckin' shot me," O'Hare said flatly, pulling bloody wood splinters out of his right calf.

"No, if I'd shot you, you'd be dead."

He looked over the two captives' heads at their boat, with the ruined control box and engine, then looked at the rifle I held cradled in my left arm. "Yeah, I suppose you're right. I wasn't gonna kill 'em, though."

I looked at the two men—boys, really, as neither looked to be more than twenty. "Who are you and what are you doing up here?"

One of them looked up at me with venom in his eyes, then seemed to recognize me and smiled. *"N' a gen kè sere, gwo moun."*

"English, motherfucker!" O'Hare boomed, standing over them and leveling his shotgun at the speaker's head. "Do you speak it?"

"I have English," the second boy said, raising his head for the first time. He grinned at me as well, ignoring the shotgun aimed at his head, and said, "You in big trouble, man."

O'Hare turned to me, lowering his deck sweeper. "You know these clowns?"

"Never seen them before in my life," I replied honestly. "But, I think I know someone who'd like to get to know them. Come with me, Bender."

We walked up to the foredeck, leaving O'Hare to watch the two thugs. "We need to call Deuce," Bender said.

"Just what I was thinking. He'll need a place to interrogate them, though, and I have a thought. You being new to the team, you might not approve, so I want to go over what's gonna happen before it does."

I explained what I had in mind and after a few minutes he surprisingly agreed. "I'm no Boy Scout, McDermitt. If shortcuts can keep people safe, I'm all in."

I took my sat-phone out of my pocket and called Deuce. After he answered, I said, "We need a dust-off, Deuce. Two of Zoe Pound's men were caught red-handed near my island by one of the local lobstermen. Do you have access to a chopper with pontoons?"

"Why can't we land at your island?" he asked.

"We're not at the island, but close by. My daughter's there and we're not going to take these guys to it."

"What'd you have in mind?"

I explained my plan to him and he chuckled softly. "Yeah, I'd kinda like to go there myself. Where should Charity pick you up?"

"About two hundred yards east of my house, you can't miss us. And bring Tony and Kumar." Tony Jacobs used to be part of Deuce's SEAL team and came over to DHS with him. I remember a different interrogation some time ago, when Tony's actions really put the fear of God into the subject. Kumar Sayef is also one of Deuce's team members and a former Delta Force special operator and linguist specializing in many Arabic dialects. Not that his linguistic skills would be needed. It was his appearance that would work.

I ended the call and told Bender to send O'Hare up here and then I called Kim. She answered on the first ring, firing off several questions. I explained that everything was alright and shortly Deuce would arrive by chopper and we were going to take the two guys in, but I'd be back within an hour to help get O'Hare off the sandbar. A partial lie, but I didn't want her to know our real plans.

She didn't like it, but I assured her everything was fine, as O'Hare approached. I ended the call and said to O'Hare, "I have someone coming that's going to take these guys off your hands."

"Cops?"

"Not exactly," I said with a grin. "I think you'll approve of what we have in mind. Your boat's stuck here for at least three more hours, until the tide comes up enough that I can pull you off that sand. Wanna go with us for the interrogation? It's not far."

He thought about it a moment and said, "Boy, I fought in the Second World War, you know. Battle of the Bulge.

Never got a scratch. Fought in Korea, too. Still carry a bullet in my shoulder from them Commie bastards. I been all around the Caribbean since then and I know a thing or two about island folks. These two are just trash, nothin' more."

"Yeah, you might be right. But, I bet you'd agree that they're superstitious trash."

His head came around and looked me straight in the eyes as a slow smile spread across his face. "You got some bad juju for them two?"

I grinned back at him. "That I do. Hope you're not the squeamish type, O'Hare. Sorry about those splinters, I didn't know what you were gonna do."

He chortled as he looked back at the two men trussed up against his gunwale. "Naw, I ain't squeamish. And these little nicks? Hell, I got worse injuries than that from just screwin' a Trinidad hooker."

After explaining the details of my idea, we went back and sat on lobster traps, drinking coffee and basically ignoring the two thugs trussed up on the deck. They whispered a word or two to one another in Haitian Creole. Apparently O'Hare spoke it as well, leaning toward me and whispering, "Bigger guy said he's scared."

I remembered the stories about O'Hare's Creole wife, Constance. *Of course he speaks the language*, I thought. All the more reason for him to come along.

"That's good," I said with a grin, looking up to the northeast, where I was just beginning to hear the heavy whump of a helicopter's blades beating the dense air at low altitude.

"Let's get 'em up and in the water," I said loudly as I stood up.

"How you want to do this?" Bender asked.

"Like this," I replied, grabbing the smaller young man by the collar of his shirt and yanking him to his feet. He seemed to be the leader of the two. I took two long strides toward the transom, dragging him stumbling along behind me, then I heaved him over the transom head first. His legs kicked frantically as he screamed, splashing into the shallow water on his side.

Bender and O'Hare did the same thing with the other guy and both quickly struggled to their feet in the knee-deep water, spitting and shouting obscenities in two languages.

The chopper came in low and fast. I looked up at the Jolly Roger on the antenna mount and knew that Charity would fly over and execute her signature climbing turn to burn off speed and land into the easterly breeze.

The chopper was a black Bell 206L Long Ranger, with dark tinted windows, no markings at all, and black pontoons in place of the normal skids. Charity landed it in the shallower water just south of where we stood by the stern of O'Hare's boat, which I saw for the first time was named *Constance*. There was no need for Charity to anchor the bird. Once it settled it was in contact with the bottom.

As the engine shut down and the blades slowed, three doors opened and Deuce got out of the copilot's side and came around the nose, sloshing through the water in jeans, combat boots and tropical khaki shirt. Tony and Kumar stepped down onto the float from the back seat on the near side. The way they were dressed didn't escape the attention of the two prisoners. Tony and Kumar both wore the traditional Islamic men's hijab and all three wore full beards, which was something new. Then I remembered Deuce's boss saying that the team should appear less military and blend in more.

Tony and Kumar stood off to the side of the chopper as Deuce came forward. He shook my hand and I introduced him to O'Hare. Deuce walked over to the wrecked bowrider and looked in the cockpit area. There was a wooden box on the deck and he lifted the lid. Inside were a half dozen American-made hand grenades.

Deuce walked over to the two captives and said, "Where did you get these?"

The smaller man looked at Deuce and spat out, "*Zafè ou!*"

O'Hare stepped toward the man and in a menacing growl surprised him by saying in Creole, "*Nonm lan reponn!*"

The shock was evident in both thugs' faces.

"How much for the little one?" Kumar shouted in thickly accented English.

I'd seen this before and barely suppressed a grin. Kumar spoke with almost no accent at all, unless need be. By cursing Deuce in his native language, the smaller thug started their little improv skit. Deuce and his tight-knit team of former Special Ops, police, and intelligence people worked on extracting information through the perceived notion that something worse than death might be in store for the subject. One of his people, the team's weapons handler, was once a stage actress and worked with the other members on how to improvise and create a perceived notion to cause an emotional response by any means necessary.

I'd told Deuce that the kid could speak English, and I was certain he in turn had given this information to his people to use against the two gangbangers if a chance presented itself.

The notion Kumar created with that simple question had exactly the hoped-for effect. It was further exacerbated when Tony turned to Kumar and began chattering in words, whistles, and clicks. The first time I'd seen this I thought it was a put-on. Now, I'm not so sure. Maybe Tony did speak some kind of Amazon pygmy language. It sounded convincing enough to me.

Kumar turned back toward us and shouted, "Five thousand American dollars if we can eat them after playing with them."

Deuce is a big man, almost as tall as me, but probably twenty pounds heavier, most of it in his wide shoulders and thick chest. His dad was Norwegian, but Deuce got more of the Viking genes than his dad. He spun around, his neck muscles bulging, and shouted through clenched teeth, "I said we'd discuss price later!"

Deuce's fierce appearance, with scraggly dark red hair and beard, and the idea now forming in the young man's mind created a bleak uncertainty and was completely evident in his face. His voice cracked as he said, "*Manje nou*?"

Until that moment, the taller of the two had been standing quietly defiant, sure that these people were the authorities and the gang leader would get them out of jail. His face went blank hearing those words and he looked to the other for guidance.

O'Hare caught onto the charade immediately and stepped up to the smaller man's face and snarled, "Yeah, they want to eat you. But not until after they have a little fun." To emphasize the point, he moved his fist to his mouth, like he was holding a turkey leg and mimicked gnawing off a huge bite.

"Get 'em on the chopper," Deuce said.

Bender and I shoved the two punks toward the chopper as Deuce walked ahead with O'Hare, talking.

I was less worried how they'd react on reaching the tiny island of Crane Key than how Deuce would. It's a couple of miles southwest of my island and I'd left a man there to die some time ago. He probably would have died anyway—he'd been stranded there for weeks and was near death when I found him. He'd murdered Deuce's dad and was the one responsible for putting the wheels in motion that had caused my wife to be murdered.

Charity landed the chopper in the skinny water on the north side of Crane Key, about a hundred feet from the little bay entrance I remembered. The chopper only had seven seats, so the two captives were just tossed on the floor and we all held them in place with our feet for the short ride.

After setting down and climbing out of the chopper, Deuce and I each grabbed one of the gangbangers and dragged them out, standing them up in the ankle-deep water.

The confusion and fear on their faces was palpable as Deuce roughly shoved them in the back toward the bay. I set off ahead of them with O'Hare and Bender. Tony and Kumar brought up the rear, chattering in both Arabic and whatever it was Tony was speaking. I was starting to believe it really was some strange dialect, because he'd break off into Arabic at times, as if teaching Kumar to speak his language.

I reached the narrow beach inside the bay and followed it into the interior. It wasn't really a bay, more like a place where rain and tide water had slowly run off of the tiny island, taking away some of the sand. I finally broke through a tangle of mangroves into a small clearing. There, leaning against a fallen palm tree, were the skeletal remains of Lester Antonio. At least, what bones were left. The intervening fifteen months since I'd last seen him had taken its toll. Some of the bones were scattered over the area, but the spine and rib cage were propped up by the dead log, with the skull leaning back, its jawbone hanging open in a grotesque and silent scream. *Crabs and buzzards*, I thought. *Plus fire ants and maybe even a feral hog.*

The two captives stopped dead in their tracks when they saw the skeleton. Deuce shouldered between them and approached the remains of his father's killer. He did what I'd told Lester I wouldn't that day when I found him. He pissed on the bones. Tony and Kumar shoved the two men into the clearing, where they fell to their knees in the sand, facing the skeleton.

Tony said something unintelligible and Kumar turned toward Deuce. "We will give you ten thousand American dollars for both of them. Can we build the cooking fire here?"

Deuce ignored him and turned to face the trembling hoodlums. He took one step closer and said over his shoulder, "If I don't get the information I want, you got a deal."

From that point, the interrogation went very well. Deuce asked each man a series of questions, getting an answer from the smaller one in English first and O'Hare translating afterward for the other man to confirm what the first had said. The information from both was pretty much the same, both wanting to be as helpful as possible.

The gang leader, Jean-Claude Lavolier, had taken a trip to Orlando several weeks earlier and when he returned, he had a very beautiful light-skinned mulatto woman with him. Everything the gang did after his return changed, as if the woman had some kind of control over Lavolier. He no longer made decisions unless consulting her first. Their drug pipeline was in disarray and in danger of collapsing, according to the smaller man. The gang members had been sent out in stolen boats to blow up reefs to draw me out in the open where I could be kidnapped.

Bender had a smug look on his face when that revelation came out. Neither man knew anything about the mulatto woman, except that she was very beautiful and thought to be very dangerous. Lavolier and the woman, known only as Erzulie, were never seen apart and it was she, not him, who'd actually done the beheading of the subordinate several weeks ago. All the gang members feared Lavolier, but those in the upper echelon feared her more.

When pressed more about the woman, the first man stammered that Erzulie was the voodoo spirit of love.

"Yeah," O'Hare said, "Nothing says romance like chopping off some guy's head."

"A mulatto spirit of love?" Charity asked, as she stepped through the narrow opening in the mangroves without a sound. Looking at Deuce she said, "Had to set the anchor, the tide is coming up. I could hear you talking all the way out by the bird."

Brushing past the two men still kneeling on the ground, she stopped next to me. "An olive-skinned beauty with smoky dark eyes that controls men using sex? Ring any bells, Jesse?"

"Can't be," I replied. "If she had half a brain she'd be back in Croatia." *Ettaleigh?* I thought. *Or whatever else she's calling herself now.* When we were in the Bahamas looking for that treasure last fall, there was a woman who'd drugged me. She'd said her name was Ettaleigh Bonamy and her family were the early settlers in the northern Bahamas, just after the American Revolution. It turned out her real name was Tena Horvac and she worked for a Croatian mobster in Miami.

"That would make sense," Deuce said. "In a twisted sort of way."

"You know who the woman is?" Bender asked.

"Part of that Croat organized crime syndicate in Miami I was telling you about," Deuce replied.

"The woman that drugged McDermitt?" he asked, turning to me and trying to hide a grin.

"Is there anyone you *didn't* tell?" I asked.

"I still don't think Chyrel told the First Lady yet," Charity said.

"Think about it, Jesse," Deuce said. "She used those drugs to control men and she failed with you. In her mind, she still has a score to settle and it probably doesn't involve any monetary gain."

"And this guy," O'Hare interrupted, jerking his thumb to the English-speaking gangster, "says this Erzulie woman is controlling Lavolier. What kind of drug was it? An aphrodisiac?"

That got the attention of everyone. "What do you know about it, O'Hare?" Deuce asked.

"My late wife was colored. A Creole woman from Montserrat. She knew quite a bit about the voodoo spirits and spells. Mostly, the spells were just a mixture of different herbs found throughout the islands." He grinned and added, "She knew a couple of herbs that when mixed right could put lead back in the dullest pencil."

"Think about it like this," Charity said. "How many beautiful, dark-eyed women do you know that can control the leader of a gang like Zoe Pound, *and* would want to kidnap you?"

"Well," I responded, realizing they were probably right. "Only one when you put it that way."

The two gangbangers were low-level soldiers, so they didn't know much about the inner workings of the gang, other than what they heard from others. With the obvious threat of being tortured, sodomized, and eaten by what they considered to be two evil Middle Eastern men, they were very eager to tell Deuce everything they knew. And they did.

After getting all the information from them he could, Deuce took out his cellphone and pulled up a photo of Tena Horvac. Holding it out so the two captives could see it, both nodded, whispering, "Erzulie."

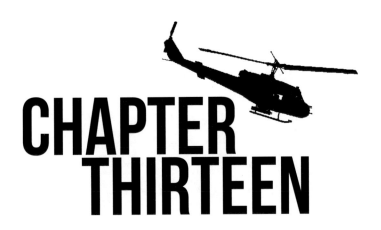

CHAPTER THIRTEEN

Thirty minutes later, Deuce dropped us where we'd left the boats anchored in the shallows south of Harbor Channel, then took off with the two men, headed back to Homestead, where they would be turned over to FDLE and most likely be back on the streets in a day or two.

I called Kim. She was very worried, but I again assured her everything was fine, that the three of us had to go with Deuce to fill out reports. I told her the tide was almost full now so we were going to get O'Hare's boat off the sandbar and I'd be home shortly.

"You can go out on the south pier with Pescador and see us," I told her.

"Just hurry," she said and ended the call.

The three of us walked around the boat, inspecting the hull as best we could, mostly by feel. O'Hare went aboard and down into the engine room and bilge, while I grabbed a mask from the *Cazador* and dove down to inspect the prop and shaft. O'Hare was satisfied that the keel was intact and there weren't any hull breaches. She still sat on the bottom and it would take a lot of pull to get the sand to release its suction-like grip. Fortunately, the propeller and shaft seemed undamaged and the stern was in water deep enough that he could use his own engine.

He tried that, racing the engine in reverse, sending a torrent of water under the hull in the hope that it would lift the boat clear and allow him to back off. When that didn't work, I started up *Cazador* and Bender pulled the anchor. Backing off the sandbar, I was able to use the bow thruster to line up behind the trawler and we tied two lines, crisscrossed, to each boat's stern cleats.

The combined thrust of the two big diesel engines did the trick and *Constance* was once more floating free. I invited O'Hare to the island for lunch and he accepted.

"Got a few nice lobster in the hold, if you want some," he offered. "Least I could do for pulling me off that sandbar and entertaining me all morning."

The channel to my house wasn't deep enough for his trawler, so he anchored it in the curve of the channel and stepped over to the *Cazador*. I started to dock the boat at the south pier, but he said, "Just dock her where you usually do. I can swim out to *Constance* when I'm ready to leave. Do it all the time."

I clicked the button on the fob to release the east door's latch and it slowly swung open. I saw Kim waiting on the dock. She and O'Hare quickly tied *Cazador* off to the dock before she jumped aboard, hugging me.

"Thank God, you're alright. What happened?"

"We caught a couple of those guys that have been fishing with explosives," I replied and then turned to introduce her to O'Hare.

After shaking the old man's hand she turned back to me and asked, "So, they're under arrest and won't be blowing up any more patch reefs? Are they the same ones from Cape Sable?"

"There's a little more to it than that," I replied as Bender led the way up to the deck. "But no, they aren't the same ones from Sable. We'll talk about it more later. Right now we have a guest for lunch."

Kim looked down at the burlap bag O'Hare was holding, then glanced out at the trawler anchored in the channel. Turning back toward O'Hare, she asked, "Are those lobster?"

"Sure are," he replied.

"They're deep now," she said. "Hard to find, free diving. Be glad to clean them for you, Captain."

The old man smiled, the cracks in his leathered face deepening as he extended the bag to her. "That's kind of ya, Miss McDermitt."

Kim quickly disappeared back down the steps to the cleaning table. She was right, lobster get a lot harder to catch this late in the season. We still get a few, but lobster for lunch is a rare treat in winter when you eat what you catch.

The Trents were coming across the clearing and waved. O'Hare leaned on the rail facing the interior and took it all in. "Y'all are a regular Robinson Crusoe family up here. What's that?" he asked, pointing at the garden.

"More than you know, O'Hare," Bender said. "They grow their own food up here. But not a single steak in sight."

I introduced O'Hare to the Trents and Carl proceeded to explain to him how the aquaculture system worked as we went down the steps and over to the garden.

"You grow fresh tomatoes?" the old man asked, eyeing about a dozen ripe ones on the plants.

"Try one," Charlie said.

O'Hare picked one from a cherry tomato plant and popped it in his mouth, relishing the freshness. He walked around the tanks, where the crawfish and catfish were raised and asked, "What's in these?" Carl went on to explain how we were raising catfish and crawfish for food, as well as the vegetables.

After a lunch of lobster and crawfish, I walked O'Hare out to the pier, offering again to take him out to his trawler lying placidly at anchor about a hundred yards down the channel.

"Like I said, I do it all the time," he replied and dove headfirst into the water.

I had to admit, for a guy who was probably in his eighties, he didn't seem so in the water. O'Hare didn't surface for a good fifteen yards and then struck out in a fast swim, making it look effortless.

Still, I waited on the pier until I saw him get aboard and start the old trawler's engine. His windlass took up the anchor line as he idled forward. The sound of the anchor seating coincided with his turning in the channel and chugging back toward me with the current.

Kim joined me on the pier as *Constance* cruised past, O'Hare waving from the wheelhouse. We both waved back and then went back up the steps to the deck, where Bender and Carl were sitting.

"Pretty spry for a guy his age," Bender quipped.

"Yeah, he is," I replied, sitting down with them.

Kim went down to the bunkhouse to get her backpack. It was an hour before she and Charlie had to leave to pick up the kids, but they were going in early so they could stop at Skeeter's to look at some tackle. A moment later, the two of them came up to the deck, told us they'd be back in a couple of hours and headed down to the docks.

"Doc called while you were pulling that tub off the bar," Carl said. "Says he found the perfect engines and emailed you the specs and drawings. With those, we should be able to come up with locations for the mounts and cut the through hulls for the shafts."

"Let's go see what he's got," I said.

The three of us went down to the *Revenge* and I powered up the laptop. I found Doc's message, downloaded the attachments and sent them to the wireless printer inside the cabinet by the TV. When the printing finished, I took the sheets out and glanced at each one as I sat down at the settee.

The engines he'd sent the specs on are built by a company called S&S Cycle. I don't know much about motorcycles, I know boats. But the specs on the engine were impressive.

"Torque peaks and pretty much maintains from forty-two hundred rpm to fifty-five hundred," I said, handing the spec sheets to Carl. "Over a hundred and forty pounds all the way."

"Whoa," he exclaimed, looking at the sheets. "And the horsepower is ridiculous. A hundred and sixty horses each? Do we really want all that power?"

"My Pap used to say that horsepower was like a specialty tool you rarely use. Better to have it and not need it than need it and not have it."

Carl glanced at the dyno charts again. "Yeah, it has a lot of bottom end, that's for sure. She'll lift up on plane at quarter throttle, more than likely."

I was looking at the mechanical diagrams and visualized the mounting brackets that would be needed, jotting some numbers on a notepad with a quick sketch. "As small as these are, we can make the cockpit larger and maybe even add some storage on either side by mounting them side by side instead of staggered fore and aft like the Cigarette. But that'd be a lot of power for a right-angle gearbox to handle."

"More room'd be nice," Carl said. "But mounting them too close would hurt maneuverability. Let me see that pad."

He took the pad and pencil from me and turned to a clean page where he quickly sketched the approximate size and shape of the boat, then drew the engines right next to one another with the shafts pointing outboard instead of to the rear. "What if we mounted them close together with the transmissions outboard of each?" He quickly drew two more boxes next to where he'd drawn the engines and slightly astern.

"Right angle gear boxes are notoriously weak," I said while he was sketching.

"No, a drive shaft with two constant velocity joints at forty-five degree angles. No belts, no chains, and it puts the output shafts to the props further outboard."

Again, I envisioned what he'd said. "Yeah, that could work. Mount a bearing between each joint to prevent any wobble, with each shaft driving a Borg Warner tranny?"

"Velvet Drive, one to one?"

I looked at him and grinned. "It'll sure turn some heads."

We worked straight through the afternoon, Bender even helped out. By the time we knocked off for the day, we'd built the engine mounts out of strong oak beams and laid out where the transmissions and shafts would run.

The whole time I was working, my mind drifted to the Croatian woman. I couldn't understand why she'd be after me. Sure, I'd been part of spoiling her chance to get the treasure, but she was an underling to Valentin Madic, who was the head of the Croat organization. Perhaps she had some stake in the outcome other than her boss's recognition for doing a good job. The idea that she'd seek any kind of revenge for anything other than money was something I couldn't get a grip on.

I'd contemplated my own inability to understand the criminal mind for some time. The mind of the enemy was much easier, as they operated primarily by political or theological ideology. One of Deuce's team, a crusty Coast Guard Senior Chief Petty Officer by the name of Bourke, said that to understand the criminal meant you had to think like one. *I have a long way to go*, I thought.

In the evening, before supper, Kim, Pescador, and I sat on the pier watching the sun set. The cold from the previous days had finally passed through and it was again tee-shirt-and-shorts weather.

"How many of them are there?" Kim asked.

She was talking about the Zoe Pound gang. "A lot," I replied. "I'm not sure exactly how many. A few hundred I guess."

"Are all of them involved in destroying the reefs?"

"Indirectly, yeah, it seems the whole gang's involved. But I doubt it's more than a dozen or so actually doing the dirty work."

"Why?"

"Because of the infrequency. I guess like any organization, they have people behind the scenes doing all sorts of jobs to support the foot soldiers."

"No," she said. "Why are they doing it?"

I'd known that one was coming. Kim has such an inquisitive mind. *How much should I tell her?* I thought. When I first met Carl, he'd advised me that in his relationship with Charlie, they kept no secrets and that was what made their relationship so strong.

"They're trying to draw me out in the open," I finally replied.

She jerked her head around, now very serious. "What for?"

She already knew a lot of what had happened on Elbow Cay last fall. I hadn't told her about the Croatian woman or the drug that she'd given me. And there was no way I was going to tell her about the effect that concoction had had on me. Some things a daughter doesn't need to know about her father. But she knew basically what had happened.

She needed to know more. At least some of it. So, I told her about Tena Horvac and her plans to take the treasure once we found it. "Apparently, she blames me for the loss of her job and the treasure and is looking for revenge."

"By sending a whole gang after you? How could she possibly control a street gang?"

"Women have always been able to get men to do things for them," I replied, hoping that would end it.

We talked a while longer and thankfully she changed the subject, telling me about a new graphite rod she saw at Skeeter's that she wanted to buy, but didn't have the money for.

"You're the one handling the books," I said. "How much are you paying yourself?"

"Nothing," Kim replied.

I turned to her and gave her a halfway grin. "I'd say you've been worth a bit more than that. I usually pay a First Mate two hundred a day when we're out and fifty a day when we're not, or six hundred a week, whichever is greater."

"That's something I've been meaning to ask you. I saw it in your old records. Why would you pay someone not to work?"

"Being ready to work at a moment's notice is important in the charter business. You never know when you might get a last-minute call from a client. I don't want a Mate to start doing work for others and not be available when I need them. When Jimmy was my Mate, we just sat around on the docks sometimes and he'd fuss around the engine room when he got bored. I probably owe you several thousand dollars right now."

Her eyes widened. "For real?"

"Yeah, go over the books tomorrow. Add up all the days you worked and all the weekdays you didn't and let me know what I owe you. Most weeks will be the six hundred minimum since we're not really chartering much."

I watched as she did the math in her head. "Wow, that's like ten thousand dollars, at least."

"And a good deal at twice the price. You've worked hard."

She smiled and leaned on my shoulder as we watched the last of the sun slip quietly into the sea.

CHAPTER FOURTEEN

We turned in shortly after supper, since we actually did have a charter the next morning. A regular client from Miami was coming down to do an underwater photo shoot and had booked me for the whole morning.

I was out of bed at zero four-hundred, with the smell of fresh coffee wafting in from the galley. After hitting the head, I let Pescador out and poured a cup, then stood looking out the window facing the island's interior. There was a light on in both the west bunkhouse and the Trents' house.

Hearing footsteps coming up the rear steps, I opened the door and Carl walked in behind Pescador. "Charlie said breakfast will be ready in ten minutes."

"Want some coffee?" I asked, seeing him eyeing the machine on the counter.

"Leaded?"

"Yeah," I replied with a grin, pouring a mug for him. Charlie had started limiting the man's caffeine intake.

He took a drink and asked, "What time you think you'll be back?"

"Not sure," I replied. "This photographer is doing something new, not just taking pictures of pretty fish. He's bringing two models with him."

"Models?"

"Yeah, underwater models. No idea what he has in mind, but he wants a deep reef with gin clear water."

Thirty minutes later, Kim and I were aboard the *Revenge* and heading northeast in Harbor Channel, while Pescador looked on from the pier. It was still two hours until sunrise, but the client was meeting us at the *Anchor* at zero six-hundred. He wanted to be set up on a reef in forty feet of water as the sun was coming up. Something about filtered light. I was planning to take them to the far side of the G Marker, where a few low, broken finger reefs extended out to a depth of forty feet. If that didn't work, there was always Looe Key, a large reef off of Big Pine, but it was further away and we might not make that by sunup.

Arriving at the *Anchor*, I saw the lights on inside and left Kim to tie up while I went to find our client, Peter Simpson. There was a rental car in the crushed-shell parking lot, a big white Crown Vic, so I figured they were inside having breakfast.

I was surprised to see Deuce's boss, Travis Stockwell, sitting at the bar, sharing a large platter of fish tacos with Rusty. "Morning, Jesse," Rusty said. "Care for some breakfast?"

"Thanks, Rusty," I said, "but we ate before we left the island." Then I turned to Travis. "What are you doing down here?" I asked, probably with a bit too much suspicion.

"Relax," he said, noting the misgiving tone in my voice. "I knew you'd be here this morning and just wanted your opinion on a couple of things."

Taking the stool next to him and accepting a mug of coffee from Rusty, I turned to the former Colonel.

"My opinion? Since when does a bird Colonel need the opinion of a fisherman?"

Stockwell had taken over as Associate Deputy Director about a year ago, when the guy that had once held that position went rogue and nearly got the President killed. We got along pretty well from the start. He's an easygoing man in his fifties, but more fit than most men half his age.

He'd served with the Army's Third Ranger Battalion in Somalia at the same time that I was there and had been retired for a few years when the DHS Secretary tapped him for his current position just above Deuce as the head of the Caribbean Counter-terrorism Command.

He turned toward me and arched an eyebrow. "Even us political appointees retire and go fishing sometimes." He had my attention then as Rusty just stood behind the bar grinning. "The fact is, my appointment was an emergency stopgap after Smith's sudden departure."

"You? Retiring? Thinking about just dropping out in the Keys, are ya?"

"That's part of what I wanted your opinion about. How do you think Deuce would like living in Washington?"

The realization of what he was asking and why Rusty was just standing there with a goofy grin on his face suddenly hit me like a broadside wave, causing me to nearly choke on my coffee.

"You're retiring and recommending Deuce for your position?"

Stockwell nodded. "He's got the right temperament for the job, his people will do anything for him and he's a bit more imposing than me."

"Right on all counts," I said. "No disrespect."

"None taken. Deuce has a way of filling a room with his presence without saying a word and when he does say something, it's short, to the point, and people listen. He's been well received the few times he's been up in Washington, and last but not least, the President likes him."

I looked over at Rusty, who was still grinning like a Cheshire cat. "Okay, what gives? You know he won't be comfortable up there, Rusty. Neither will Jules."

"He's also recommending you to take over Deuce's team," Rusty blurted out, laughing, as Kim came through the door.

"Not a chance," I said as Kim approached the bar.

"Not a chance of wh—?" she started to say, but I interrupted her.

"Wait a minute," I said, turning to Travis. "How'd you know I'd be here this morning?"

He smiled slowly. "All the other team members check in twice a day, but you're sort of in a different classification and I'd never ask you to do that. So, we monitor your website's calendar. You never charter two days in a row, rarely more than two a week, and the dates are booked weeks in advance."

"There've been plenty of times that I've booked a client and didn't update the site."

"Not lately," Travis said, glancing at Kim. "No doubt Miss McDermitt's influence, I presume?"

I introduced her to Travis and she sat on the stool on the opposite side of me. Rusty had a mug of coffee and a plate in front of her before she sat down, and though she'd already eaten, she took two fish tacos from the tray.

"You also refuel after you get back in from a charter, which is wise. Your boat holds seven hundred gallons of diesel fuel. Rusty's tank here only holds a thousand and you're the only boat that buys diesel from him. Since diesel can be used in a truck bomb, like Oklahoma City, bulk deliveries are monitored. If you forget to mark your calendar as booked, a fuel delivery here means you're going somewhere."

"And you think I'd be interested in taking over Deuce's job watching when people buy fuel?"

"You know that's not part of his job, Jesse. That's what low-level statisticians in the basement of the Pentagon do."

Kim put down the taco she was eating, wiped her mouth and said, "Would Dad have to deal with politicians? Cause if he would, that's, well, it's just not gonna work, and besides, you can't offer enough to change that. We like our life just the way it is, right, Dad?"

I grinned at my daughter, "I couldn't have said it better, kiddo."

"Well, that's out of the way, then," Travis said with his palms up. "You are the logical successor, all the people in the team like you, but if you're not interested, well, I made the offer. So that takes care of the official reason for my visit." He smiled and leaned toward me. "Now, tell me about living down here."

Just then the door opened and two young women walked in, followed by my client and his co-diver. I got up and met Peter halfway across the bar, shaking his hand.

"Good to see you again, Jesse. You remember Tom, don't you?"

Tom Schweitzer was a long-time dive client and was now working as Peter's underwater photography assistant. I shook his hand and he introduced me to the two women, Annette and Mitzi. The two girls headed straight for the taco platter.

"Where are you taking us, Jesse?" Peter asked. "I have something a little different in mind today."

"I thought we'd stop on the offshore side of G Marker for starters and if the water or light isn't good for you, we can go to the finger reefs on Looe Key."

"G Marker should work perfectly," Peter said thoughtfully. "I've dived it a time or two. I think the relief on Looe Key will be too much anyway. I want low relief, like a patch reef would provide. How soon should we leave?"

"Still an hour before daylight," I replied, motioning toward the bar and coffeemaker. "It's only twenty minutes to get there. Have a cup of coffee and I'll stow your gear aboard."

"I'll get it, Dad," Kim said as she nodded to the two men. "Good to see you again, Mister Simpson. Tom." Then she was out the door.

"She's going to allow you to retire early," Peter said.

I led the way to the bar, where Annette and Mitzi had already started in on the fish tacos and coffee. Both looked to be in their early twenties. Annette had shoulder-length blond hair and Mitzi, longer dark hair. Both were rail thin and God only knows where they were putting the food, because they were wolfing it down like they'd been starved for days.

"Got room for a passenger?" Travis asked when I sat down next to him, the two girls having taken up my and Kim's stools.

"I'm not interested in any more sales pitches, Colonel."

"I know," he said. "Wouldn't think of it. I just happen to have two whole days free and really would like to see how you live down here."

"You dive?"

"Yeah, I'm certified," he replied. "Not to the level you or some of the other team members are, probably not even as capable as your daughter, but I'm comfortable in the water."

"You're hired for the day," I said, sliding a dollar to him. "Kim has some admin work to do and you can help Peter and Tom, freeing her up to do that while we're out, instead of waiting and doing it tonight."

He picked up the dollar, stuck it in his pocket and said, "That's it? No resumes? No interviews?"

"Down here, we like to do business on a man's word and a handshake."

"You have a swab, then," he replied, holding out his hand, which I took. "But, I think next time I'll want a raise."

I laughed and clapped him on the shoulder. "Come on, I have all the gear you'll need." Then I turned to Peter and said, "We'll be ready to go in fifteen minutes, Peter. Or any time after that that you're ready."

As Travis and I walked out of the bar, Kim was just stepping aboard with the last dive bag from Peter's van. We helped her stow it aboard and I explained that the

Colonel would be assisting Peter and Tom today, freeing her up to do some accounting chores and try to book another empty spot we had on the calendar.

"And be sure to mark it booked when you fill it," I said, grinning at Travis. "Don't want Big Brother to lose track of us."

Ten minutes later, we were idling through the canal to open water. The powerful spotlight on the roof reflected off the low early morning fog hugging the water, illuminating the boats tied up along both sides from above and below. Stockwell was wrong about mine being the only boat that bought diesel here. With winter fully upon us, Rusty's little marina was full to capacity. Most had no intention of going out, they just liked living on their boats in a warmer climate, but all fueled up on arrival and a few had diesel engines. Rusty had a guy that sold him diesel at cut-rate prices, whenever his tanker truck had leftover fuel after making his usual deliveries. It was just fifty or a hundred gallons now and then, but it kept his tank topped off most of the time.

I knew the fog would end just beyond the canal, and the forecast called for a cloudless day. With Kim entertaining the four guests in the cabin, Travis took her usual seat in the second chair and looked longingly at the boats tied up in the canal. He leaned over to try to see the instruments, but eight feet above the water, little light spilled onto the bridge.

I reached up to the console above the windshield, toggled the switch for the red overhead lights and pointed to the angled console in front of him. "Radar screen on top, sonar screen below it. Switch on the radar and set it to a five-mile range and set the sonar to forward scan."

With the subdued light, he had to lean closer and put on a pair of reading glasses to make out the controls, but soon had the radar up and running, the image on the screen distorted by all the trees along the edges of Rusty's property.

The sonar was sweeping forward, showing the bottom contours ahead of us. Travis looked over my plane with an appraising eye as we passed by it. *Island Hopper* was tethered on the canal bank near the mouth of the canal, an overhead light pole illuminating its bright red aluminum skin and the nose art I had a friend paint on the cowling. It was in the old WWII bomber style, but instead of the pretty girl straddling a bomb, she was lying back on a leaning palm tree, with a green flash sunset in the background and *Island Hopper* scrawled below it.

When we cleared the small jetty, the low fog disappeared and the radar image cleared up, showing nothing ahead in the darkness. I idled forward another fifty feet or so, then pushed the throttles slowly forward to the halfway point. The boat settled slightly in the stern, the big propellers pushing all the water out from beneath the hull and lifting the bow, accelerating upward as well as forward. In a few seconds the long foredeck came back down as the big boat stepped up on top of the water, planing out on the mirror smooth surface.

"Whoa," Stockwell sighed. "That's a shitload of power. What's a boat like this set a man back?"

"About half a million," I replied honestly, knowing that if anyone was able to, the man sitting beside me probably knew my finances better than anyone else could. Probably better than me. "A bit more when you add in specialty stuff."

"So the term 'boat bum' is a misnomer? Still, I can see the attraction to the lifestyle. You do this only once a week or so?"

Was he trying to feel out how honest I'd be? He'd already alluded to the fact that he knew my schedule. *Probably even knows how much I paid for fuel*, I thought. No, with all the information that crosses his desk, the daily comings and goings of a part-time transporter wouldn't be high up in his memory.

"As little as possible," I replied. "Only because I enjoy being out on the water, more than anything else. I came into some money some time back and do this because I enjoy it. So, I can be very selective about who I take out and who I tell to piss up a rope."

He laughed and said, "Well, I for one appreciate your selectivity. Those two models are a lot easier on the eyes than any Senate subcommittee member."

"Yeah," I replied, "and probably younger than your own kids."

"Never married, no kids."

"Really?"

"I was engaged a couple of times, but they couldn't deal with Army life and I just never had much of a desire to get married."

I steered due south, knowing the opening in the reef ahead like it was a paved road. When the sonar picked it up slightly to port, I turned the wheel a little and reduced power. Pointing at the sonar display, I said, "The opening in the reef is about forty feet wide and twenty deep, plenty of room for us, but it's always a good idea to approach narrow passages slowly, in case the tide brought something in and wedged it in the opening."

Not seeing anything on the 3-D digital display and sweeping the surface with the spotlight, I pushed the throttles back up and we went through the opening into deep water. The truth is, I'd never been able to decide which I liked better. The vastness of the deep blue water on the south side of the islands, or the crystal clear, filtered water percolating into the backcountry of Florida Bay from the Everglades. Each held its own attraction for me.

Passing the thirty-foot line on the plotter, I turned to the west, pulled up G Marker on the GPS memory and selected it. I switched on the autopilot, so the computer would steer a course that would take us straight to G Marker, veering out away from the reef line. On modern nautical charts it's called Marker 22, having been changed sometime in the early eighties from G Marker, but local fishermen and divers still refer to it by its old name.

"Is that where we're going?" Travis asked, pointing ahead and slightly north to a green marker light.

"No, that's Marker 49A. G Marker is a few miles further. The red light."

"I guess you learn all these things over time?"

"The less time it takes, the better," I replied. "What you don't know can get you in trouble fast out here. Reach in that chart locker by your leg and pull out the one marked eleven-four-forty-two."

Once he'd found the right one and unrolled it across his knees, I switched the overhead from red to white and leaned over toward him. "We're about here," I said, pointing to a spot south of the Seven Mile Bridge. "Where we're going is G Marker, here. It's the one marked with a twenty-two, due south of Spanish Harbor."

He looked at the knotmeter, checked the scale on the chart and said, "Less than half an hour?"

"Give or take a few minutes. The client asked for a reef in forty feet of water with low relief. There's quite a few that fit the bill, but for his level of photography, water clarity is real important, so that narrowed it down to just a few spots."

"The two women will be modeling underwater? In what? Scuba gear?"

"I don't have any idea what he's got in mind. He's one of those creative types, so it should be a pretty interesting day."

I heard jazz coming up from the salon and turned the topside speakers up just loud enough to create a pleasant background to the steady swish of the bow wave. I set the radar alarm for two miles and swallowed the last of my coffee. Leaning back, I put my feet up on the dash next to the wheel and clasped my hands behind my head. "If you're serious about retiring, you can't find a better place to put everything behind you than right here."

"Yeah, I'm quickly seeing just what you mean," Travis said as he took a drink from his coffee mug and looked out over the foredeck at the water. The waning moon was nearing the horizon far ahead of us, causing the surface of the water to sparkle.

"How old are you, Travis?"

"I'll be fifty-five in July. You?"

"Forty-six come next month," I replied. "You miss it?"

He looked over at me pensively. "The military? Yeah, all the time." He turned and looked out to the starboard side as the early morning traffic crossed the Seven Mile Bridge in the distance.

Forty minutes and few words later, we came down off plane, idling slowly across the deeper part of the reef a hundred feet off the marker tower. I switched on the stern-mounted underwater lights and they lit up the water all around us. Peter, Tom and the two models looked down, pointing, and discussed things for a minute, then Peter called up that the spot looked perfect.

Kim took Travis forward, showing him how to release the brake on the anchor chain, and it rattled out of the well, the anchor dropping to the sandy bottom. I reversed the engines, idling backward with the current until Kim signaled that we had enough rode out and set the brake on the winch. Once I felt the heavy Danforth bite into the sand, I gunned the engines, setting it deep, and then shut them down. We were anchored and ready to dive, just as the first rays of the sun peeked over the horizon. Peter and Tom were suited up in lightweight wet suits, and with the cockpit lights now turned on I noticed for the first time that the two women were wearing, of all things, evening gowns.

I helped Travis get his gear together and Kim helped the two divers set theirs up on the four-seat bench I'd had built, which anchored in the fighting chair mount. I was puzzled about the evening wear, but neither Peter nor Tom offered any explanation.

When everyone was suited up and ready, Peter turned to Travis and explained, "Your and Tom's primary job is to keep the girls on air using your octopus and to move them and their dresses around as I direct you. Just watch for my hand signals."

"They're wearing evening gowns underwater?" Travis asked, incredulous.

Peter winked and smiled, saying, "You'll see."

Annette and Mitzi each wore long, flowing pastel gowns. Annette's was strapless, pale blue below the waist with a tight-fitting dark blue bodice, while Mitzi's was a yellow-and-white number with a plunging neckline, cut very low in the back with a halter strap tied around the back of her neck. Each woman wore matching gloves that almost reached the elbow and carried high-heel shoes.

"An interesting day, you said?" Travis quipped, as Tom did a giant stride entry from the swim platform.

Peter handed Tom the camera equipment and stepped off beside him. Turning, he pulled his mask down around his neck and said, "Hand me the light bar, please." Kim unstrapped the unwieldy mechanism from the top of the bench and handed it down to him.

To the two women, Peter said, "Wait until we're on the bottom and set up, then come down with Travis, sharing his second regulator, just like we discussed yesterday."

Annette and Mitzi stood on the platform with Travis, looking down into the water, and nodded. In a luxury yacht commercial it would look normal, but on a working dive boat, the two fashionably dressed ladies standing beside a diver looked kind of comical. A few minutes after the two divers descended, there was a flash of light from below and Annette said, "They're ready for us."

Travis went in first and the two women knelt down and rolled forward head first, entering the water with hardly a ripple, the long gowns flowing up around them as they both somersaulted and came up on either side of him. They moved in the water like they went swimming while fully clothed all the time.

"We'll each take your arm," Mitzi said to Travis, taking his left one and treading water. "We'll trade your second regulator back and forth as we go down. Don't worry, we've both done this a few times and we won't use much of your air. But you'll have to guide us to where Peter directs you, since neither of us will be able to see very well." A moment later, they disappeared below the surface, the chiffon gowns billowing behind them.

"I think I could live here all my life and never see anything stranger," Kim said.

"Don't say that," I replied with a grin. "A stranger thing is always just around the corner down here. Go get the computer set up for editing. I'll keep an eye on things."

I went back up to the bridge, where I had a better view, and turned off the underwater lights. Looking down, I could clearly see the three divers, and I couldn't help thinking that the models in those flowing gowns looked just like giant fly fishing lures. But they both seemed very comfortable in the water, allowing Travis and Tom to move them around in front of the bright light bar, which was attracting quite a few brightly colored reef fish. Soon, the divers swam away and the strobes on the light bar began to flash.

I watched as Tom and Travis moved the women around the reef edge and Peter photographed first one and then the other as they slowly drifted upward in the current. The women were breathing off each diver's octopus rig between shoots. From above, it looked kind of weird, but Peter's the artist. The sun was above the horizon now and I poured another cup of coffee from the thermos, sitting back to think about Stockwell's earlier announcement and plans.

He was right about Deuce. His easygoing manner and his ability to instill confidence in others made him perfect to take over Stockwell's position as the political liaison between the leadership in Washington and the teams in the field. With the new team being spun up to work out of Key Largo and Deuce presently overseeing their training, no doubt working right alongside them, he'd be in a much better position to know each person's strengths and weaknesses.

The wild card was Jules. They'd only been married less than a year and she'd only been north of Palm Beach a few times in her life. She's an island girl who loves the water and she knows the backcountry better than anyone I could think of. *Adapt to life in Washington?* I wondered.

Deuce had been slowly acclimating to his new lifestyle here in the subtropics himself. They'd bought a Whitby ketch and lived aboard at Rusty's little marina. Hell, he'd even grown his hair and beard out and was wearing boat shoes. I wasn't sure if he'd relish being in Washington full-time. But, when it came right down to it, he'd go where he was told and do what was needed of him. He'd probably accept the position. Not out of any desire for advancement. Deuce wasn't like that. He'd do it out of the realization that he was the logical man for the job and his desire to serve to the best of his ability. Nothing more.

Then there was Stockwell. Was he ready to leave the city life behind or was he just pulling my leg? *No*, I thought, *he's not the leg-pulling type.* If he felt it necessary to send someone else down here, even himself, he'd just do it and if he said he was retiring and considering living down here, that's exactly what he was doing. A Colonel's pension wouldn't go far, though. Maybe he'd done some wise investing over the years.

After forty minutes under water, the lights on the bottom winked off and the divers slowly surfaced to swap out tanks. Kim had fresh tanks ready and waiting and together we exchanged the empties without the divers even getting out of the water. I checked each one's depth gauge and none of them had a red line over thirty-five feet, so I reset the maximum depth indicator to zero on all three consoles. A second dive to that depth wouldn't require a decompression stop, but I suggested they do a safety stop at ten feet after the next one, just in case. Peter and Tom readily agreed.

Thirty minutes after they'd gone back down and Kim had returned to the salon to work on the computer, the urgent beeping of the radar alarm brought me out of my thoughts. It was set to alert me if another boat came within a mile.

My first instinct was to look out to sea, east to west, where any large ships might be coming too close to the reef. Seeing nothing, I checked the radar, which showed a small boat closing fast from the southeast, where the sun was now well above the horizon. Looking that way, I couldn't make it out in the blinding glare of the sun on the water. The radar showed it to be less than a mile away.

Damned idiots, I thought. Though I couldn't see them, they had the sun to their backs, and my boat, with its blue hull, white decks and the big red-and-white diver down flag flying above the roof, should be visible for twice that distance.

I snatched the mic to the marine band radio and hailed them. "Vessel approaching the dive boat *Gaspar's Revenge*, anchored south of Marker Twenty-Two, I have divers down. Change your course and slow down."

There was no response, so I repeated the call, checking to make sure I was on the hailing channel. Again, no response. The boat was within a few hundred yards according to the radar, but still invisible in the glare and coming on quickly. They were approaching way too fast and directly out of the sun. *Something's not right*, I thought as I opened the overhead locker and took out my 9mm Sig Sauer P226 in its clip-on holster. I quickly checked the magazine and chambered a round before slipping it into my waistband at my back and pulling my tee shirt over it.

Why would a small boat be coming out of the southeast? There's no land that way except ... Haiti! Impossible! That's seven hundred miles of open ocean. The only other possibility was that they came out of one of the islands in the Keys and were intentionally approaching out of the sun.

Once on the deck in the cockpit, I stepped up onto the starboard gunwale and shielded my eyes, straining to make out the approaching boat. I could hear the sound of the outboard approaching, but still couldn't see it. I waved my arms and pointed out to sea several times, trying to direct them away from my divers.

Suddenly, a twenty-foot runabout went screaming by less than thirty feet away with two black men on board. As I reached for my Sig I saw the man in the back of the boat throw something toward me, splashing into the water ten feet away. It was followed instantly by another as the driver pointed a gun at me and started shooting.

Instinctively, I knew he had no chance of hitting me and little chance of even hitting the *Revenge*, so I aimed carefully, but didn't return fire.

Suddenly the boat rocked to port, knocking me off balance and into the water as two geysers shot up from the depths. The runabout never slowed down, speeding off around the marker and heading back toward the islands. I swam quickly to the dive platform empty-handed, having dropped my gun when hitting the water. Kim came running out of the salon and I shouted for her to get back inside as I levered myself up onto the platform.

"What's going on, Dad?" Kim shouted, leaning over the transom.

"Just get back inside!" I yelled, quickly throwing one leg after the other over the transom, rolling across it and heading to the storage cabinets. She started to protest, but I shoved her inside, locking the hatch from the inside and closing it. I grabbed a mask from the cabinet and in two quick strides, I was over the side and putting the mask on underwater.

Quickly tilting my head back, I broke the seal around my cheeks and exhaled through my nose to clear the water. Then, jackknifing my body, I started kicking for the bottom thirty-five feet below. The two women were drifting near the base of the reef, either dead or knocked out. One of the divers was swimming to them and another was holding the sides of his head, but swimming to the inert third diver. I recognized the equipment on the diver headed toward the women as my own and knew it was Stockwell.

I started swimming after Stockwell, diving deeper and from above him. As he reached Mitzi, I came down right next to him. Pointing to Annette who was twenty feet away, I grabbed Mitzi under the arms and with my lungs starving for air, I pushed off the bottom with all I had. In the back of my mind I recognized that the sound of the boat's propeller was getting fainter and headed away.

My lungs were burning from being down too long and as I kicked frantically for the surface I started to release the air in my lungs. Breaking the surface, gasping for air, I took Mitzi in a cross-body drag, kicking toward the stern of the *Revenge* about twenty feet away.

Stockwell surfaced with Annette in tow. Wearing fins, he quickly passed me, pulling her inert body behind him. Reaching the dive platform, he quickly shed his gear and climbed up, pulling Annette up behind him. I reached the platform and Stockwell pulled Mitzi up onto it with Annette before helping me up onto it.

Together we pulled both women through the transom door. Neither was breathing and we found no pulse, so we started CPR. Hearing splashing from behind the boat, I looked back and saw both Tom and Peter swimming under their own power toward the dive platform. As I started to lower my mouth to Mitzi's once more, she began spitting up foamy, pink seawater. I left her there and banged on the hatch for Kim to open it. When she did, I told her to pull Mitzi inside the salon and wrap her in a blanket.

"She's probably in shock and suffering an embolism," I added as I quickly climbed up to the bridge and started the engines.

I engaged the windlass, but it seemed to take forever for it to drag the boat forward before the change in its pitch told me the anchor had come free. When I heard the rattle of the chain on the roller, I glanced back and saw Tom closing the transom door and Travis still bent over Mitzi's body. Peter was collapsed in the corner, but waving off Tom's help.

I engaged the transmissions and pushed both throttles to the stops. The *Revenge* responded instantly, surging forward and up, climbing on top of the water as I spun the wheel to the right. I straightened out, heading east. Once she reached planing speed the hull broke the surface bond of the water and we quickly accelerated to over forty-five knots.

I glanced back down to the cockpit and saw that Tom and Travis were both working on Annette, who still lay motionless on the deck. I turned back and checked the radar as I reached for the radio mic. I saw the runabout on the screen. It was headed due east about two miles ahead. I keyed the mic. "*Dockside*! *Dockside*! This is *Gaspar's Revenge* with an emergency!"

Seconds later a voice came back over the speaker. "*Gaspar's Revenge*, this is *Dockside*. How can we help?"

"I'm coming in with injured divers. CPR is being performed on one, another has a possible embolism, and there are three others that are awake, condition unknown."

"Contacting Fisherman's Hospital now, *Gaspar's Revenge*. Come straight to the fuel dock, we'll have transportation waiting for you. What happened, Jesse?"

It was then that I recognized the voice. Robin used to work at *Dockside* until about a year ago, but left suddenly. "Those idiots from Miami just threw grenades at us, Robin." Somberly, I added, "I had five divers in the water."

I glanced back down at the cockpit. Nobody was there and Kim was climbing up to the bridge. "How are they?"

"Not good, Dad," she replied, sitting down in the second seat. "Mister Simpson can't hear anything and is bleeding from one ear. Mitzi and Annette are both awake, but coughing up blood."

She saw me glance at the radar and checked it herself, looking at me with a concerned expression. The other boat was only a mile ahead, but we were coming up to Sombrero Key light and they were angling to go on the south side of it. The straighter course to Knights Key Inlet or Sister Creek would take us well to the north of it.

Every fiber of my being wanted to chase them down and crush them under the bow, but I eased the wheel to the left, putting the light on our starboard bow. Kim switched the sonar to forward scan and looked around to check where we were.

"*Dockside*," I said, keying the mic again, "our ETA is less than ten minutes."

"Roger, Jesse. Ambulances are on the way."

"Are they going to be okay?" Kim asked.

"I don't know," I replied. "I hope so. I just don't know."

The intensity of the concussion from a grenade is magnified underwater. Peter had no doubt ruptured an eardrum and likely the others had as well. The two women coughing up blood indicated a serious embolism. At thirty-five feet the pressure was more than double that on the surface and to compensate the external pressure, air is delivered through the regulator at the same pressure. Essentially, a breath at that shallow depth held the same volume of air as two breaths on the surface. If a diver came up too fast while holding their breath, the air in their lungs would expand, causing an embolism, or air bubble, that could block blood flow to part of the body, or worse, enter the heart and stop all blood circulation.

Another voice came over the speaker, "*Gaspar's Revenge*, this is Monroe County Deputy Martin Phillips."

"Go ahead, Deputy Phillips."

"Did I understand you to say you were attacked? I'm motoring into Sister Creek now."

"Head back out!" I said. "Two black men in an eighteen-foot yellow runabout heading east, just passing Sombrero Key light. You can be on them in five minutes. Be careful, they're armed with handguns and grenades."

"Roger that," he responded. "Any idea where they're headed?"

"No idea, but if you had a stolen boat report in the last couple of hours, they're probably heading back to where they left their car before stealing it."

"Yes, we did. A deputy is there now. We'll take it from here, *Gaspar's Revenge*."

A moment later, I could just make out the deputy's boat coming out of Sister Creek dead ahead, coming up on plane, blue lights flashing. I waited until the radar picked him out of the background scatter and picked up the mic again.

"Deputy Phillips, this is *Gaspar's Revenge*."

He responded and looking at the two blips on the radar, I said, "On your radar, at a heading of about one hundred and thirty degrees, a mile past East Washerwoman. Do you see him?"

"Roger, *Gaspar's Revenge*. Are you certain that's the boat that attacked you?"

"Absolutely," I replied. "It's the only other boat on my screen in the area and I've had a fix on it since they attacked us."

"We've got him, thanks for your help."

I hung up the mic and concentrated on the approach, which was coming up at almost fifty knots now. As much as I hated to, I was going to go up the creek a lot faster than is prudent or allowed. It's a no wake zone, but I was going to be up on plane all the way into Boot Key Harbor.

I made the turn and lined up the green and red markers. As I neared the wide mouth of the creek, I brought the speed down to thirty knots, preparing for the few blind turns just beyond.

Making our way up the creek, I cringed at each noise behind us. The sound of boats on either side banging against their docks. No doubt there were at least a few people on their phones calling the sheriff's office already.

I slowed to twenty knots as I came to the opening into the harbor and hoped there wouldn't be anyone heading out from around the blind turn. I spun the wheel and the *Revenge* responded, turning hard right and heeling over, kicking up spray to the port side.

Nothing in the channel, I pushed the throttles, keeping the big boat on plane all the way to *Dockside*'s fuel dock at the east end of the harbor. I could see the red flashing lights of several ambulances as I brought the boat down off plane and approached the dock. Kim climbed down and went to the bow, ready to toss a line to one of the men on the dock.

Minutes later, we were tied up and moving the divers to the waiting ambulances. The EMTs loaded Mitzi into the first ambulance. She'd lost consciousness. It took off for the short half-mile ride to Fisherman's Hospital. Or possibly a much longer ride to a hyperbaric chamber in either Key West or Islamorada.

Stockwell declined transport, saying he was fine except for a little ringing in his ears. "I was furthest away from both explosions. The grenades fell between the girls and the photographer, closer to the girls, not ten feet away from them."

Annette was loaded into the second ambulance in a stretcher, awake and answering the questions from the EMT. It spun out, spraying crushed coral as its tires lost traction. They grabbed the asphalt of the road with a screech and the ambulance roared away, siren wailing. Tom and Peter both climbed into the third ambulance on their own and it followed after the other two.

"Do they have a chamber at the hospital here?" Stockwell asked.

"No," I replied. "Nearest ones are the Army's Underwater Warfare School on Fleming Key and Mariner's Hospital on Islamorada. Both are about forty miles away."

In the distance, we could hear the first ambulance's siren fading as it headed north, away from Fisherman's Hospital. A moment later, the sound of the second one faded away to the north, also.

"They're taking the women to Islamorada," Kim said as the sound of an approaching outboard grew louder behind us.

I turned to see a Monroe County Sheriff's patrol boat idling up to the dock behind the *Revenge*. It had the run-about in tow and there were two uniformed deputies on board. The two black men were handcuffed and sitting on the deck in the open cockpit area ahead of the center console.

I couldn't believe my eyes. Less than twenty-four hours earlier, the two men O'Hare had run over had been in Deuce's custody, flying north in a chopper. Now the smaller of the two and another young black man were right here, handcuffed once more.

I turned to Travis and said, "Follow my lead and be ready to show your badge."

I walked toward the patrol boat as the deputies were tying off. *What was the thug's name again?* I thought. *Gabriel something?*

The punks looked up as the two deputies hoisted them to their feet and the smaller man saw me looking down at him, smiling. The hardness in his face turned to fear.

"Hello, Gabe. Long time, no see."

"He doesn't speak English," one of the deputies said, stepping up to the dock with Gabriel, now visibly shaken. The deputy was young, maybe twenty or twenty-one. But I'd served with younger men and they were more than competent.

"You know him?" the deputy asked.

Noticing the name tag on the young man's uniform, I stuck out my hand. "Good job, Deputy Phillips. I'm Captain McDermitt of the *Revenge*." I pumped his hand and said, "Gabe here speaks and understands English just fine. We'll have a word with him, if you don't mind."

"Now hold on, McDermitt," Phillips said, releasing my hand. "This is police business."

Travis stepped forward and held up his identification for the deputy to see. "I'm Associate Deputy Director Travis Stockwell, Deputy. With the Department of Homeland Security, Caribbean Counterterrorism Command. We only require a few minutes with your prisoner."

Without waiting for permission, Stockwell took Gabriel by the arm and steered him toward the *Revenge*. I just shrugged my shoulders at the deputy and turned to follow Stockwell.

Kim was standing by the transom as we approached. "Kim, why don't you go get a cheeseburger from inside. Make it three, with a big bag of fries. Introduce yourself to Robin and tell her to put it on my tab."

When she left, I stepped down into the cockpit, yanking Gabriel by the collar and jerking him down with me. I shoved him forcefully into the salon. "Welcome aboard, Gabe."

Inside, I put him on the couch as Travis came in. "Director Stockwell, this punk was in Commander Livingston's custody not even a day ago. Any idea how he's back out so fast?"

Stockwell played along. "I'll find out, Captain." He picked his phone up from the settee table and made a call.

I leaned toward the Haitian man, putting my left hand on the cushion next to his head. Inches from his face, I whispered in as menacing a tone as I could, "You have less than a minute to answer this one question, Gabe.

And your answer better match the one the Director's getting, or we're going for a little boat ride. Up to a certain tiny island where a cook fire will already be going, and some good ole Arab boys are just dying to play with you. Who got you out so fast?"

CHAPTER FIFTEEN

Having returned Gabe to the custody of Deputy Phillips, satisfied with the answers he provided, the three of us sat at a covered table behind *Dockside*, eating greasy cheeseburgers and fries.

My thoughts were on how all this was affecting my daughter. In the few months she's been with me, she's witnessed more than most kids ought to. She'd handled things in an adult manner, but I was worried about how it would affect her in the long term. The teen years should be about fun and friends.

Phillips came up the walk and broke my thought. "Crabtree is taking the prisoners in," Phillips said. "Dispatch received over a dozen calls from people on Sister Creek."

"Just tell Sheriff Roth to ask the residents to submit any claims directly to him and I'll pay for any damages."

"Mind if I sit down?"

Stockwell and I moved our chairs apart, closer to Kim on the other side of the table, and Phillips pulled one from another table and sat down in it. Looking at Stockwell, he asked, "What's the federal government's involvement here? Especially someone from the top end?"

Travis put down his burger and looked at Phillips a second before answering, "I'm just visiting, Deputy. The only involvement DHS has in this is that one of your prisoners was in our custody in Homestead less than twenty-four hours ago."

"That's a pretty quick release," Phillips offered. Stockwell didn't respond, so he turned to me. "That's pretty much what the sheriff said you'd say, Captain McDermitt. How're you involved with the feds?"

"The Colonel and I go way back," I replied, nodding toward Travis. "We served in Somalia at the same time." *Enough truth in that*, I thought.

"Like I said," Stockwell interjected, "I'm just here to get away from Washington for a couple days of diving. Thinking about retiring here."

"And you, ma'am?" he asked Kim, who was sitting back and quietly munching on a French fry.

"She's my daughter," I replied. "And First Mate on *Gaspar's Revenge*."

Seeming satisfied, Phillips stood up. "Dispatch hasn't had any calls of serious damage, Captain. Mostly just complaints. Y'all have a nice day."

As he walked away, Kim attempted to hide watching him. I leaned back in my chair, blocking his retreat and said to Stockwell, "How was an attorney able to convince a judge to release Gabriel with just one phone call? The guy's nothing but a pawn in the organization."

Travis looked out over the harbor, with its dozens of sail and power boats swinging on uniformly spaced mooring balls, and thought for a moment. "We're looking into it. Actually, Miss Koshinski is. I got a text from her a few minutes ago. The attorney isn't a cheap one. He was hired by Zoe Pound and the judge is being investigated for bribery by FDLE."

I didn't need any more than that. "Let's go." The only reason Zoe Pound would spring a foot soldier so quickly, was because he had information for the gang. Where I lived.

I'd just spotted Jimmy and Angie climbing up to the sundeck of her houseboat in a nearby slip. As we walked along the dock to where the *Revenge* was tied at the end, I stopped and turned to Kim.

"I want you to stay here with Angie and Jimmy." Stockwell went on ahead, coming to the same conclusion I had. "That guy knows where we live and he knows where we were today. I want you to stay here for a bit. Once I'm sure everything's okay at home, I'll come and get you. Or Angie can give you a ride up to Old Bridge and you can meet Charlie there, when she picks up the kids. Just appease the old man, huh?"

She smiled and said, "You're not that old, Dad. Okay, but stay in touch?"

"I will," I said. Then I looked up to where Jimmy and Angie were sitting. "Ahoy the boat."

Angie turned her head and looked down, smiling. "Hi, Jesse. Hey, Kim."

"Mind if I hang out with you guys for a little while?" Kim asked. "Dad has some business to take care of."

"Sure, come on up," Angie replied, as Jimmy moved quickly to hide what I figured was his bag of pot.

I gave him a stern look. He just waved and said, "Yeah, man, we're just enjoyin' some rays. Nothing else."

I've known Jimmy for quite a few years now. His use of pot notwithstanding, he's a hardworking man and I never had any trouble when he worked for me. He always arrived for work sober and left the stuff ashore. This was his not-so-subtle way of telling me he wasn't going to involve my daughter in anything I'd kick his ass about later.

When I started to turn away, Kim said, "Hey, Dad, I forgot to tell you, I booked a charter for Friday. A new client, but I think you'll like them."

I stopped mid-turn and looked back at her. One charter a week is enough in my mind. *But, a Friday charter*, I thought. *Linda will be here Friday.*

"Who?" I asked.

"Some guys from a nonprofit group up the coast called Homes for Warriors," she replied with a smile. "Mister Landeros had them chartered out of Key Largo, but the charter boat blew a head gasket and will be down. He emailed to see if we'd take them at no charge."

I winked at her and said, "You're the boss."

Trotting over to where Travis stood holding the forward rail with one hand and the stern line in the other, I said, "Shove off when I get the engines started." Then I jumped aboard, climbed to the bridge and started the big diesels, which settled into a steady rumble.

I nodded to Travis, and he flipped the line over the dock cleat and tossed the end of it into the cockpit, leaving it tied to the boat's stern cleat, but free of the dock. He then shoved the boat away from the dock before jumping aboard.

As I engaged the transmissions in opposite directions and the *Revenge* started spinning on her own axis, I looked down to see Travis coiling the dock line and stowing it. A moment later, he climbed up to the bridge and took the second seat.

"You know your way around a boat?" I asked.

"Helped my dad out when I was a kid. He ran a tug on the Missouri River. How many people are on your island right now?"

I glanced at my watch. "Charlie probably hasn't left to pick up the kids yet and Trent and Bender are probably still there." He took out his cellphone and I explained that there was only one spot on the island that ever got a signal and unless Bender was on the deck at the top of the front steps he wouldn't be able to reach him.

"These are the newest sat-phones, all the team has them now. Looks and works just like an iPhone, but if there's no cell signal, it has a satellite override built in."

Leaving the harbor through the west inlet, I brought the *Revenge* up on plane and turned due north, headed for the twin spans of the new Seven Mile Bridge and the old bridge to Pigeon Key next to it. I listened to the one-sided conversation as Travis explained to Bender that Gabriel had already been released and somehow Zoe Pound knew where we'd be today.

Stockwell ducked a little as he ended the call and we passed under the old twenty-foot-high span, clearing it by a good five feet. I turned into Knights Key Channel, dodging around the shoal water, then turned out of the channel and set a course northwest into East Bahia Honda Channel.

Setting the GPS for Horseshoe Bank and engaging the autopilot, I asked Stockwell, "Are you armed?"

"Just my service pistol," he replied.

"Wait here. The boat's on autopilot. Just dodge anything floating in the water and it'll come back on course by itself."

I went down to my stateroom and punched in the code to release the bunk, raising it up out of the way. I grabbed a Penn Senator reel case and two longer fly rod cases. Lowering the bunk until the lock clicked, I headed back up to the bridge, handing the fly rod cases to Travis before climbing up and taking over at the helm.

Pointing to one of the longer cases, I said, "Open it."

He grinned at me and said, "But I didn't get you anything."

Opening the case, his grin broadened. Inside was every old Soldier's best friend, an M16A1. Travis lifted it out and I took the case and set it on the port bench. Flipping the rifle over to the left side, he noticed the three positions on the selector switch. He looked up and asked, "Full auto?" I nodded and he looked to the other case, which I'd placed on the deck in front of the bench. "Same thing?"

I shook my head. "Mine's bigger." This caused him to laugh, lessening the tension.

After arriving back at the island and finding everything secure, I sat down with Stockwell and Bender at one of the two heavy outdoor tables next to the bunkhouses. Bender said that Charlie and Carl had gone to town early, to do some shopping before picking up the kids. That explained why Pescador was still here.

"Do you mind if I stay a couple days?" Stockwell asked. "I can have one or two from Deuce's team come down."

Normally, I'd reject such an offer without a thought. Being able to move this way or that quickly had worked well for quite a few years now. Having others around had only slowed me down. Looking around the little island, I began to wonder if I'd done the right thing in setting all this up. I'd built it for this very reason. A place where my friends could come to relax and escape reality for a day or two, or a place to prepare and wage war from. It wasn't easy to find, only a dot on a nautical chart with no name, similar to many others around here.

Now, I had my family to think of. My daughter was here and my other daughter would be here in a few days with her husband and my grandson. I'd also gotten closer to Carl, Charlie, and the kids since Kim's arrival and considered them family, as well. Deuce was up on the mainland training a bunch of new door kickers and around here, everything had been quiet for over five months.

"They won't come today," I said as my own sat-phone chirped in my pocket. "You're welcome as long as you like." Taking my sat-phone out, I saw that it was Kim and stood up, flipping it open.

After I answered, she said, "Deputy Phillips is here looking for you."

"What's he want?"

"One of the models died," she said.

I put my hand out and leaned against the big stone fireplace and grill, hanging my head. "Who?"

"Annette," Kim replied. "Mitzi's in the chamber. Tom and Mister Simpson were treated at Fisherman's and released. They're going up to Mariner's in a few minutes."

"Thanks for letting me know," I said, shaking it off. I'd lost men in battle a few times, but never a civilian diver that I was in charge of. "Everything's fine here. Can Angie give you a ride to Wooden Bridge? Charlie's leaving in a few minutes."

"Actually, Dad, that's the other thing. Marty's shift ends in an hour. He offered to bring me home."

"Who's Marty?"

"Deputy Phillips."

"Oh?"

"Well," she said, dragging the word out, "if it's okay with you, he'll wait until I can get a shower and change clothes. He wants to take me to dinner."

Not something I was ready for. I hadn't been an active participant in raising her and had no idea how the father of a teenage daughter was expected to handle dating.

"Tell *Marty* to stop by and see Rusty before he picks you up at *Dockside*. He'll have something for the deputy to read. After that, if he wants to take you out for dinner, we'll talk about it when you get here."

"Dad, I'll be eighteen in five months and I'm leaving for college soon after that."

"I know," I said "I'd just like to meet any young man that wants to take you out. I know it's old fashioned, but it's how I was brought up."

"You already met him."

"As Deputy Phillips," I said. "Not as a young man coming to take my daughter out on a date."

"Alright," she said. "We'll see you in a couple of hours."

I went back over to the table and sat down. "One of the models died. That changes everything, doesn't it?"

"Yes, it does," Bender said. "Use of a weapon of mass destruction in commission of a homicide. That makes it a federal case now."

I turned to Travis, "That deputy will be bringing my daughter home in a little while. How soon can a few of your guys get here?"

"Who do you want?" Travis asked, taking out his cellphone and starting an email to Deuce. "They can be here in less than an hour. I'd suggest moving your daughter someplace safe, but I know you'll override that and keep her close to you."

I had no idea why Horvac wanted to find me nor if there was any connection at all to Beech. But I don't believe in coincidences. And I don't like waiting. Whatever was going to happen, it would be soon and I wanted to be ready and I wanted Kim safe. The safest place would be with me and the men Travis would send.

"Andrew, Tony, Art, and Donnie," I finally replied.

"Hinkle?" Bender asked. "Aussie's a loner. Why him?"

"For just that reason," I replied. "He's at his best alone."

Travis finished his email and sent it. A moment later when his phone pinged, he looked at the message and said, "They'll be here within the hour. Chyrel's coming, too. She'll handle communication. What's your schedule for the rest of the week?"

"You don't know?" I asked.

He grinned and arched an eyebrow. "Not everything."

"I have a charter on Friday, then my other daughter and her family are coming here on Saturday."

"You might want to think about cancelling both," Travis said. "At least until we get a handle on what we're up against. I'm also going to contact the Secretary. Since this involves us, I'm going to suggest DHS take the lead. When he gives the green light, both teams will be ready to move into action."

I thought about that a moment. With two antiterrorism teams to draw on, this could all be over very quickly. The group in my Friday charter were from a nonprofit organization that helps injured servicemen and women by remodeling homes and providing activities to acclimate them to civilian life. I'd hate to disappoint them, and few other charter boats could afford to do a charter for free.

"No, I'm not gonna cancel either one. The charter is through a service-related-injury nonprofit. Those guys have had enough disappointment. And this weekend will be the first time I've seen Eve in a long time and the first time I meet my grandson."

"The daughter that's married to the lawyer?"

"Yeah," I replied. "Haven't been in contact with him since that night a few months back."

The truth is, I was looking forward to both the charter and the little family reunion and was hoping both went well.

"Let's do this, then," Stockwell said. "If we don't have a good resolution to this Zoe Pound thing by Friday, you hire a couple more crewmen besides me. If need be, some *friends* might be spending the weekend at your *fish camp* when your family arrives."

"Just how do you figure the Secretary can justify taking the lead?" I asked Travis. "The team is supposed to be deployed against terrorism."

"There was a bit of a change in the CCC's mission statement a few months ago. It hasn't been overly publicized, but the CCC has been redesignated as a police force. Still to be called upon against known terrorist targets, but able to work freely on American soil. It happened a few weeks after the takedown in Key West."

Stockwell was referring to the arrest of Dimitri Darchevsky last year, when about a dozen of the team's spec ops people moved to take the Russian down after an assassination attempt on the President.

I sat back down at the table next to Travis. "Just how does a Miami gang being directed by a Croatian psychopath equal terrorism?"

"They've been using grenades, a weapon of mass destruction, right?" I nodded and he continued. "They've been dropping these grenades on fragile coral reefs, knowing you wouldn't stand for it and would come out of what they perceived as you hiding."

"I still don't get the connection to terrorism," I said.

"There are a number of types of terrorism. Those reefs are old and fragile, right?" I nodded again. "And pretty important to the environment, wouldn't you say?"

"Environmental terrorists?"

"For lack of a better word, yes. Or ecoterrorists. Thousands of people come down here every year. This area depends on that environmental balance with tourism. I'm sure the Secretary will agree."

"Do what you have to, Travis," I said, standing up. "Bender and I will get the quarters ready."

Setting up the bunkhouse wasn't a difficult task. All the linens, blankets, and pillows were stored in a single closet in each bunkhouse. Kim would have a roommate for a while, but she and Chyrel got along well. Bender took care of the eastern bunkhouse for the men and while getting a bunk set up for Chyrel in the other bunkhouse, I thought about what Stockwell had said.

Reefs are very old. Most corals only add an inch or so a year to the hard calcium skeleton they live out their lives attached to. Individual polyps live only a couple of years and it takes thousands of them to create a formation that covers a single square foot of area.

They live mostly in warm shallow water, where their tiny tentacles gather microscopic food particles as they drift past the colony in the currents. The reefs are part of the reason the water in the Keys is so clear. The destruction of a small area of a reef, whether it's by a grenade, a boat running aground, or just uneducated divers kicking the polyps with their fins or dragging equipment across them, takes many years to recover. Some never do, leaving behind the ghostly white skeleton most people think of when coral is mentioned.

I try to do everything I can to ensure the safety of not only my divers, but the environment they visit. I never allow heavy gloves and as long as the water temperature is above eighty degrees, I discourage the use of wet suits. Exposed bare skin usually keeps divers from touching anything.

After getting the bunkhouse set up, we didn't have long to wait. Soon, the heavy beating of a helicopter flying low could be heard from the northeast.

Moments later, Charity gently settled the black Huey in the center of the clearing and as the whine of the engine subsided, the doors slid open.

Tony was out first, reaching back and grabbing his duffle and gear bags. Donnie Hinkle jumped out beside him, gear bags in hand, and the two men started walking toward us, Pescador trotting up to Tony for an ear scratch.

Hinkle is a former SEAL sniper, a lanky, dark-haired Australian with an odd sense of humor. He's not really a loner, as Bender said. Shooters just have a different mindset and are usually the quiet type.

Art Newman and Andy Bourke came around the front of the chopper as Charity climbed out of the pilot's seat. I first met Art and Tony the day I met Deuce a year and a half ago. They'd accompanied Deuce to find the place his dad wanted his ashes scattered. They were both with Deuce's SEAL team at the time and about to transfer to DHS.

Art and Tony were both in their early thirties and Art was always ready with a quick joke. Like Deuce, he'd grown his hair since I last saw him and now wore it slicked back and tied in a ponytail. His short, powerful frame belied his catlike reflexes.

Andrew Bourke is the old man of the bunch. A former Senior Chief Petty Officer in the Coast Guard's Maritime Enforcement, he drills the younger men and women in the team on small boat boarding tactics. The same age as me, he's a bit shorter but the same weight, with broad shoulders, barrel chest, sandy blond hair and a bushy mustache. He has an easy way about him and can always be relied on in tough situations. Quiet most of the time, but when he speaks in his deep, rich baritone voice he gets people's attention without having to raise it.

I shook each man's hand in turn. I hadn't seen Art in quite a while and he was amazed at the progress on the little island. Tony was quick to point out the aquaculture system and explained how it worked. Tony had spent a lot of time working on it with Carl. Noticing the many fruit trees growing around the edge of the perimeter, Art said, "You can damned near stay off the grid here."

"That's the idea," I replied. "Y'all store your gear in the east bunkhouse. Hey, I thought Chyrel was coming with you."

"She had to pack some electronic equipment," Charity said. "She's driving down and bringing her little boat. Should be here before dark."

"Alright," Stockwell said, "stow your gear and we'll go over everything in a few minutes."

Once the team had their gear put away, we gathered around the tables and Travis brought everyone up to speed on what was going on and who we were up against. When he was done, he read an email to the group from the Homeland Security Secretary, directing him to take charge of the investigation and bring those responsible for destroying the reefs into custody.

"Is there anything you'd like to add, Jesse?" Travis asked, when he'd finished the short briefing.

"My youngest daughter is living here with me now," I began, glancing at my watch. "Should be back in less than an hour. She knows a good bit about what's going on and I'll fill her in on the rest. I hope this thing can be resolved quickly, because my other daughter and her family are due here on Saturday."

"If we're still here Saturday, mate," Hinkle began in his lyrical Australian accent, "yer family won't even notice."

"What's your assessment, Mister Bender," Travis asked.

Bender stood up at the far end of the table. "Jesse was wrong about two things earlier," he began. "If Tena Horvac has firm control of the gang's leadership, she won't wait until tomorrow. This is a woman who thrives on dangerous situations, and the prospect of losing a dozen or more of the gang's lower ranks won't dissuade her one little bit. They'll move tonight. Also, from everything I've read and learned, she isn't a psychopath, but a sociopath with Messalina complex tendencies, probably stemming from both physical and sexual abuse as an adolescent."

"Messa what?" I asked.

"It's a psychological disorder more commonly called nymphomania," Bender replied.

Bourke suppressed a laugh, but Charity was unable. "Yeah," she said, between snorts, "that describes Etta-leigh, alright."

I stood up quickly. The laughter and grins disappeared. "What exactly do you base this opinion on?" I asked Bender.

"Sit down, Jesse," Travis said. "He meant nothing personal. The rest of you, act professional here. Jesse, Paul has a degree in forensic psychology."

I slowly sat back down. "Forensic psychology?"

"It's the application of psychological techniques and principles to situations involving violations of the law that are criminal in nature and understanding the criminal mind," Bender replied.

Bourke leaned over to me and said, "Think like a criminal."

Late one night a few months ago, Bourke and I sat on the bridge of the *Revenge*, trying to fathom the reasoning behind why someone was trying to kill us. We agreed that we were just unable to think like a criminal. Bourke looked back to Bender and asked, "So you think they'll attack here tonight?"

"If Deuce and the rest of the team don't find them in Miami, yes, they will. And not according to any logical time table. Don't try to determine cloud cover, moon phase, tide, or anything else. They'll move as soon as they know their two men failed earlier today."

The sound of two outboards approaching brought everyone to their feet, reaching for handguns. I recognized the sound of Charlie's boat slowly approaching from the south, dodging the shallow sandbars and reef heads. The other one sounded like twin outboards, coming into Harbor Channel at the east end.

"Two boats," I said. "The one coming from the south is Carl and Charlie, with their two kids. They're about ten minutes out. The other might be a Monroe Sheriff's patrol boat coming up Harbor Channel. Closer, less than five minutes. Donnie, grab your scope. You can see the channel from the waterline, just beyond the fire pit."

Hinkle was gone in a flash and in seconds came out of the bunkhouse with his rifle uncased and slung over his shoulder. In seconds he disappeared into the mangroves on the northeast side of the clearing.

A tense moment later he returned, waving us off from the tree line. "Sheriff's boat with two people aboard," he shouted as he walked up to the group.

"That'll be my daughter and Deputy Phillips," I said.

CHAPTER SIXTEEN

The group became scarce, unpacking in the bunkhouse and walking out to the north pier. I took Kim, Carl, and Charlie aside at the dock and explained what I could to them. Carl had already seen the chopper come in, as they were within sight of the island long before the deputy's boat got close enough to see it.

"How many men do you have here?" was all he asked, as their two kids carried boxes of groceries up to the house.

"Besides Bender, five more, and I think Charity is planning to stay over."

Carl looked at his wife and a silent message seemed to pass between them. "We'll stay," Charlie said. "Probably safer here than anywhere else. I'll get started on dinner."

Charlie was a soft-spoken and practical woman. When something needed to be done, she just did it. Lately, I'd come to rely on her counsel about my teen daughter. Charlie is quite a bit younger than Carl, and little Patty and Carl Junior were her only children. Jimmy's girlfriend, Angie, is Carl's daughter from a previous marriage and though there were only ten years between them, Charlie helped her through a difficult stage of life.

Regardless of what Bender said, I still felt confident that Deuce would take them down in Miami. Failing that, if they came at all, it would be tomorrow. Very late tonight at the earliest and that was only if the landlubbers could find their way. So I was ready for Kim's question when it came.

"Will it be okay if I go out with Marty? We won't be late."

"Why don't you go get cleaned up while *Marty* and I have a talk," I said, glancing over at the young man in the patrol boat.

She went up to the main house for a shower and the Trents headed for their house to start supper, leaving me alone on the pier with the deputy, who was still sitting uncomfortably in his boat.

I walked toward him, Pescador at my heels, and said, "Deputy?"

He stood up in the boat and stammered at first, trying to find the right words. Finally he managed to say, "I went to see Mister Thurman, like you said. He didn't know what I was there for and neither did I, really. We talked about what happened this morning trying to figure out why you thought I should see him and I mentioned I had asked Kim out."

"And?"

"He showed me a letter that was framed," he replied. "'The Rules for Dating a Marine's Daughter,' he called them."

"You do understand that badge on your chest is the only reason we're even talking?" I said. "And that badge won't matter to me when it comes to Kim's well-being. I hope you paid particular attention to rule number six."

He grinned and said, "Absolutely, sir. All of them. Your daughter is safe with me."

"How old are you?"

"I'll be twenty in a month, sir," he replied. "My dad's a good friend of the sheriff and I went through the academy after graduating high school. I've only been with the department for a little over a year."

"Ben Phillips?"

"Yes, sir. Dad pulled a few strings to get me hired on."

Ben is a well-known fishing guide who lives and works out of Ramrod Key. I'd met him a few times and thought him to be a good man.

"Walk with me, Deputy," I said and started up the steps to the deck, Pescador bounding ahead. He climbed quickly from the big center console, adjusting his uniform and catching up to me. As we reached the back steps and started down to the clearing, he noticed the helicopter.

"Holy crap! You have your own chopper?"

"It's not mine," I replied as Bender and Stockwell stood up from the table and started toward us.

As we approached, Stockwell stuck out his hand. "How are you, Deputy Phillips?"

The young man quickly made the connection between the unmarked black chopper and the fed he'd met earlier in the day, but was obviously struggling to remember the name.

"Travis Stockwell," Travis said, shaking the deputy's hand. "And this is Paul Bender, one of my men."

The deputy shook hands with Bender as the others seemed to appear from nowhere, drifting out of the tree line and the bunkhouse and walking casually toward us.

Phillips eyes moved over the approaching group of four men and a woman, also noting the bunkhouses. "This is a DHS compound of some kind?"

"Something like that," I said. "Being a law enforcement officer, I don't have to tell you about operational security. These people are here due to a potential threat in the Keys from a Miami gang. You've heard about the people using explosives on the reefs?"

His mind was quick. Looking at the group in front of him and then at me, he said, "Grenades is what I've been hearing from some local fishermen."

"That isn't public knowledge," Bender said.

"Yeah," I replied, "it pretty much is down here. Secrets don't last long in a small town."

"Why's local law enforcement involved?" Charity asked.

I introduced Phillips to everyone and explained that he would be escorting my daughter off island for supper.

"If she wants to eat out," Bourke offered, "one of us could take her. No need to involve the locals."

"It's not official," I explained. "It's social."

"Ahh," Tony said, grinning. "You're dating Kim?"

"With Mister McDermitt's permission," Phillips replied.

Tony stepped closer to the young man, his dark black scalp glistening with a light sweat. He put his arm around Phillips's shoulder, squeezing it with the nubs of two fingers he lost on an op in Cuba last year. "She's like a baby sister to all of us here. Anything happens to her besides a nice meal at a nice restaurant, I'll be first in line after Jesse."

"They'll be alright, Tony," I said. Then I turned to Phillips and looked hard into his eyes. "You will be armed at all times, right?"

"Armed?"

I quickly explained the situation with Zoe Pound to the deputy, telling him that no action was expected over the next few hours, but I'd consider it a favor if he remained armed while going out with my daughter. "She'll be armed, too."

"She will?" the young man replied as Kim came walking across the clearing. She was dressed in jeans and wore a clean and pressed denim shirt. I don't even own an iron, so I had no idea how she'd accomplished that.

"Yes," I replied, "She will."

"Ready?" she asked Phillips, hugging my arm and kissing me on the cheek.

"What time will you bring my daughter home, Deputy?"

"Early, sir," he replied, extending his hand. "It was a pleasure meeting you earlier."

I walked them to the north pier and helped untie. "Early is twenty-one hundred," I said. "Late is twenty-one oh one."

"Yes, sir," Phillips replied, starting the engines. I watched as the boat idled down the short canal from the house.

Returning to the group, we all sat down at the tables and I listened as the twin outboards opened up in Harbor Channel, heading east.

"I just got an email from Deuce," Travis said. "Both teams, combined with officers from FDLE and Miami-Dade, moved on the home of Zoe Pound's leader, Jean-Claude Lavolier, their clubhouse, and a known warehouse belonging to the gang. A short firefight ensued at the clubhouse, and three of the gang were killed before the rest surrendered. Grayson was wounded slightly, just grazed by a bullet."

Scott Grayson had been a Staff Sergeant in the Marine Corps when he was tapped to join Deuce's team. A tall black man, he had the physique of a body builder, yet defied the stereotype and had been a Combat Diving Instructor in the Corps. Powerful muscles aren't a prerequisite for combat divers since underwater, the divers are weightless.

"Lavolier wasn't at any of the locations, nor was Horvac. The house had a small staff, there were only a few people at the clubhouse, and aside from eighty kilos of cocaine found at the warehouse, it was empty."

Hinkle let out a low whistle. "Eighty keys? And nobody to watch over it? Somethin' seriously wrong there, mate."

"A complete disregard for everything the gang's been involved with for years," Bender said. "They're on their way here."

A part of me still couldn't comprehend the why of it. Any sane person would have been long gone since Elbow Cay and never looked back. It's like Bourke and I had discussed—there's just no rhyme or reason to the thought process of the criminal mind. I looked from Bourke to Bender and then to Stockwell. Apparently, Bourke and I weren't the only ones to discuss the best way to understand the way bad guys think. Probably a big reason why

Bender didn't have to spend as much time training as the others. His primary job with the team was his expertise in understanding the criminal mind. *Forensic Psychologist*, I thought.

"Paul," I said, "how will they come? Will they just come hell bent for leather? Or methodical?"

Bender grinned. "Yeah, at first. Finding this place after dark will be a bitch, though." Turning to Stockwell, he asked, "Did Deuce get any intel on how long ago Lavolier left his compound? How many men?"

Stockwell nodded. "They missed him by minutes. Ten to twelve men with him and Horvac."

Bender considered it and looked at his watch. The sun was nearing the end of its daily dance across the sky, already lighting the high, puffy clouds to the east with a soft orange hue.

"Two hours driving time, an hour to organize a plan and steal a boat. They'll come fast after that, but like I said, finding this place after the sun goes down will be the hard part. An hour at least to get here by boat. Twenty-two hundred at the absolute earliest. More than likely after midnight."

"We go dark at sunset," I said. "One-hour watch starts once Kim gets back, two on at all times. Until then, no approach is invisible from the end of the piers. Everybody relax and catch something to restock the food supply. Charlie and Carl will have supper ready in an hour."

"I already told Deuce to have six men return to Homestead and come directly to Marathon by air. They'll land within the hour and wait there as backup."

I nodded. "Probably won't be needed. Eight of us and only a dozen of them."

We discussed options, countermeasures, and possible intangibles for another twenty minutes. Charity went back to the chopper and returned with a small case, passing out communication earwigs to everyone.

"Where do you want me, mate?" Hinkle asked.

"Hope you brought a mosquito net, Donnie," I replied. "Follow me."

The group split up, some heading for the main house, where snorkeling equipment was stored in the dock area, while others went to the bunkhouse, where several kept their own rods and reels for when they stayed over on the island. We lived mostly off the sea and what vegetables and fruit we grew. Having more people on the island meant everyone had to pitch in to keep up the food stock.

As Hinkle and I walked toward the main house, Charity trotted up beside me. "Think Kim would mind some company?" she asked. "I'm staying for a while."

Without waiting for an answer, she stopped at the chopper and grabbed a Go Bag, then turned and went back to the west bunkhouse. When Hinkle and I reached the end of the south pier, I pointed west. "See that island?"

He nodded. "Where's the approaches?"

I pointed to the northeast. "Harbor channel runs almost straight for three miles. That's the only deep-water approach and except for the light on Upper Harbor Key and a few crab traps, it's unmarked. A boat big enough to carry ten to twelve men can only come that way."

He looked toward the channel and back to the south end of the mangrove-covered island west of the pier. "Looks to be a couple hundred meters from here and a lot of range with no obstructions. Right enough, even at night. Any other approaches?"

I pointed due south toward the gap between Water Key and Howe Key. "That way's shorter, but you have to know the water. There's a lot of sandbars and cuts, navigable in a small boat, but dangerous at night."

Pointing toward the interior, I said, "Water on the north and west sides of the island is only deep near the island itself. Beyond the pier up there it gets shallower. The only way to get back there is by running right along the mangroves where it's a little deeper due to the current. Even a flats boat couldn't make it at low tide and when the tide's full, you'd have to pole across most of the north flats. Odds are, they'll come from Harbor Channel." Pointing back to the island, I added, "Last month, I built a small platform on the south end of that little island. From there, both approaches are visible for over a mile."

He grinned and nodded. "Be just like back home in the outback." Pulling out a small spotting scope, he scoured the nearby island. "I don't see no platform, mate." Lowering the scope, he added, "Seeing as you built it, though, I wouldn't expect to."

"It's level with the surrounding mangroves about ten meters in from the south tip. In a ghillie suit, you'll be invisible. None of my boats have shallow enough draft to get over to it, so take a change of shoes."

"I'll get my gear. Doncha worry, mate. I'll be more than comfortable."

Hinkle trotted up the pier and I stood there a minute, looking out over the water. An artist couldn't paint a more serene scene. *Why were there so many people that wanted to muck up the water?* I thought. Everywhere down here, people were wanting to take beautiful, undisturbed landscape and put up condos, build roads and bridges, and develop the whole area with tee shirt shops and bars to grab the tourist dollars. I guess I'm slightly guilty of that myself, but at least my little island wasn't built into some ungainly, concrete monstrosity.

Leaving the pier, I went to the Trents' house to see if they needed anything. Charlie said they had everything under control and we'd be having fresh catfish. When I went back out, Stockwell was sitting at the table with Charity. He appeared to be doing all the talking, as he slid what looked like a manila folder across the table. She nodded and folded it into an inside pocket of her flight vest. They stopped talking when I approached.

Travis looked up at me from the table. "When the deputy brings your daughter home, it would probably be wise for him to stay here."

"Yeah, I was gonna suggest that," I agreed. "I know he knows his way around the water down near the bigger islands, but it's real easy to get lost up here in the backcountry, if you don't know the way really well."

"That's what I was thinking. If he ran across a boat full of Haitians, a fast exit wouldn't be a good idea. Do you know when they'll be back?"

"No later than twenty-one hundred," I replied.

After supper, I went out to the north pier with Pescador as the others settled in for the night, most opting to get some sleep while they could. Sitting at the end of the pier, I called Linda.

"I was just about to call you," she said. "Are you and Kim sitting on the pier?"

"Me and Pescador are. Kim is out on a date."

"A date? Good for her. Who's the lucky guy?"

I went on to tell her about Deputy Phillips and of course I had to tell her how they came to meet, recounting the events of this morning.

"Yes, it was brought to my attention shortly after it happened. Three of my officers were with Deuce and his team about an hour ago. I'm sorry to hear about the girl. Who was she?"

"A model my client had hired. They'd apparently worked together before. They seemed pretty good in the water."

"And the other one?"

"In the chamber at Mariner's," I replied. "She should be alright, though. My clients were treated at Fisherman's and released. They went up to Mariner's a few hours ago. Where are you right now?"

"Looking right over your head from my office."

"You have a sunset view? The commissioner must like you. Not quite the same as being here, I bet."

"I'll be there before it sets a second time. Pick me up at Rusty's?"

"You sure you want to be here for this family reunion? I have no idea how it's gonna turn out."

"Yes," Linda replied. "I want to meet your grandson."

We talked a few minutes longer as we watched the sun go down from our different vantage points. We didn't discuss what might or might not happen tonight, though I could tell it weighed heavy on her mind as well as my own.

CHAPTER SEVENTEEN

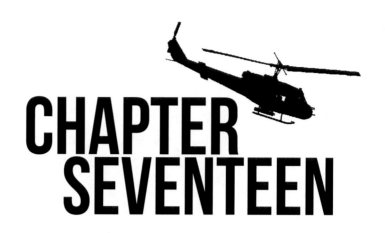

I'd better get you home," Marty said. He and Kim had just finished their giant-sized pizza at No Name Pub, but they hadn't gone directly there. Kim had insisted they first go to Picnic Island in Newfound Harbor to watch the sunset. Being in a sheriff's department patrol boat, a number of other boats quickly left the tiny island as soon as they idled up. In the middle of the harbor, it was known to be a party spot. Just a few trees and a long sandbar, it was frequented mostly by younger people.

Walking out of the restaurant, Kim pointed out the dollar she and her dad had signed and stapled to the ceiling near the door. As they walked back to Old Wooden Bridge Marina where they'd left the boat, Kim said, "Do we have to go back so early?"

"I promised your dad I'd have you home by nine. So, if I ever want to take you out again, that's just what I'm gonna do."

"Are you asking me out again?"

Marty looked at her in the moonlight. At seventeen she was a lot prettier than any girl he'd ever met. He'd guessed her to be older when they'd first met earlier in the day. He'd only learned her age when reviewing the witness statements after her dad and the fed dragged his prisoner off. Only two years older than her, he'd learned she'd graduated high school a year early, while they ate and talked. She also said she would be starting college in the fall, but would be around through at least the spring.

"Yeah," Marty replied. "If you'd like to go out again, that is."

"I would," Kim replied as she took his arm. "But next time, can you wear, like, regular clothes?"

Marty looked down at his uniform and grinned. "It's a deal."

At the marina, Kim untied the lines while he started the two big outboards. Minutes later, they idled out of the marina and turned north, moving with the current under No Name Bridge. It was only eight o'clock, but he wanted to make sure he wasn't late. Something about the way Kim's dad carried himself told him that those rules Mister Thurman had shown him weren't just a joke.

Clearing the bridge, Marty continued straight toward the red and green markers showing the entrance to Big Spanish Channel, east of Porpoise Key. The shorter route would be to the northwest, through the shallow cuts and sandbars between Annette and Howe Keys. During daylight, that's the way he'd go, but the cuts aren't marked and the last thing he wanted was to be late getting Kim home because he ran up on a sandbar. *No*, he thought, *Mister McDermitt wouldn't accept that excuse.*

Half an hour later, as Marty made the turn into Harbor Channel, he noticed a dive charter boat, illuminated by the rising full moon, running outside the Content Keys in the deeper water of the Gulf. It was running with no lights. *Probably a drug runner*, he thought. Being off duty and having Kim with him, he never even considered going after the boat.

Arriving at the dock ten minutes before nine, he expected Kim's dad to be standing there and was glad he wasn't. That meant the man trusted him. He'd heard of Jesse McDermitt many times. Known to be a no-nonsense man who liked his solitude, he was rumored to have ties to a government agency, which Marty now knew to be true. He certainly didn't want to cross the man.

Marty shut off the engines and as he and Kim were tying off, he heard a splashing sound coming from the west. Stepping up to the pier, he looked out over the water and saw someone sloshing quickly through the shallow water toward the west shore, where the caretaker's house was.

"Who's that?" he asked Kim as they walked up the pier.

"I don't know. I wonder why none of the lights are on."

As they crossed the deck in near total darkness, their eyes grew accustomed to it. *Something doesn't seem right*, Marty thought.

True, he'd only been a deputy since last year, but he'd learned quickly from his partner. There were no lights on anywhere on the island that he could see. He figured there was no electricity from the mainland, like No Name Key, but surely they must have some sort of power supply. When they reached the steps at the opposite side, he could clearly hear the pumps running on the island's vegetable-growing system. *So, why no lights?* he wondered.

At the top of the steps leading from the deck down to ground level, he stopped, extending his left arm to block Kim from proceeding. "Something's not right. Wait here a minute, okay?"

As Marty started down the steps, he drew his sidearm, holding it out to the side, aimed downward. Just as he reached the bottom of the steps, he saw a shadow move out of the trees on the west side, coming toward him. He dropped to one knee and aimed his Glock toward the approaching figure.

"Police!" he shouted. "Show me your hands!" The person stopped, raising his hands, and Marty saw he held a long object in his right hand.

"Easy, mate," the man said. "I'm Agent Hinkle with DHS. Is that Deputy Phillips?"

Holstering his sidearm, Marty stood up and said, "Yeah, where is everyone?"

"What I came over here to find out, mate," Hinkle answered as he walked over to the deputy. Marty noticed the object he was carrying was a rifle with a long scope attached. "Jesse had me on that island over yonder to watch the approaches and suddenly all the talk over our communication system just stopped and I couldn't get anyone to answer. I heard a couple of groans, so I came right over."

Kim suddenly screamed and both men ran up the steps in the moonlight to find Kim knelt beside her dad's dog, who was lying on the deck to the right of the steps.

She lifted the dog's huge head, holding the muzzle close to her face. "He's alive," Kim said. "And doesn't look like he's hurt anywhere, just knocked out. Where's Dad?"

The deputy looked at Hinkle and noticed the night vision goggles covering his eyes as the former SEAL sniper turned and looked out over the island. "What can you see?"

"Nobody. Nothing moving," Hinkle replied, looking around the interior of the island from the elevated deck. "Wait! Over there by the old fire pit, someone's moving."

Hinkle started down the steps and Marty turned to Kim. "Your dad said you were armed. Is that right?" Kim nodded. "Good. Stay up here and look after the dog. We'll scout around and see what's happened."

"Pescador will be alright," Kim said, drawing her Sig Sauer P229 from her purse. "I'm going with you. This is my home and you can't stop me."

Kim took off down the steps after Hinkle, Marty following close behind her. Remembering things her dad had taught her, staying low and close to the tree line, she began working her way west toward the Trents' house. She could barely see her dad's friend doing the same thing around the east side of the island. Halfway to the small house, Marty caught up with her as she knelt by an orange tree.

"How did you know something was wrong?" she whispered.

"I don't know," the young deputy replied, moving ahead of her toward the house. "Stay behind me."

When they reached the house, Kim slowly opened the door. The heavy drapes were all closed over the windows, but a single small candle in the kitchen area shone with enough light to see Carl and Charlie lying on the floor.

Kim rushed to the smaller of the two bedrooms and found the two children asleep in their beds. At least she hoped they were asleep. Crossing the room quickly, she put the back of her hand in front of Patty's face and was relieved to feel her warm breath as she exhaled. Moving to Carl Junior's bed, she found him to be sleeping as well.

"These two are okay," Marty said, rising from beside Carl's inert form as Kim came out of the bedroom. "They seem to be sleeping. Just like the dog."

"Same with their kids," Kim replied. "We have to find my dad. He'll know what to do."

Exiting the tiny structure, they followed the tree line toward the two bunkhouses and nearly tripped over someone lying on the ground in the shadows, ten feet from the first building.

Marty knelt down and examined the man, putting a hand against his throat. He was wearing the same night vision goggles Hinkle had. The man had a strong pulse, was breathing and appeared unhurt. "It's the black man with the shaved head and missing fingers," he whispered to Kim. "He's wearing night vision."

Marty gently removed the goggles from Tony's head and put them on, adjusting them to fit his head. He looked around the clearing. The image was distorted, everything appearing in shades of gray and green. He saw Hinkle rising up from another person lying on the ground on the opposite side of the clearing. Remembering that Hinkle had said something about a communication device, he began searching Tony's pockets for a radio. Finding nothing, he looked closer at the man's face with the night vision.

Turning the man's head, he saw what looked like a hearing aid on his left ear and removed it. Wiping it off, he put it in his ear. Adjusting the clip around the back of his ear, he heard nothing. "Agent Hinkle, can you hear me?"

A voice came over the tiny device in his ear, sounding like the man was standing right next to him and whispering in his ear. It was disorienting, as he could hear nothing in the other ear.

"You found Tony? Is he alright?"

"Yeah, just knocked out. Same with the caretaker and his family. I have this guy's night vision too."

"Good on ya, mate. Check the bunkhouse. Charity went to bed a couple hours ago and Chyrel was setting up her computers. Should be the only ones in there."

"Roger that," Marty replied. Turning, he said, "Stay behind me, Kim."

They moved quickly to the bunkhouse and opened the door. Through the night vision, he could see what appeared to be an office of some kind. There were two desks, one with a computer tower beside it and the other with a laptop open on the desk next to a half-eaten meal. A woman with wavy blond hair sat slumped back in the chair in front of the keyboard.

Looking around the tiny room, he saw two sets of bunk beds, one occupied. He moved quickly to the bed, while Kim followed and went to the woman at the desk. There was just enough moonlight filtering around the cracks in the drapes for her to see.

"This is Chyrel," Kim whispered. "Asleep like the others."

"The woman pilot is over here in the bed," Marty whispered back. "Same thing, sleeping."

Over his earwig, Marty heard Hinkle say, "Art and Colonel Stockwell are out cold, too. Looks like the Colonel was sitting at the table here and fell backwards. Got a nasty gash in his head, but looks like he's alright. There's a thermos on the table and two mugs of coffee, both still warm. I'm going to the other bunkhouse. You check the other half of that one, but it's probably empty."

Kim and Marty slipped out the door and moved behind the small bunkhouse to the opposite end. Entering quickly, both of them with guns still drawn, Marty looked around and saw that it was totally empty, the beds all bare.

Back outside, they joined up with Hinkle coming out of the other bunkhouse. "Paul, Art, and Andrew, all knocked out," Hinkle reported. "What the bloody hell is going on here?"

"Dad must be in the main house," Kim said and began running across the clearing in the moonlight.

"Kim, wait!" Marty shouted, but she wasn't having any of it. He ran after her and caught up to her at the bottom of the steps, grabbing her arm and stopping her. "Let me go first," he whispered.

Moving ahead of Kim, he started up the steps. Halfway up, he heard a low rumbling sound coming from the top of the steps. Through the night vision, he saw the dog move slowly into view, its head bowed, lips pulled back in a menacing snarl and the hair all along its back standing straight up. Marty knew this wasn't good. "How well do you know that dog?" he whispered over his shoulder, never taking his eyes off the big animal.

Kim looked up to the top of the steps and saw Pescador standing there in the moonlight, his back arched and ready to attack. She stepped around Marty and called his name. "Pescador, it's me."

To Marty's relief, the dog immediately lifted his head to the sound of Kim's voice and sat down. Kim went ahead of Marty and scratched the dog's ear. "Pescador, this is my friend, Marty. Where's Dad?"

She moved past him to the door of the house and opened it, disappearing inside. Marty followed, stepping quickly around the dog, who sniffed his leg as he passed.

As he went through the door after Kim, he nearly bumped into her, coming back out. "He's not here," she said.

Running across the deck, she leaned over the rail and shouted into the darkness, "Where's my dad?"

"He's not out on the pier," Marty heard Hinkle reply over the earwig. "But I did find something. Meet me at the tables, mate."

"Come on," Marty said. "Agent Hinkle found something."

As Marty and Kim rushed down the back steps, Pescador slowly followed. A light came on in the Trents' house and Kim could hear one of the children crying.

"Go," she said to Marty. "I'll check on them."

Walking through the door into the Trents' kitchen, Kim saw Charlie coming out of the bedroom, holding the little girl, and Carl sitting at a table, holding his head.

"Are you guys alright?"

Carl looked up, his eyes bloodshot. "Yeah, what the devil happened?"

Charlie got Patty quieted and Carl Junior came into the room, rubbing his eyes. "We just finished putting the dishes away," Charlie said. "Most everyone went to bed right after supper, but Jesse and Travis rolled up their sleeves and helped, so we got it done pretty fast. When Chyrel got here, they went out and helped her unload. I made a plate of leftovers for her and when I came back in, I just collapsed on the floor."

Carl Junior went to his dad and climbed onto his lap before Carl spoke. "I found Charlie on the floor and went to her, but then I just went black."

Marty opened the door and leaned in. "Everyone's waking up. Everything okay here?"

"Yeah, I think so," Kim said.

"Yeah, we're okay, Marty," Carl said. "When'd you get here?"

"Captain Trent?" Marty stepped fully into the room. "I didn't recognize you earlier. Kim and I just got back from supper."

Carl looked confused for a moment, then seemed to shake it off and stood up. "The others?"

"Knocked out, like you."

"Go ahead," Charlie said. "We're all fine. Give us a minute to get the kids back to bed and we'll come out and help."

Kim joined Marty and they went out to the clearing together. The little light escaping from the curtains did little to illuminate the area, but a full moon had just risen above the trees and it was lighter.

They saw Hinkle standing by the table talking to Travis and walked over to them as the others started coming out of the bunkhouses. As they walked up, Marty noticed what looked like a propane tank standing on the table.

"Fentanyl," Travis said. "That explains it."

"Ain't that the stuff the Russians used a coupla years ago?" Hinkle said. "The Dubrovka Theater?"

"Yeah," Travis replied as Kim and Marty stepped up to the table. "A hundred and thirty hostages and all forty terrorists were killed by it. Where'd you find this?"

"Floating on the bank next to the foot of the pier, Colonel."

Travis stood up and wobbled a little, as the rest of the team gathered around them. "Heavier than air gas," he said. "Must have been someone in scuba gear who released it on the north side, letting the breeze carry it over the whole island. Who was first to wake up?"

"The dog," Marty replied. "Up on the deck."

"Makes sense," Bourke offered. "Had he been down here, he'd have been out longer. The rest of us were already asleep and didn't even notice it. How long were you knocked out?"

Art checked his watch and said, "Tony and I just started our watch twenty-four minutes ago. I don't remember anything after my first circuit out to the north pier and back to where Donnie found me, and I woke up just a few minutes ago."

"So we were only out for fifteen or twenty minutes," Travis said. "They can't have gone far."

"The dive boat!" Kim said.

"What dive boat?"

"When Marty and I turned into Harbor Channel, there was a dive boat running without lights out beyond the Contents. The water's deeper out there and it was headed east." She crossed her arms and looked from Travis to the others. Choking back a sob, she asked, "Where's my dad?"

Travis got up and walked over to where Kim stood, gently guiding her to the bench and sitting her down. "We'll find Jesse, Kim. You have my word on that."

Charity sat down and put her arm around the girl. "We will."

Travis looked at Chyrel. "Get Deuce on the horn." Turning to Marty, he said, "Deputy, can you contact the sheriff? We need eyes in the sky. Did you see the dive boat as well?"

"Yes, sir, I'll give dispatch a description and we'll have choppers up out of Marathon, Key Largo, and Key West right away."

Travis reached into his pocket and took out a business card, handing it to Marty. "Give the sheriff my number. Have him call me right away."

"Yes, sir," Marty replied, taking the card and running across the clearing.

Travis slowly turned around toward Bender. "They came early, Paul. And covertly."

"They must have had a plan ahead of time. It's only twenty-one-thirty. Lavolier and Horvac couldn't possibly have moved that fast. In fact, they should only have arrived in Marathon by now."

"Andrew," Travis said, "Get on the horn to the Coast Guard. Let them know one of our agents has been kidnapped."

"Linda!" Kim said. "Somebody has to call her."

"Do you have her number?" Tony asked calmly, sitting next to Charity with a nod of his head toward the chopper. "We'll call her together. Charity has to get up in the air."

As Charity rose and headed toward the chopper, Tony helped Kim to her feet and started toward Chyrel's office, which was now all lit up.

"Donnie, go with Andrew in the chopper," Travis ordered and then turned to Bourke. "Andrew, coordinate with the Coast Guard and the sheriff's birds from the air. Have the sheriff's office pass the boat's description to every law enforcement agency between here and Miami."

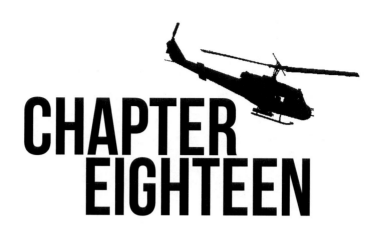

CHAPTER EIGHTEEN

I'm here in Marathon now." Deuce was talking to Chyrel using the video function on his sat-phone. "We just landed."

Stockwell's face appeared next to Chyrel sitting down at the desk. "Jesse's been kidnapped, Deuce."

"What? How? When?"

"We found an eighteen-liter tank of fentanyl by the north pier. They came ashore somehow and released the gas, letting the wind carry it across the island. It knocked everyone out."

"Is anyone hurt? That's dangerous stuff."

On the tiny screen, Deuce could see Art step into the office behind Stockwell. "Colonel, we found the spot where they came ashore. Looks like three men in either canoes or kayaks. A pair of fins were stuffed in a nearby mangrove root where they beached two boats."

"No," Stockwell replied after a moment's thought. "Nobody hurt and it doesn't appear that anything else has been disturbed. Everyone here's a little groggy, but alright. Canoes or kayaks would have been seen—way too much water to cross with no cover. My guess is a scuba diver or snorkeler carried the canister over and was picked up, along with Jesse, by the small boats. The effects of the gas only lasted about fifteen minutes."

"That's about how long it'd take to paddle ashore from deeper water. They must have had a larger boat out there."

Stockwell described the dive boat Kim had seen, relaying the information as she sat on the bunk talking on Tony's sat-phone. Outside, he could hear the Huey starting up.

"We have a Monroe Deputy out here, a friend of Jesse's daughter. He's relaying the information to the sheriff's office and says they'll have helos up out of Marathon, Key West, and Key Largo in minutes."

"We're still at the airport," Deuce replied. "Heading out to the jet now. We'll be in the air about the same time."

"Wait, Deuce," Stockwell said. "The sheriff's chopper has to be taking off from there. The jet's useless out here, except as command and control."

"Roger that, Colonel. We'll locate and join the sheriff's chopper. It won't have room for all of us, so I suggest we put the jet up with its long range radar. I can put two men aboard to coordinate the chopper search. We refueled when we landed, so they can stay aloft for hours."

"Good idea," Stockwell replied. "The rest of you join with the sheriff's helo and head due north. Charity is lifting off now with Donnie and Andrew aboard and will be headed east. We find the boat and converge, force it to stop and board it from the birds."

Within minutes, the G-5 was rolling down the taxiway with priority clearance. Deuce quickly found the sheriff's chopper with the help of someone with the airport's fixed-base operator. Identifying himself to the deputy on board, he soon got the okay from the sheriff's office and the chopper was in the air.

Sitting in the copilot's seat, Deuce adjusted the headset's mic boom. "Head due north. We're looking for a dive boat about thirty feet, with a full hard top, open on the sides."

"Roger," the pilot replied. "But you know that describes about half the hundred or more dive boats that operate out of this area."

"How many of them will be out at this time?"

"A lot more than you'd think. Night diving is pretty popular in the backcountry. Still lobster season for another six weeks."

His phone pinged a message. It was from Bourke, asking him the frequency the sheriff's chopper was on. He glanced at the radio mounted in the dash and typed in the numbers, sending the message to both Bourke and Kumar Sayef aboard the Gulfstream. A moment later, Bourke's baritone voice boomed through the headset, "CCC Air Two to sheriff's helo."

Expecting it, Deuce grabbed the mic before the pilot could. "Andrew, this is Deuce. Where are you?"

"Just lifted off the island, bearing zero niner zero at one thousand feet."

"We're headed due north," Deuce responded. "Should intercept you in four minutes."

"CCC Air One, we're aloft," Kumar's voice came over the headset from the Gulfstream. "We'll begin circling counterclockwise at ten thousand feet, searching by radar. Deuce, Goodman can already see a half dozen small craft on the bay."

Kumar Sayef was a Delta Force First Sergeant, before being hired by DHS for his linguistic skills. With him was Ralph Goodman, a former Maritime Enforcement Specialist Petty Officer with the Coast Guard and airborne electronics technician.

"Deuce, this is Ralph," Goodman's voice interrupted. "We now have twenty-one possible bogeys, most all of them in the size range you described. If you take a heading of three four zero you'll be over the first one in two minutes. Andrew, turn to a heading of zero seven niner two miles out—you'll see the second nearest one. We'll just have to eliminate them one by one."

That's a lot of boats, Deuce thought. Knowing the search could take all night, he called Director Stockwell. "A lot of boats out here, Colonel. Do you have any better description?"

In the background he heard Kim's voice. "It had a white top that ran all the way to the stern and it was running without lights. Big bow flares like the *Revenge*."

"Dive boat dead ahead," the pilot said.

Looking out through the windshield, Deuce soon saw the boat. It was anchored, with lots of lights on. Seconds later, they came to a hover ahead of the boat. It had a white top that only covered the bridge and half of the deck.

"I know that boat," the pilot said. "It's Jeff Rockport, he's a fisherman. Runs a charter boat out of Crawl Key."

"That's not it," Deuce said and keyed the mic. "No joy, Ralph. Open cockpit fisherman. He's anchored up."

Goodman gave him a new heading and the chopper turned, flying off toward the next boat. For the next two hours, the two choppers, augmented by two more from Key West and Key Largo, painstakingly checked one boat after another, all taking direction from the men in the Gulfstream.

"Agent Livingston?" the pilot said.

Deuce knew what he was about to say. He'd been watching the fuel gauge and knew they were running low. "Head back to the airport," he told the pilot. "We'll refuel and get back out here."

Taking his sat-phone from his pocket, he called Stockwell with the news. "We're bingo fuel, Colonel. Returning to Marathon."

"Roger that, Deuce. Charity is headed there in a few minutes. They're checking one more boat first. The other two choppers will have to pull off in a few minutes as well. The Coast Guard and sheriff have three patrol boats in the area, with more coming. The patrol boats are intercepting three more boats that Kumar identified as possible bogeys. It's been three hours, Deuce. They could be anywhere."

"How's Kim?"

"As expected. Nervous. But she's pulled the VHF radio from one of the boats and is hooking it up here. We'll be on in just a minute. Agent Rosales is en route, arriving at Marathon airport in minutes. Charity is picking her up and bringing her here."

"The sun will be up in four hours, Colonel. There'll be a lot more boats out there before then. It's like looking for a needle in a haystack out here."

CHAPTER NINETEEN

Linda Rosales pulled into the entrance to Marathon airport, the tires on the department's big sedan protesting with an audible screech. She didn't bother with finding a parking spot and sped past the main parking area into the passenger pickup and cab stand area. She came to a sudden stop behind two taxis, Cheapo and Keys Hopper. Placing an FDLE placard under the wiper blade, she hurried through the first terminal entrance and looked around.

The airport was small, with only a single departure and arrival gate, manned by a sleepy-looking TSA agent. She flashed her badge and asked where the sheriff's helicopter would be refueling. He gave her directions and she hurried through the security area and out onto the tarmac. Turning left, she could hear a helicopter starting up and picked up her pace.

Approaching the FBO under the yellow lights that illuminated the parking apron, a sheriff's helicopter lifted off and turned toward the taxiway. Just beyond where it had taken off from, she saw a black helicopter with dark windows and hurried toward it.

When she got there, the fuel truck operator was just finishing fueling. She'd only met a few people connected with Deuce's counterterrorism team, but these were obviously part of it. Two very serious-looking men, one who looked like a blond bear and another man dressed in full black, were talking with a tall, short-haired woman a few years younger than herself. *Charity Styles*, Linda thought, remembering meeting her briefly a few months earlier on Elbow Cay.

As she approached, the big man turned to her and spoke with a deep voice, like he was in a barrel. "I'm Andrew Bourke," the man said, extending his hand and shaking hers. "You've met our pilot, Charity Styles, and this is Donnie Hinkle. We'll take you to the island before resuming the search."

"I haven't talked to anyone since Kim called me, two hours ago."

"Climb aboard, Linda," Charity said, shaking Linda's hand. "We're ready to go. Tony's with her and we'll fill you in on the way out there."

Linda climbed in back of the Huey and turned to the other man. "Have you heard anything more?" As Charity started the engine, he pointed to the headset he was wearing and another on the bulkhead in front of her. She put on the headset and repeated the question.

"A lot of boats out there," the man named Hinkle explained in a lyrical Australian accent. "But don't worry, love. We'll find him."

The big helicopter rose into the air, the nose dropping as soon as they were airborne. It moved quickly along the short taxiway, gaining speed. Charity made a climbing turn over the runway and then flew out over the water, turning northwest.

Linda could just make out the sheriff's chopper heading northeast with its spotlight piercing the black sky creating a circle of light on the water below. The moon was past its zenith and starting down toward the western horizon, where she could see a bright star just about to fade into the sea.

Is that Neptune? she thought. *No, too late in the night.* She remembered Rusty telling them, while they were on Cape Sable, that the King of the Sea fell into the ocean just a few hours after sunset this time of year.

She couldn't help but think that if Jesse were here, he'd know what star it was. In the darkness of the chopper she shed a quiet tear born of fear. Wiping her eyes with a handkerchief from her purse, she sat forward in the seat, looking ahead with anticipation.

Charity quickly gave her the details of the previous evening and the search up to now. Linda had met quite a few men over the years, but none that she thought were as tough as Jesse. Not tough in a valiant, or violent sort of way. He had an inner strength that had borne him through a lot of tough things in his life. *This one isn't any different*, she assured herself.

The flight to Jesse's island only took a few minutes. The little mangrove-covered key stood out against the dark islands and black sea surrounding it, like a ship floating on the water. Lights emanated from all four structures, filling the center of the island with enough light to see the ground. Torches were burning on the four corners of the island, marking the inside edge of the dense mangroves that surrounded the fringe.

As they descended toward it, she could easily make out Jesse's flags flying on the flagpole, illuminated by a solar-powered light mounted on top of the pole. She'd never seen it from the air, only from the boats. On the water's surface it was nearly impossible to tell it from the dozens of others scattered over hundreds of square miles. From the air, however, it was hard to miss. Seeing the flags, Charity adjusted course to approach the island into the north wind.

Looking down as they flew over the side of the house, Linda could see someone on the deck, headed down the front steps and wondered who it was and how many people were here.

"We'll only be on the ground for a second, Linda," a voice said over the headphones she wore. Andrew turned in the front seat and faced her. "We'll find him. You have my word."

CHAPTER TWENTY

Travis watched as Hinkle slid the door open as the chopper touched lightly down. He quickly jumped to the ground and helped a tall auburn-haired woman to the ground and quickly climbed back in. The woman ran toward the group at the tables. Stockwell gave a thumbs up to Charity when she was clear, and the chopper took off.

Travis stepped away from the rest of the group and extended his hand. "Agent Rosales, I'm Travis Stockwell."

Stockwell? Linda thought, taking his outstretched hand. *What's the head of the whole command doing here?* "Heard a lot about you Director. Where's Kim?"

"In the bunkhouse with Chyrel. Please, it's just Travis."

She nodded. "Linda, then. Any more news?"

The sound of the receding chopper had faded and the silence on the island was deafening. Pescador came trotting across the clearing and sat down in front of her, looking up expectantly.

Linda glanced down at Jesse's dog. Somehow, she sensed that he knew Jesse was in trouble. "He'll be alright," she assured the dog, with a scratch behind his right ear.

Walking into the bunkhouse with Travis, Linda saw Chyrel sitting at her desk, the main computer showing video feeds from half a dozen cameras while a smaller monitor held a satellite image of all of south Florida and the Keys, with dozens of red and green dots in the Gulf and Florida Bay east of their location.

Kim got up from where she was sitting on a disheveled bunk and met Linda halfway across the tiny room. "They're going to find your dad," she said as Kim melted into her arms, sobbing. She tilted the girl's head back. Her eyes were wet and bloodshot. "Jesse's been up against a lot tougher people than this."

"Can we go outside?" Kim asked.

"Sure. The night air will do you good."

The two of them left the bunkhouse, walking without aim and ending up on the north pier. "I saw someone up on the deck when we flew in," Linda said.

"That was Art. Art Newman, Tony's partner. He was checking the boats. They plan to get out on the water in the morning, if the helicopters don't find Dad. It's a lot of water out there."

"You said the dive boat you saw was heading east?"

"Yeah, Mister Stockwell said they probably came across the flats underwater and in canoes from a bigger boat. The dive boat me and Marty saw—that's the sheriff's deputy I was with. Anyway, it was going east, just outside the Contents." Kim pointed north, where lumps of blackness rose up slightly higher than the far horizon, lit up with stars.

"Here," Linda said, pointing to the end of the pier. "Let's sit down for a minute."

Sitting there with their legs dangling, Linda looked at Kim. "Let's try something. I want you to stare out over the water past the islands to the deeper water where you saw the boat."

Kim looked far out over the water to the north as Linda pointed and swept her hand from the bigger islands northwest of them over to the light flashing at regular intervals on Harbor Key Bank.

"Now, let your eyes follow the deeper water you know is out there. You know the water. Follow it to the lighthouse thing over there. When you get to the light, close your eyes and visualize the boat. Try to let your mind just go blank and see it." Linda spoke quietly, soothingly.

Kim slowly turned her head, her eyes tracing the deep water she knew to be only half a mile out there. She stopped at the light and closed her eyes. She'd fished and snorkeled all around there many times and was really learning her way through all the small channels and eddies created by the islands themselves as the tide surged in and out of the backcountry twice every day. She could see the boat clearly now in the moonlight her mind recreated. It was all white, with a long roof that extended beyond the foot of the bridge to the transom.

"Damn!" Kim exclaimed suddenly.

"What is it?"

"The boat was inside the light on the Bank, running the narrow channel between the light and Marker Fifty-Five! They don't know the water! It's deeper on the outside!"

"How is that significant?"

"The light's built on a shoal. They thought it was another marker and they had to go between it and the channel marker to get to deeper water. Dad would have called them landlubbers. They don't know the water! That's why they were going east. They might not have continued east after that at all. Maybe they turned and went north or west, or anything in between. They could be anywhere and everyone's searching just to the east."

"Come on!" Linda said, getting quickly to her feet.

The two ran back to the bunkhouse. When Kim explained what she'd suddenly remembered to Stockwell, he turned to Tony, "You're the Squid. What do you think?"

"People who don't know boats and aren't familiar with local waters and markers do all kinds of stupid stuff, Colonel. What she described, and I'm guessing she knows the waters around this island as well as Jesse himself—well, it makes perfect sense in a completely ignorant way. There's no reason for them to run between the light and the marker. It's there to warn, not as a navigation marker. In fact, it's more dangerous, just like Kim said. Unless they're inexperienced in these waters and assumed that was the pass to deeper water. We should expand the search area."

Tony looked at his watch and realized it had been almost seven hours since Jesse had disappeared. "A boat like both she and the deputy described with wide bow flares? It's meant for open water and is probably capable of at least twenty, maybe thirty knots. It could be more than two hundred miles north or west, just as easy as a hundred miles east. A boat like Jesse's could be more than three hundred miles away."

Stockwell visibly winced. He turned to Chyrel and told her to get Kumar on. "He's already on," she replied and clicked a few keys on the keyboard. One of the images went to full screen and changed to the inside of the Gulfstream, circling far overhead. Even with its extended range, it had to be getting low on fuel.

"Kumar," Travis said into the desk mic. "Expand your radar search to three hundred miles in all directions."

"Okay," Kumar's voice came over the desk mounted speakers. "That's a huge chunk of ocean. Half of Florida, most of Cuba and the northern Bahamas. What do you need?"

"Shit," was all Travis could come up with. He looked at the laptop screen, and the satellite image zoomed out showing a good portion of the Gulf of Mexico, the northern Caribbean, and most of Florida. It took a moment for the computer to communicate with the radar system on the G-5 and the satellite in geosynchronous orbit. Suddenly hundreds of red dots began to appear on the screen. A box in the corner showed a counter, registering 238 small craft. Dejected, Travis turned to Tony and asked, "Three hundred miles?"

"At wide open throttle, yeah."

"It didn't look like a fast boat, not very new," Kim said. "And it looked heavy, like it was struggling to stay on plane."

"Fifteen knots?" Tony asked. "Then a hundred miles."

Travis leaned toward the mic. "Set to one hundred miles and give me a count on watercraft?"

"Goodman wants to know, all watercraft, or just the size range we're looking for?"

"He can be that specific?" Travis asked.

Goodman leaned into the picture and nodded. "Yes, sir, with experience and practice, the return echoes can be differentiated between sizes and I can program the computer to ignore obviously large echoes. To a degree."

"Just the size we're looking for, Ralph."

Goodman leaned back out of the picture and Kumar shifted his gaze to the side, apparently watching the readout on the computer screen.

Kumar whistled softly. "I never would have thought there'd be so many. Over a hundred, Colonel." As the laptop screen zoomed back in and displayed the new count, Kumar added, "Most are in the area around the Keys."

"I'm sure you already thought of it, Travis, but what about his cellphone?" Linda asked.

Tony held up Jesse's cell. "Art found it in a tackle box on his skiff."

Travis slowly paced the narrow space between the desk and the bunks. "Linda, this is way too much area and too many boats. They have to land somewhere. I think it's time to add Jesse's face to the APB. Maybe a local cop will see them."

"I'll get on it," Linda replied somberly, understanding the meaning and taking out her Blackberry. "I can get it done a lot faster than you or the sheriff."

"You're giving up?" Kim asked Travis.

"No! We'll keep looking. But we have to look from the center outward, regardless of how far outward they might be. We now have six choppers up from the sheriff's department, Coast Guard, DEA, and Fish and Wildlife. Plus twenty boats from those agencies and I don't know how it happened, but dozens of civilian boats are hailing the Coast Guard that they're putting out to join the search."

CHAPTER TWENTY-ONE

A sudden jarring to my left ribcage woke me up. As I started to struggle against the bindings on my wrists, I heard a hissing sound and drifted back into blackness. Before the inkiness enveloped me completely, I filed something in my memory. As groggy as I was, I knew that I was on a boat. The darkness drifted back over my mind and my head slumped back to the deck.

It seemed like minutes later I woke again. My eyes stung and the back of my throat was dry. I held perfectly still, remembering that I was bound and on a boat. I tried to take stock without moving. Besides my eyes and throat, I had a roaring headache. I didn't think it was from a blow, though. It felt more like a hangover. At least I couldn't feel pain anywhere else. My feet were also bound and there was a hood or a bag over my head.

It felt like I was in the open. There was a slight breeze on my lower legs. Whatever was on my head didn't seem to be a heavy material and if it were daylight I could have probably see light through it. So I assumed it was dark. That narrowed the time span I was out to no more than ten or eleven hours.

By the sound of the bow wave and the movement of the boat I didn't think we were going very fast. Less than twenty knots, I'd guess. The boat seemed to be struggling just to do that. I've been on a few boats, and this one was big and sluggish as it wallowed between the waves, sort of top heavy. The steady, low hum and vibration beneath the deck told me I was on a diesel-powered boat. Probably an old trawler or early model sports fisherman, maybe a motor yacht. Sniffing the air, I thought, *No, it smells more like a working boat.*

How long was I out? I wondered. It'd take at least an hour to get to water this deep at the speed the scow was going. The area for quite a few miles in any direction from my island was comparatively shallow. It stayed shallow going east and got shallower in Florida Bay before reaching the mainland. That meant any direction between northwest and northeast. Northwest was the Gulf of Mexico and there's no way this boat was crossing that much water. We were headed toward the west coast of Florida somewhere.

Muffled voices came from above and forward that I couldn't make out. I was pretty sure it wasn't anyone that I knew or had met. One was speaking with a slow drawl, like Texas or Oklahoma. The other had a thick accent. A Creole accent.

Haitians.

But how? The last thing I could remember before waking up on this tub was helping Chyrel set up her equipment in the bunkhouse. When Charlie brought her a plate of food and told me there was a thermos on the table, I'd walked out to where Travis sat and poured a cup. We talked for a few minutes. Tony and Art had just woken from a short nap. They had first watch. I must have blacked out a little before twenty-one hundred.

Kim!

She was supposed to be back by then. I gently tested the bindings on my wrists.

Useless.

Every fiber of my body screamed for me to act. But act against who? And how? I had no idea where I was, how long I'd been out, or how many men were even on this boat. Twenty years ago I would have struggled against the restraints anyway, got knocked out again and struggled more when I came to. Stubbornness is a hard thing to work out of some people. I did have a pretty good idea how many of them would die, if Kim had been hurt in any way.

Every damned one of them.

Lying perfectly still, I waited, biding my time. We'd get where we were going sooner or later and that would be the time to act. Until then, I had to think. There were at least two men on board. I usually don't worry about two-on-one fights. Strike first and strike hard. Then it becomes a one-on-one fight.

It must have been about twenty-thirty when I blacked out, no later than twenty-forty-five. Then I remembered the hissing sound from when I woke up earlier. A gas? Had to be. Some kind of odorless knockout gas. Assuming they just waltzed ashore after releasing the gas....

Wait, I thought suddenly. *Tony and Art went all the way around the perimeter of the island, going opposite di-*

rections. They'd been all the way out on the north pier and were halfway to the south pier on the return. I remembered hearing them whispering on their earwigs. Mine was turned off, but I could still hear them.

Nobody had waltzed ashore. They'd have seen or heard something. How did the Haitians release the gas? Did it knock everyone out, or was there a firefight? Considering the boat I was on and the fact I was on it at all, it meant there was no firefight. So I had to have been out since just before twenty-one hundred.

An hour to get in and out after the gas was released and another hour to get to where we were now, in deep water. *In deep shit, McDermitt*, I chastised myself. *You were trained by the best for many years to anticipate and adapt to unconventional happenings on the battlefield!*

But my home's not supposed to be a battlefield. "Head on a swivel!" I could hear Deuce's dad yell inside my head. I'd wanted to believe I could live out my days in peace just a few years ago.

I'd love it if people would just leave me alone.

Didn't matter.

What mattered was getting out of this. I was out cold for at least two hours and awake now for fifteen minutes, making it at least twenty-three hundred, but not yet dawn. I calculated we would have come at least twenty to twenty-five miles and no more than two hundred. We were somewhere between Cape Sable and my hometown of Fort Myers.

Yeah, I said to myself, *or the middle of the freaking Gulf.*

As if by my own will, I heard and felt a change in the pitch of the engine. We were slowing and the wave action was decreasing. We were nearing shore. Somewhere on the southwest coast of Florida.

Good for me, I thought. *For them? Not so good. They'll come for me soon.*

In the distance, I heard more voices. Though I couldn't make out what they were saying, the tone of at least one seemed annoyed. The engine came down to an idle and two heavy thumps came from forward, near the bow, as the sound of the engine died.

"Fend her off, you stupid pricks," the Texan shouted.

I heard a stomping sound from directly above where I was lying. "Hey, wake up down there! You're here, bring him up."

I sensed movement just a few feet away and slightly above me. Someone groaned and springs creaked as though they were lying on a bunk and sat up.

A sharp kick in the lower back from a bare foot cleared the last cobwebs from my mind. *Wait for the opening*, I reminded myself.

"*Kanpe sou de pye ou, kochon!* On you feet!"

"Untie his feet, dumbass," the Texan drawled, his voice full of scorn and sarcasm. "That dude's gotta weigh two twenty. You two skinnies ain't gonna lift his ass up there."

The ladder from the bridge creaked and someone jumped from it to the deck where I lay. "You dumb shit! You stepped on my finger!"

More voices from close by. Orders were given in Creole as the boat bumped what sounded like a bare wood dock for the second time.

Snugging her up, I thought, feeling someone tugging at the bindings on my ankles, and suddenly they were free.

"Pick his ass up," Tex said. "If he ain't awake yet, maybe a quick swim will do the trick."

Hands grabbed me under the arms and two men jerked me to my feet. I pretended to collapse and they jerked me upright, where I wobbled for a moment, waiting. The dock grew silent and I sensed rather than felt the people out there all step away from the boat as one unit.

"Remove the bag from his head. I want to know you brought the right one." A woman's voice, one that I did recognize.

The hood was quickly pulled off and I let my head drop, but my eyes were open and my mind clear. It was dark. I knew that as soon as I looked up, I could learn at least two things and I might only have a few seconds to figure them out. First, how many people I was up against and second, how long I'd been out.

I'd stopped wearing a watch some time ago, except to dive. I found little use for it these days. The sun, moon and stars were my clock, along with the rise and fall of the tides.

The deck of the boat I could see was wood, the gunwales fiberglass, both stained from time and neglect. The bright work was tarnished and green, with more stains streaking the fiberglass from the mounts. Not a trawler. A really old and worn-out sports fisherman.

A hand grabbed my hair and yanked my head back, where I could finally see the stars. As fate would have it, my first glimpse of the night sky was to the north.

Polaris wasn't in the right place. I've seen it every night for the last seven years from my island or nearby. Always in exactly the same spot in the night sky, never moving. As my friend Rusty would say, "Timeless and predictable." It was just slightly higher now, confirming I was north of my island. By the position of the stars around it, I realized I'd been out for five hours and it was another three or four hours before dawn. I was somewhere about seventy-five miles north of my island. The Ten Thousand Islands.

I stomped hard on the instep of the man holding my hair and pivoted. I'd put on a pair of heavy boots after supper and the combination of crushing and twisting on the top of the man's bare foot with my heavy rubber sole was more than he could bear.

As he screamed in pain, he released his grip on both my hair and shoulder, I continued the pivot, sweeping the legs out from under the other man. As he crashed to the deck on his head, I put my shoulder squarely into the first man's gut and shoved hard.

One-on-one, here. Five more on the dock.

Before I could move, Tex grabbed my hair again and I felt cold, flat steel against my throat as my head was jerked back. "You so much as move, and I'll mix your blood with a thousand fishes' in the bilge." I stopped struggling. He could kill me with just a twitch of his wrist.

"Know what this knife is, dip wad? It's called a Ka-Bar, a Marine fighting knife, and I can kill you a thousand different ways with it. You understand me?" I nodded my head slightly. Whether or not this man really was a Marine didn't matter. The steel mattered.

Tena Horvac stepped forward to the edge of the deck. "Don't kill him yet."

The moon was full on her face now. I'd met her briefly many months earlier and had been quite taken with how beautiful she was then. That was in full daylight.

By the light of the moon she was even more so. But her beauty was tainted by the knowledge that she was one sick, deranged bitch.

"Put him in the shack," Horvac said. "Make sure he's tied securely and it's locked. I'll deal with him in the morning."

A man stepped up next to her. He was dressed a little better than the others, but still he wore gang colors. He had a gold front tooth and what looked like a Mr. T starter kit around his neck. I recognized him from the pictures I'd found on the Internet.

"Why not just kill him here and now, Erzulie?"

"That would be too easy," Horvac cooed, caressing Lavolier's arm. The man became visibly weak in the knees and started breathing heavily at the touch of her hand. I noticed even under his baggy pants he had an erection. *Poor son of a bitch*, I thought. *You're dead and don't even know it yet.*

Two of the gangbangers held semi-autos leveled at my belly as two others reached for me and dragged me up onto the makeshift pier. It was little more than posts sunk into the muck with a floating deck attached to them. It appeared to be made of wood pallets and thirty-gallon plastic drums, lashed underneath, half filled with water. I'd seen this construction technique in a lot of third-world countries.

One of the guns prodded me in the back, shoving me down the pier toward shore. The two men with the guns behind me were joined by a few of the others, while Horvac and Lavolier led the way. On shore, I was forced up a path cutting diagonally up a small limestone cliff to high ground.

Reaching the top, no more than ten or twelve feet above the water, I heard the boat's engine start up and it begin idling back out to deeper water.

"Pleasure doing business with ya!" I heard Tex yell.

The limestone was a dead giveaway. I knew there was a cove just to the north of here where snook came by the hundreds at high tide to feed on the smaller fish every fall. They were hiding out on Panther Key in the Ten Thousand Islands. Just across Gullivan Bay from here is the resort town of Marco Island. I could just see the faint glow from the town on the horizon.

The procession wound along a path inland through the pine forest for a couple hundred yards. Soon, we came into a clearing where there were a number of simple wooden structures. I could hear a generator running and there were lights in two of the buildings. More people were there, milling about, but none looked at Horvac.

They're afraid of her, I thought. What was it Gabriel had called her? The voodoo spirit of love? Spirits are highly feared among voodoo practitioners, especially the uneducated ones. The men here at this camp weren't gangbangers, like Lavolier and Gabriel. These were the poorest of the poor, Haitian refugees. The mere mention of a spirit would cow them into submission. Mix that with what I knew about the woman's affinity for herbs and pharmaceuticals and it was no wonder they trembled in her presence. Zoe Pound was probably using them for slave labor, to harvest pot in the surrounding forest.

One of the gangbangers shoved me toward a small building on the outskirts of the small settlement. "In dere, white boy!"

Another man opened the shed door, which I noticed was solidly built, and I was pushed inside, tripping over a piece of wood and falling to the ground. The door closed and I was enveloped in pitch darkness as everyone walked away, laughing. All but Horvac. While I couldn't make out what she was saying, I could tell by the sultry sound of her voice that Lavolier would be busy for a while. Maybe some of the others as well.

They'd neglected to tie my feet. I rolled over and got my knees under me, then managed to stand up. Slowly, my eyes became adjusted to the near total darkness. I could smell wood smoke. A tiny amount of light leaked through the eaves of the roof overhang.

First, I needed to get my hands free and then find some kind of weapon or a way to communicate. I looked around the shed and couldn't see anything. I started to move toward the back wall and ran into something hanging from the rafters. It swung slowly back and forth.

I moved around whatever it was and nearly tripped on another piece of wood. The smell of smoke grew stronger and I realized I was in some sort of smokehouse. Probably a deer hindquarter was hanging there. I backed up to the wall and felt around. The boards and studs were smooth. I couldn't find any protruding nails or splinters.

Dropping to my knees again, I slowly rolled to my left shoulder and lay down on my side. As kids, an old friend and I used to play Houdini and see if we could get loose from being tied up. My reach made it easy. At six three, my arms and legs are pretty long.

Rolling onto my back and lifting my lower body with my feet tucked close to my ass, I rolled my shoulders forward. It wasn't easy, because they'd tied my hands very well, but eventually I worked my hips between my elbows and was sitting forward. After that, it was just a simple matter of rolling onto my side and working my legs, one at a time, between my outstretched arms.

That accomplished, I had my hands in front of me. Biting and chewing on the restraints, I realized it was leather and the knots were on the underside, where I couldn't get to them with my teeth.

Nor could I get my hands in my pockets, but I could feel what was in them. As far as I knew they hadn't searched me. A laser bore sight was in my cargo pocket with my wallet. It's used to sight a rifle fairly accurately without firing a shot. Insert it in the barrel and where the laser pointed was where the round would hit. Just adjust the sights until they're on the red dot. I wasn't sure how I could use it. Maybe I could blind one or two of the gang whenever they came for me.

I dropped to my knees and began searching the floor of the shed. Odds were they used scrap lumber for the fire whenever they had any, along with hardwoods. Scrap lumber meant imbedded nails that would be burned out of the wood. It took a long time, nearly an hour, but I found a bent sixteen-penny nail and started to work on the bindings.

Getting the crooked, rusty nail point against one of the straps proved to be harder than I thought. I finally got the nail started through the strap and using a hunk of burnt wood on the ground to press the nail against, it poked through the strap, gouging my left wrist. I was bleeding, but couldn't stop working. I'd have to be more careful and repeat the process over and over, poking holes as close to the same spot as I could to weaken the leather enough to where I could chew through it. Rope would have been easier.

An hour later, exhausted, covered in sweat and black soot, I parted the leather and I was free. Confined, but free.

Didn't matter, I could fight. I went straight to the back wall of the smokehouse and tested each board in the vertical siding. It wasn't regular siding, but a lot thicker. Probably made from pressure-treated two-by-twelves. Busting through that was out of the question. The corner posts were six-by-six lumber, buried in the sand.

I dropped to my knees and started digging, pushing the loose sand as far as I could, knowing it would fall back in. I stopped every few minutes to listen for the sound of approaching footsteps.

Finally, my hands reached the bottom of the boards. Enlarging the hole and working furiously, I moved more and more sand and soot. Middle of February and every square inch of my clothes and skin was drenched in sweat and covered with chalky soot.

After nearly an hour of digging and removing a few large hunks of limestone, I slid my head and shoulders into the hole. I had to lay flat on my back and wiggle my way through, but I got my head up on the other side. I kicked with my feet and pushed more sand away from the other side until my feet were low enough inside the smokehouse to slide my legs under the wall.

I quietly slipped into the dense forest behind the smokehouse. I was free. I had an idea how to communicate, but it relied on a few things that the odds were heavily stacked against. I grew up just sixty miles north of here and fished the Ten Thousand Islands many times with Pap. With Mam too, a few times, and later with several friends and girlfriends.

I knew there used to be a low ridge just north of here, about the middle of the island. It had been burned off in some long ago fire and the limestone made plant recovery very slow. I'd camped here a lot of nights. The ridge had been bare from the time I was eight to when I left for Boot Camp and would likely be bare still today.

If I could get there, I might be able to send a signal, if anyone was looking for it. *If there's even anyone looking for me*, I thought. I didn't know what had happened on the island. There might not even be anyone looking for a couple of days. I pushed that thought to the back of my mind where it could kindle the rage I might need later on.

Deuce's team has access to a multimillion dollar surveillance satellite. Chyrel told me about a year ago how it worked. It was actually designated for use by the FBI, but since all the alphabet soup agencies fell under the umbrella of DHS since 9/11, Stockwell could authorize the usage time and movement. Somehow, it could be held in a stationary spot above a fixed place on the ground, or moved around thousands of miles up in the sky. Chyrel explained how, but like with so many of her other explanations, my eyes crossed and I just nodded. I'm not a rocket scientist and don't need to be. If she said it worked, it worked.

If everything was okay on the island, Chyrel would be given control of the satellite. I remember her saying that it took hours to get it in the right position sometimes, depending on where it was located. But once there, the computers could hold it in place so its expensive camera array could look straight down at a spot on the ground and literally count the blades of grass growing out of a crack in a sidewalk. I was hoping she was zoomed out a little further than that.

As the sky began to turn purple in the southeast, I reached the bare spot I remembered as a kid. The raw limestone sand prevented just about anything from taking root and was still bare. I found the most level spot I could and lay down on my back. This was going to be the longest shot I'd ever made. But first, I had to find the right star to shoot.

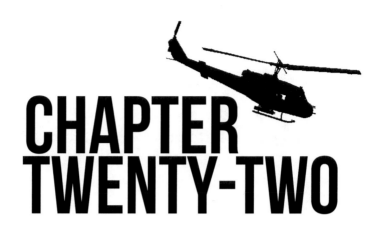

CHAPTER TWENTY-TWO

Tony stood next to Travis, watching the monitors. Chyrel had a direct feed from the onboard cameras of eight helicopters now, and every few minutes one would come up on a boat. Some were smaller pleasure boats, heading out for a day of fishing. Those they skipped over almost immediately. Some were way larger than the boat they were looking for, cargo ships coming and going from several ports along the coast. Occasionally, the size was right, but not the configuration.

It was a process of elimination and each boat they eliminated had a corresponding light on Chyrel's laptop that changed from red to green. Less than thirty percent were green.

"It'll be daylight soon," Tony quietly noted.

"I know. You're anxious to get out there and help search."

"Wouldn't be much help, but at least we'll be on the water and out there when one of the choppers finds the right boat."

Travis glanced over at Kim and Linda. They'd been talking for the last hour and had fallen asleep, Kim leaning on Linda's shoulder. When he looked back, Tony could see the dejection in the man's eyes.

Only Deuce and a couple others knew Stockwell was planning to retire. He'd spent nearly forty years serving his country in one way or another. Every minute that passed reduced the chances of finding Jesse and both men knew it. It had already been nine hours and they were nearly mainlining coffee.

The guys in the choppers had it worse, staring at a small circle of light on the water for hours on end. As far as Tony knew, the Colonel had succeeded in every aspect of his professional career. Not finding a kidnapped comrade at the end of it was something he'd never be able to get over.

"Nobody expected this, Colonel."

"No," Travis said, quietly looking down at his hands. "But I should have anticipated every possibility. I failed him."

Tony looked back at the video feeds as a boat entered the cone of light from one of the helicopters. It was Deuce and they were low on fuel again. Chyrel had joined the telemetry feed of each chopper to the video and they could see how much fuel each bird had. The boat in the middle of the light circle became larger. Again, it wasn't the right kind of boat. It was another sailboat.

As the two men watched, something on the other screen to his right caught Tony's eye. He leaned closer, not sure what he'd seen. Aside from a short nap and being knocked out for fifteen minutes or so, he hadn't slept in over twenty-four hours.

He saw it again. One of the red lights that represented an uninspected boat flashed on and off. "What the...?"

Chyrel glanced to where Tony was looking and saw the flashing light. Her fingers flew across the keyboard as Travis stepped around Tony for a better view. "Not a glitch," she said. "Everything checks out."

"This is a real-time satellite image?" Travis asked. She nodded and he put his finger on the flashing red light. "If it's not a glitch, why is this boat on dry land?"

The three of them watched the flashing light. Suddenly Travis exclaimed, "Morse code!"

"Standard SOS!" Tony added as Kim and Linda rose from the bunk and moved to join them in front of the monitors. "Followed by something else. Dot dash dash dash, then dash dash."

"JM!" Travis exclaimed.

Linda's hand flew to her mouth. "Jesse!"

The same series of flashes continued, but Travis was already in motion. "Chyrel, get the coordinates where that's coming from."

Reaching for the mic, he saw Deuce's chopper pull off the sailboat. They were closest, only forty miles away. Then Travis realized they barely had enough fuel to make either Homestead or Marathon. Knowing Deuce the way he did, he knew he'd order the chopper to go in, even if it meant not being able to get back out. He scanned the other video feeds. Two birds were already headed to Marathon and two more would have to refuel pretty soon. Charity had just landed at Marathon and would be back in the air once they took on fuel. Only the two DEA helos had enough fuel to get there and get out. They'd just refueled at the Naval Station on Boca Chica and were currently west of Key West.

Travis ordered the DEA helicopters to head toward the southwest coast of the mainland, then read off the coordinates Chyrel handed him. They were more than a hundred and twenty miles away, checking out a large number of boats near the Dry Tortugas.

Travis turned to Tony and handed him the paper. "Get Paul up. You, him, and Art get ready. Take the Cigarette."

As Tony started toward the door, Linda grabbed his elbow. "I'm going with you."

"With all due respect," Tony replied, "your handgun's gonna be pretty useless where we're going."

"Dad gave me the combination to his war chest," Kim suggested. "Where he keeps his guns. That's what he calls it."

"Go!" Linda said to Tony. "I'll be ready before you get underway."

He quickly left, leaving the door standing open. Linda turned to Kim and said, "I know you want to, but you're not going. So get that out of your head. Now, take me to Jesse's guns." The two of them ran out of the bunkhouse after Tony.

Travis picked up the mic. He ordered the remaining choppers to pull off their search and go immediately to the nearest place they could refuel. He then ordered any of the surface craft who had enough fuel to make Marco Island to respond.

Deuce's voice came back over the radio. "What do you have, Colonel?"

"A signal from Jesse. He's on an island just east of Marco. I have two DEA birds headed there plus Tony, Art, and Agent Rosales in the Cigarette. I want you to fly to Homestead, refuel and get there as fast as possible, as backup. That's an order, Deuce." After a couple seconds, he quietly added, "Maybe the last one I'll give you."

Deuce didn't hear that last part. Travis had released the mic's key. After several seconds of silence, Deuce finally responded, but without conviction. "Aye, aye, sir. We can make Homestead and be near Marco in ninety minutes."

One by one, the surface craft responded that they didn't have enough fuel, except one.

"Colonel, this is Deputy Phillips. I can make it."

"Deputy Phillips, are you alone?"

"Yes, sir," the young man replied. "But I know that area really well and I'm less than an hour away. I can get there with fuel to spare."

"Roger that, Deputy. Agents Newman, Jacobs, and Rosales are leaving here in just a minute in Jesse's Cigarette. They'll arrive there a little after you, along with two DEA helicopters. Tony Jacobs is in charge. You're alone on the water out there, son. Your call."

There was only a moment of silence. "Which island, sir? I'm throttling up and headed north."

"Have you ever heard of Panther Key?" Travis asked over the mic. Releasing it he asked, "Chyrel, is there any way you can signal Jesse back from that thing?"

The deputy replied before he finished. "Yes, sir, good snook in the fall and a ridge perfect for camping. I'm on my way!"

Chyrel was already typing, while she said, "Depends on how clear Jesse's eyesight and the sky are. It has lights that I can probably flash on and off."

Travis sat down with a pad and pencil. It'd been a long time since he'd learned Morse code and he struggled, erasing nearly as much as he wrote. Finally, he handed her the pad. "Flash the lights five times, wait five seconds and send this twice."

Chyrel bent over the keyboard and logged into the satellite's mechanical system, which controlled the lights used in navigation should it ever need to be retrieved for servicing. When she finished, she looked up at Travis. "What did it say?"

"'How many?'" Travis replied and bent toward the laptop's monitor. The flashing had stopped. He picked up the notepad and waited. Suddenly, the light flashed five times again, stopped and began flashing another message. He wrote down the series of dots and dashes. It was a long message.

Travis sat down and started to work again. "Flash five times and wait while I figure this out and write the next message." It took several minutes this time. When he finished, he handed it to her and she began manipulating the light system controls again. "I can't believe this is actually working," he said to himself.

When she finished, Travis sat ready to take the message when Jesse responded. The message was long, but he was remembering more and he recognized many letters instantly. When he stopped writing, he picked up the mic with a grave expression.

Charity's voice came through the speaker, hailing Goodman on the radio. "We're taking off in just a minute, Ralph. Where to next?"

Travis cut in. "Charity, we found Jesse. He's near Marco Island and needs help. Get in the air as quickly as possible. Contact Tony and drop your passengers on his boat."

Travis then advised the two DEA choppers that two boats would arrive at the coordinates given and that there probably wouldn't be a landing zone when they arrived. They were to provide cover and support to the agents in the boats. Then he activated the earwig he'd been wearing all night. He'd turned it off an hour ago to save the battery.

"Tony, this is Travis."

"Just about to leave, Colonel," he heard Tony respond.

"Be advised, Charity is leaving Marathon momentarily and will rendezvous with you while underway. Deputy Phillips is already halfway there and will get there before you. Two DEA choppers can provide support, but Deuce has to refuel and will get there thirty minutes after you arrive."

"Yes, sir," Tony replied. "Any further communication from Jesse?"

Travis keyed the mic. "Yes, he said there are ten to twelve combatants on the island and more than twenty noncombatant refugees. He began to say something else, but it was interrupted. Nothing more in several minutes. Engage only if fired upon."

CHAPTER TWENTY-THREE

Kim and Linda stepped aboard the *Revenge* and made their way quickly to the forward stateroom. Kim unlocked and raised the bunk. "What are you comfortable with?"

Under the bunk, Linda saw only rod and reel cases from several different manufacturers. "An assault rifle would be perfect, but whatever he has that's longer than my arm."

Kim grabbed one of the cases and pulled it out. Opening it, she handed Linda an M16A1, perfectly cleaned and oiled, with two loaded magazines taped together. In a reel case, she took out two more boxes of ammo, twenty rounds in each box, and handed them to her. Linda stuffed the extra ammunition in her pants pockets and Kim started to reach for another long case. Linda stopped her. "I said you're not going."

As Kim started to protest, they heard the engines of the go-fast boat start up and Linda said forcefully, "No!"

Returning quickly through the salon to the cockpit, Linda stepped easily over the other boat as the door slowly swung open. As Art cast off the lines and Tony engaged the engines, Linda turned to Kim and said, "We'll be coming back with your dad before lunch. You have my word on that, Kim."

The sleek racing boat idled out of the short channel from Jesse's house and turned left into the main channel. Art climbed into the other molded front seat and buckled in, while Linda and Paul did the same in the rear of the boat in the two seats amidships.

Art quickly fired up the GPS and radar, while Tony stood up, steering the boat. With the moon at his back, he aimed the boat toward the flashing light three miles ahead. The sky to the east was just beginning to change the low faraway clouds from gray to a burnt orange.

"Red sky at morn," Tony said.

"Sailor be warned," both Linda and Art said simultaneously.

"That supposed to mean something?" Paul asked Linda.

"Might be some bad weather moving in," she replied.

"Radar's clear!" Art said. "GPS and plotter are active!"

"Clear and active," Tony responded as he sat down and quickly buckled in. "Tighten your straps!"

Tony pushed both throttles slowly forward, but only halfway, not wanting the engines to cavitate and overrev. The two big racing engines roared as the boat accelerated, planing within seconds. Relying on the navigation system like an airline pilot at night, Tony looked more at the radar and plotter, only occasionally glancing at the water ahead for anything floating. It was an incoming tide and the water should be clean and clear. Several previous trips through the narrow Harbor Channel remained on the plotter as thin blue lines. He had only to keep the boat within the lines to avoid the shallows.

"Approaching Harbor Key Bank!" Tony shouted over the halfhearted roar of the engines.

Linda leaned forward against the restraints, looking for the knotmeter among all the gauges. She assumed it'd be the largest, but those were oil pressure and engine temperature. She found it, not a knotmeter, but a speedometer, just like a car. It showed their speed at sixty miles per hour. She'd never gone this fast on the water before. The long, sleek hull and the two men at the controls made it look effortless.

"Is this as fast as it goes?" Linda shouted from the back.

Tony and Art looked back in unison for only a second, before returning their attention to the screens and instruments.

"No, it's not," Art said, without taking his eyes off the many instruments on his side of the console.

Tony looked back quickly once more, yelling, "Hang on!"

The light tower flashed past on the left and Tony pushed the throttles all the way to the stops. They were in thirty feet of water and had nothing ahead of them but deeper water. The boat rocketed forward, nearly pinning all three to their seats.

When the force of the acceleration subsided, the boat flying at top speed across the flat water, Linda was able to lean forward again. They were going over a hundred miles per hour. She'd never gone this fast anywhere but an airplane. Although she hadn't been to Mass in nearly a decade, she quickly crossed herself and asked God to deliver them in time.

"You had to ask," Paul mumbled.

Five miles behind the Cigarette, *Gaspar's Revenge* slowly came up on plane.

CHAPTER TWENTY-FOUR

Seeing the star I'd been aiming at pulse five times, I was dumbstruck, but knew immediately that I'd gotten through. The laser sight emits a narrow, focused beam of intense light that is invisible until it hits something. Up close, like a hundred yards away, the red dot is a tiny pinpoint. At a thousand yards, moisture in the air disturbs the narrow beam, refracting it so that the dot is slightly larger than the size of a BB, but it's still very intense. Pilots have been momentarily blinded by idiots shining laser pointers at airliners from a mile or more away, not realizing that it's a violation of federal law.

The satellite was fifteen thousand miles away. I figured by then, the beam would be a lot wider, but hopefully intense enough to be seen. That is, if anyone knew I was missing, if they were looking and if the camera was looking at a wide enough area to see my signal. A lot of ifs.

Once I'd arrived at the bare outcrop, I'd lain still for ten minutes, staring straight up. The only star in the sky that doesn't move is Polaris. Any star directly overhead will slowly move toward the western horizon. With the sun still below the eastern horizon, I was counting on it illuminating the satellite enough to be seen. Finally, I noticed one star that was slowly being chased down by another and passed by a third. A stationary star, directly overhead.

Though it doesn't have sights like a rifle, the bore sight is long and narrow, made to slide into a rifle barrel, so I aimed along its length and began tapping the power switch.

Was it the right satellite? Was anyone even looking? These and a dozen other questions went through my head as I tapped the same message, over and over. Just five letters, the first three were easily recognizable, even for people who didn't know Morse code. SOS, followed by JM.

Seeing the satellite pulse, I stopped and waited. After a moment, it began pulsing again. Not much of a pulse, but as clear as the early morning air is, I could make out the rhythmic changes in intensity. "How many?"

Aiming the bore sight once more, I began tapping. Finishing the message, I could hear shouts from the refugee camp. They'd discovered that I had escaped.

The sky was getting lighter, meaning the satellite would be invisible in just a matter of minutes. I could barely make out the pulse now. "Two by air, seven by sea."

My friends were on the way. I aimed again. Time was short. The satellite was nearly invisible in the quickly lightening sky and I could hear someone coming. Halfway through the message, I heard a yell from just forty or fifty feet away.

I stuck the bore sight in my pocket and scrambled for the far side of the clearing, away from the camp. I wasn't even sure I was aiming at the right spot in the sky, anyway.

A shot rang out and sand kicked up from the ground just ahead of me as I charged through saw palmetto and scrub oak. More shouts as I twisted and turned, altering my course several times. The forest was thick and I made my way north to the far end of the small island. If I could get to the water, the rising tide would help carry me inland, among the many tidal islands that make up the Ten Thousand Islands area.

The problem with that was that it was a maze of tiny mangrove islands, with narrow cuts between them, deep enough in some places for a small boat to navigate. The twice-daily rise and fall of the tides brought clean oxygenated water in and took dirty, nutrient-rich water out. A lot of people had become lost out there.

A better idea would be to stay on Panther Key, where my friends could find me. It'd also be the less likely of the two options that the gang would think I'd do, so that's the one I chose.

Crashing through the brush, I could hear them behind me. My arms and legs were cut and bleeding in dozens of places. They don't call it saw palmetto because you can see it. They grow close to the ground, the trunks sometimes running for twenty feet, snaking in and around each other, no more than a couple feet off the ground. The fronds grow to ten feet in places, the branches flat, with jagged thorns that resemble saw teeth along the edges. They can slice through clothes and skin alike. I finally descended the north end of the limestone outcropping, sliding down a short cliff to the water.

Some geological event way before the time of the Tequesta Indians' arrival here had pushed the limestone up, exposing it to the elements. Over time, the water had worn it down. These outcroppings could still be found in many places around Florida. More in the northern and central parts of the states, but a few are still visible in what's left of the Glades. No Name Key is one such outcropping, as is Panther Key.

Finding a suitably sized hunk of limestone, I raised it over my head, waiting. I wanted to make sure my pursuers were close enough to hear it, but far enough away that they'd not expect to see me after jumping in. When I judged they were close enough, I heaved the rock as high and far as I could. It splashed into the water with a loud, satisfying plunk.

Turning quickly, I made my way along the mangrove bank, moving west, away from the spot I'd slid down the cliff. I wanted to work my way around the mangrove-lined shoreline to where the boat had arrived on the southern end of the small island. My plan was simple. Get a gun from one of these punks and use it.

I froze when I heard the pursuers at the top of the small cliff, a few loose rocks tumbling down to the water. From there, it was only fifty feet across the quickly moving water to the next, much smaller island. I hunkered down in the water and pressed myself into the mangrove roots and watched.

At one point, one of the two men, the one whose foot I'd stomped on, looked directly at me. I was deep in the shadows of the mangroves and though the sun was coming up and it was plenty light, he apparently didn't see me. I realized that my face and hair were probably streaked with black soot, making me nearly invisible among the dense roots in the gathering light.

The two men turned and went away. I knew they'd keep looking, probably send a couple of men to the next island. I had to move. My friends wouldn't be here for at least an hour, if I guessed right. Seven by sea could mean one of two things. The Cigarette could only hold six, so they were either coming in two boats or all of them aboard the *Revenge*. Hopefully, they already had a boat out looking and would rendezvous with *Fire in the Hull*, which would be leaving now. With no place to land, two by air must have meant choppers providing cover. More than enough to take these idiots down.

Behind me, on the narrow beach, I heard a twig snap.

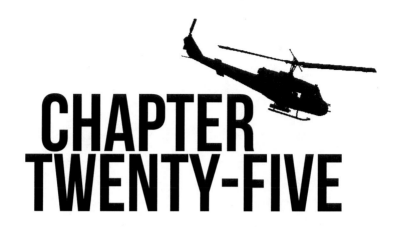

CHAPTER TWENTY-FIVE

Charity ordered the fuel guy away from the chopper as she started the engine. He'd only filled the tanks a little more than halfway. Being only ninety miles to where they were going and another seventy-five to Homestead, it would have to be enough.

Lifting off, she ignored the rules to follow the taxiway and runway, pushing the cyclic forward and making a beeline for the coordinates Stockwell had given her. In the back of her mind was the file he'd handed her and how that was going to impact her life. She pushed those thoughts from her mind, concentrating on the mission at hand.

Bourke and Hinkle were making themselves ready for the transfer, Hinkle breaking his rifle down and packing it in the shockproof case he carried it in. They'd made transfers from chopper to boat many times and even though this one would be at a much higher speed, they felt confident in their ability, as well as the abilities of their teammates.

"I have the Cigarette on radar," Charity said over the intercom. "ETA is twenty minutes."

Bourke replied in his usual calm, deep voice. "If I don't get the chance to say it later, thanks for getting us on board safely."

Charity looked at the big man in the copilot's seat and nodded. She liked his easygoing way. Ten years older than her, in many ways he was like her older brother, steadfast and wise. Always the calm voice in any situation. His instruction during small boat boarding training had always soothed any anxiety she felt, like now. Hovering over a boat and dropping people into it was one thing, but doing it while underway took a lot of composure.

They'd never done it at speeds above forty knots, though. She was glad that it was Tony at the helm, knowing he'd be talking constantly when they came over the boat. Her job was to match their speed and let Art guide her with hand signals. Tony would be talking more to Bourke and Hinkle, giving a running report on water conditions ahead of him in a way the two men on the chopper could relate, to time their leap into the Cigarette's cockpit perfectly.

She was flying low, only a hundred feet off the water. The images on her radar scope were headed back toward shore, so picking out the superfast boat heading away was easy. Only one other boat was heading north, about ten miles behind Tony and on the same course. A moment later, it came into view a few miles ahead.

"Is that—" Bourke began to say.

Charity finished his question. "Jesse's boat?" The chopper closed on the *Revenge*, going more than seventy knots faster, then flashed on past. "Sure is."

"That was his daughter at the helm!" Bourke exclaimed, reaching for the radio.

Charity put her hand on his and glanced over. "What are you going to do? Order her to go back? Something tells me she's already been told that. Forget it, this thing will be over before she gets there and she's not going to listen to reason."

Bourke didn't know much about teen girls. He had a son once and had moved so fast through his own adolescence, he couldn't remember. He looked at Charity and she grinned. Something he didn't see often. "You know I'm right, big guy."

Bourke nodded, unbuckled his harness, and climbed past her to the rear compartment of the Huey. They'd be over the boat in just a few more minutes.

Charity turned on her earwig. "Tony, can you hear me?"

"Weak and broken," came the static-filled reply. They were still almost five miles away, which was the outside, unobstructed range of the devices.

"Five miles out. Rate of closure is forty-five knots."

"Roger, Charity," Tony replied, much clearer now. "Slowing to seventy knots. Damned sea is flat as glass. Never seen it so calm. We'll have to get Jesse to bring us all out here tomorrow and catch some fish."

Charity knew he was trying to diffuse the situation Jesse was in, not just for her, but everyone else. Tony was like that, but he didn't have to. Jesse had been captured on the island and brought out here against his will. The fact that he'd been able to signal Stockwell meant he was somehow free. Her only concern was if he'd leave anyone alive. She'd seen firsthand how quickly he could react against anyone that crossed him. No threats, no intimidating tactics, no attempt at mediation. Just swift but calculated action.

Charity pulled back slightly on the cyclic while decreasing the collective, causing the chopper's nose to come up slightly, bleeding off airspeed as it descended. She looked back at Bourke and nodded.

Unlatching the port side door, Bourke slid it open, the roar of the air swirling in around the two men as the bird slowed. He and Hinkle both had their equipment tightly secured to their bodies and were ready. Being the biggest, Bourke would go first, so he sat down and slid his legs out the door. The wind caught his pant legs and the snapping sound of the loose clothing added to the cacophony inside the helicopter.

She slowed more, putting the bird into a crablike angle with the nose pointing slightly to the right of their direction of flight. She heard Tony talking to Bourke, but was concentrating more on Art's hand signals.

"Over the boat in ten seconds," Charity said over the intercom.

"Roger that, mate," came Hinkle's reply as he and Bourke unplugged the comm link cables from their helmets.

Hinkle sat down right behind Bourke, helping the larger man steady himself as he slid further out the door and put his feet on the left skid.

No longer even looking where she was going, Charity followed Art's signals. He was standing in front of the left seat, with Agent Rosales between the seats and Bender strapped in on the port side.

The cockpit looked a lot bigger when she'd been on the boat itself. Now it appeared much too small. Art continued to signal her forward with his left hand, the other palm out, toward Bourke. When he clenched his left fist, she held the controls steady, flying at seventy knots just five feet above the boat.

Though she couldn't see him, she heard the light thud as he dropped almost eight feet to the deck of the boat and she felt the bird lighten and she moved slightly off target. Art patiently guided her back to the right spot over the boat and gave the second signal. A second later, Art gave her a thumbs up and she peeled off, setting a course for Homestead.

CHAPTER TWENTY-SIX

Tony was looking far out ahead as the boat rocketed across the water's surface. Nearly as fast as the helicopters that were following behind them, the Cigarette ate up the miles of ocean quickly. He liked the go-fast boat. When they used it in training, he'd take her out on the Gulf afterward to blow the cobwebs out of the engines.

Art kept his eyes on the radar screen, which let him know about any boats in their path. There were a lot of them out here. Halfway to their destination, Art switched the radar to full scan to see where the choppers were. He picked them up easily, two echoes flying close together just north of Key West, and a third one more than ten miles behind and closing. He also saw that there was a boat back there on the same course. Stockwell hadn't mentioned any other boats heading out.

Art studied the echo and determined that whatever boat it was, it was pretty fast, traveling at nearly fifty knots. Jesse's big boat was the only one he knew of in the area that was as big as the echo return indicated and could make that kind of speed. He doubted even the sheriff's patrol boats were that fast.

As the chopper came closer he forgot about the boat on the radar. "Charity's about ten miles back and closing fast," Art said.

As Tony began a gradual deceleration, Art unbuckled his harness and turned around, putting his knees against the bottom of the seat and leaning forward over the backrest to keep his head out of the slipstream. "Get ready!" he shouted to Linda. "You'll need to move up here between us in just a minute."

Linda nodded and unbuckled her harness, sliding forward in the seat. Standing up fully at this speed would probably lift her out of the cockpit, so she intended to scramble forward on her hands and knees.

"Paul," Art said, "slide over to the outside seat and strap in. I know you haven't done this yet, but you're the wide receiver. When Andrew hits the deck, grab him and hang on. He'll turn around and grab Donnie when he jumps. Don't let him go until both are on board. Got it?"

Paul nodded, unbuckling his harness and sliding over. He strapped himself in, pulling the lap belt as tight as he could, but leaving the shoulder harness unbuckled.

Tony held his hand to the side of his head, covering his ear. "Roger, Charity," he said, hearing her voice over his earwig. Then in a calm voice, like they weren't still traveling faster than any legal speed on land, Tony said, "Slowing to seventy knots. Damned sea is flat as glass. Never seen it so calm. We'll have to get Jesse to bring us all out here tomorrow and catch some fish."

A moment later the beating of the helicopter's rotors all but drowned out the sound of the engines, now throttled back to almost three quarters. Art motioned Linda forward and she scrambled on all fours between the two front seats, then turned around on her knees.

Three minutes later, Linda was sandwiched between Bourke and Bender, amazed at how easy these men made it look. Hinkle sat down in the starboard rear seat, assembling his rifle, as Tony pushed the throttles to the stops once more.

"Welcome aboard," Tony said, glancing in the small mirror on the console at Bourke. "Might have a few sprinkles in a little while. Glad you got here before it started."

Picking up the sheriff's patrol boat on the radar, Art reached for the radio mic. The patrol boat seemed to be drifting about ten miles ahead, maybe a mile from the coast.

"Deputy Phillips," Art said into the mic, "this is Agent Newman. Do you copy?"

A moment passed and Marty's voice came over the speaker. "Hi, Agent Newman. I only got here a few minutes ago. Didn't expect you for a while longer."

"We caught a tail wind," Art said. "We'll rendezvous where you are, and two of our people will join you."

"Roger that. Standing by."

Another voice came over the radio then. "Marty? What are you doing out here?"

"That's Kim!" Linda exclaimed.

"Yeah," Bourke said, turning to Linda, his voice competing with the roar from the powerful engines right behind them. "We flew over her a little ways back. She's on

Jesse's fishing boat, but she won't get here for another twenty minutes or so."

"Kim?" the young deputy's voice asked over the radio. "What are you doing out here?"

"I asked you first."

"I'm doing my job. Where are you?"

A few seconds ticked by before Kim replied. "About twenty miles south of you."

"I order you to turn back," Marty said.

Bourke remembered the short conversation he'd had with Charity and laughed out loud. "Yeah, that's gonna work real good, kid," he said to nobody in particular.

"She's got her dad's backbone, that's for sure," Tony added.

There was silence on the radio for a few seconds, then Kim came back on. "Not happening, Marty. *Revenge* out."

The young man tried to hail her a couple more times, but she didn't answer. Tony started to slow down as they neared the patrol boat, finally reversing the engines and coming to a stop alongside.

"I hope she turned back," the deputy said.

"She won't, mate," Hinkle said as he vaulted over to the deputy's boat. "Just as stubborn as her old man, I'd expect." Art joined Hinkle on the deputy's boat. He'd cross-trained with him and his spotter, and the two had worked well together.

Tony handed Linda the extra earwig he'd snagged late last night. "Stick this in your ear and adjust it to fit. You stay with me. Like a second skin. Understand? Jesse'll kick my ass if you get hurt, and I'm pretty sure you'd do it if I told you to stay on the boat. So I'm just mitigating my way out of two ass kickings."

Looking around at everyone, Tony said, "We have as many as a dozen hostiles and maybe twice that number of refugees here. Probably forced labor to grow weed, housed in a makeshift camp maybe two hundred yards inshore. We only engage if fired on."

Turning to the young man, he said, "Deputy, this'll probably be over before Kim gets here. If it's not, you'll be out here to stop her. That's a third ass kicking I want to avoid."

Phillips started to protest and Tony stopped him with a single look. "This is Collier County, Deputy. You're outside of your jurisdiction, but you can help us before she gets here. Satellite imaging shows elevated ground three hundred yards from the camp, not far from the northern tip of the island. You said you're familiar with the area. Know where that is and how to get to it unseen?"

"Sure do," Phillips replied. "I can get there through the cuts and channels from the north. Take maybe ten or twelve minutes to get there from here."

"Good," Tony said. "That's enough time to put Donnie and Art ashore and get back out here." Tony quickly outlined the plan and the patrol boat sped off.

CHAPTER TWENTY-SEVEN

I was in a different structure when I woke up for the third time. My head was severely pounding, a lot worse than from the gas. I'd been clobbered. Once more, I had my hands and feet tied, sitting up in a straight-backed chair. Light through an open window told me that I hadn't been out long. The sky was still gray outside. With my head hanging down, the floor was the first thing to come into focus. I wasn't blindfolded and two of the gangbangers were in the room with me, standing by the door with assault rifles slung on their shoulders. The room itself was nearly devoid of furnishings and decoration, but had a wood floor and was fairly clean. A bed was pushed up against one wall and a cheap table and two chairs were against the opposite wall.

Remembering my earlier escape, I'd been just about to turn around, hunkered down in those mangroves, when I was clocked from behind. It couldn't have been the two I saw on the cliff, so it was one of the others. *As soon as I get loose*, I thought, *I'm gonna knock out every damned one of these assholes.* I was getting old, my reflexes were slowing down, and I was becoming lazy with too much relaxing island time. I'd neglected my daily runs and swims and it was taking its toll. I was getting soft. Ten years ago, anyone sneaking up behind me was being lured into a trap.

There was a scuffling sound outside the door. When it opened, Lavolier strode into the room. His eyes spoke of the arrogance he felt as he walked around the room and back, eyeing me like a cat would a mouse. He was dressed in off-the-rack camo pants and a long-sleeved tan shirt.

"You don't look so tough, *wou kaka.*"

I stared him straight in the eye, my anger slowly building.

"Erzulie say you a rich man. A very rich man."

Ah, the money from the treasure, I thought. The number one motivator among criminals, according to Bender.

Lavolier, typical of many islanders, was a dark-skinned black man with light-colored eyes. He came toward me. Grabbing my hair and forcing my head back, he placed a knife against my throat. "Just another chickenshit white boy," he said.

My eyes never left his as I growled, "You'll look real cute when I shove that blade up your ass."

"Enough!"

Lavolier released my hair and wheeled. "I wasn't going to hurt him. Just wanted to scare him a little."

"Men like Jesse McDermitt don't scare easy," Horvac said as she walked into the room. She had her hair pulled back in a tight ponytail and was wearing jeans, boots, and a lightweight tropical work shirt. Miami chic. The two men guarding me lowered their gaze, averting their eyes from the voodoo spirit. "Men like him scare other men."

"He's not so scary," Lavolier replied.

Horvac went to the table, set her black leather briefcase down and opened it up. "It doesn't matter how frightening he appears just now," she said calmly, lifting out the false bottom and placing it on the table. "Tell the others to leave."

Lavolier nodded to the two guards and they hurried out the door, obviously happy to be away from the woman. "You giving him the same *wason* you gave me?"

"Not exactly," she said, handing him a small flask. "This is yours. Drink only half."

The man took it from her and quickly twisted off the cap. He began drinking the concoction instantly, swaying as he chugged it down. "His will be a bit stronger and mixed with a serum that will prevent him from telling me a lie."

Turning to me, I could see his eyes already clouding with animal lust. "You gonna like Erzulie's *wason*, white boy." He grabbed his crotch and added, "Might make your *pati gason* as big as mine."

She mixed several ingredients into a second flask, put the cap on and shook it for a moment, as she turned around. "I doubt that, *cheri*," she said, embracing him from behind and rubbing her hand across his belly. The man's knees began to shake as soon as she touched him, and his whole body trembled.

Her eyes smoldered as she looked at me. "You will tell me what I want to know, Jesse. You will want to please me. And once I've taken from you what I want, I'll put your head on a pole for spurning me."

Gliding toward me, she let her hand lightly caress Lavolier's shoulder and arm. Lavolier nearly collapsed on the floor. "Hold his head back, *cheri*," she said over her shoulder, never taking her eyes off mine. "And pinch his nose shut."

Lavolier went around behind me, yanking my head back by the hair as the first raindrops could be heard falling on the tin roof of the little shack. Not the soft, misty rain like several days ago, but big, fat raindrops that told of an approaching storm. I was the only one that knew what kind of storm it would be, though.

As Lavolier squeezed my nose, Horvac straddled my legs and forced a twisted rag into my mouth. Pulling it down, my jaw opened and she poured the sweet, sticky liquid into my mouth. I coughed, spewing most of it on her blouse and both of their faces. The sight of her breasts showing through the wet blouse caused Lavolier to pull back harder as she poured more. I couldn't do anything but swallow or drown on the stuff, so I swallowed it in big gulps. My lungs strained to take a breath, but she kept pouring until the flask was empty.

Tossing aside the empty flask, she looked at Lavolier's face just above mine. Their eyes met and she leaned toward him, licking the stray drops from his cheek. Releasing my hair, the two embraced passionately, Horvac grinding her hips into my lap, as I gasped and fought for breath.

Ignoring me, she stepped back, focused on the tall black man behind me. "Turn his chair around," she ordered. "He'll want to watch this."

My chair scraped roughly on the bare wood floor as he turned me to face the small bed. *These are some sick minds*, I thought, wrestling against the bindings.

With her back to me, Horvac stripped out of her wet blouse. I noticed the full tattoo on her bare back, angel's wings. A part of my mind realized it was new, since I'd seen her in a bikini top. Another part of my mind was fixed on the seductive imagery as her back muscles extended and flexed while she removed her boots. The angel's wings seemed real.

A distant flicker from outside the window was like a flashbulb going off on the set of a cheap porn movie. But it wasn't a camera, as the flash was followed a moment later with the rolling sound of thunder.

The concoction she'd given me spread quickly throughout my body. Rain started pouring down, beating hard on the tin roof. More flashes streaked across the wall, dancing around the room, and though I couldn't see it, I knew lightning was flashing diagonally across the sky. The accompanying thunder claps now followed in shorter and shorter intervals, no longer rolling, but cracking like a gunshot. The storm was getting closer.

I didn't want to, but I watched.

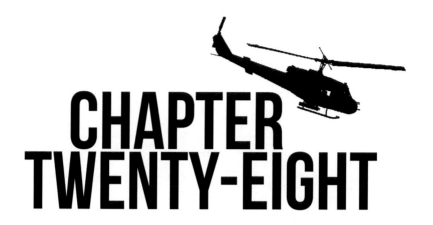

CHAPTER TWENTY-EIGHT

"We're on shore," Tony heard Art say over his earwig. "Moving toward the rock."

"Kid drives that boat like it's a bloody sports car," Hinkle chimed in.

Tony looked back at Paul and Andrew in the cockpit, then over at Linda in the left seat. They all nodded. "We're moving, Art. Choppers are ten minutes out."

He engaged the twin engines, bumping the throttles up to slightly more than an idle, while in the east, lightning flashed across the Everglades and a wall of water could be seen moving up from the southeast. "Looks like we're gonna get wet," Tony said quietly, a wry grin creasing the corners of his mouth. "Good weather for SEALs."

They slowly idled forward, Linda scanning the southern tip of the small island with a pair of binoculars. Still, the floating pier was hard to spot. "There!" she exclaimed. "A little to the left."

"Guide me!" Tony shouted, pushing the throttles halfway. His words were nearly drowned out by the throaty roar of the engines and the sudden downpour of rain.

The brightly colored boat looked completely out of place in the muted gray sea and dark green backdrop of the northern Everglades, now enveloped in a late winter thunderstorm. As if it were a panther, the boat leaped out of the water and pounced forward. It was a short trip, lasting only a minute.

"Straight ahead! See it?" Linda asked, looking through the binoculars.

The boat's wipers were on full and barely cleared the windshield before it was covered by the rain again. Tony strained to look through it and finally surrendered, standing up fully and holding the top of the wheel. He saw the line of posts sticking out of the water and angled toward them, the pelting rain stinging his eyes. He pulled back on the throttles and the boat slowed as it neared the pier.

There was nobody on the narrow beach and the makeshift pier was empty of both boats and people. They approached cautiously, all but Tony with their weapons out and ready. Linda carried Jesse's M16, while Paul carried only his side arm. The big Coast Guardsman had an MP5 submachine gun strapped around his neck and shoulder, sweeping it across the beach with his right hand. Tony carried the same weapon and both men had side arms in holsters, strapped high on their thighs.

Paul was first off the boat, tying the stern line off to one of the posts. Andrew was next, looping his line around a cleat just forward of the windshield and tying it off to another post. Tony quickly shut down the engines, then he and Linda jumped to the pier together.

With Tony and Andrew leading the way, each covering one side of the beach ahead, the four quickly moved toward shore. Reaching the end of the pier, Paul moved to the right, knelt in the sand and aimed up at the top of the ten-foot-high cliff. The others moved toward the angled path and quickly started up it, under Paul's cover.

Reaching the top, Andrew peeled off to the left and took cover next to an old rusted barrel while Tony and Linda knelt behind a palm tree on the right. Tony motioned Paul to come up.

"Want to just take the path?" Andrew asked Tony as Paul reached the top. "Ain't gonna be anyone outside in this weather."

Tony nodded and Andrew moved quickly up the path toward the camp. Paul followed, with Linda and Tony bringing up the rear.

Andrew raised his fist and dropped to one knee on the edge of the path, Paul taking a position a few yards back and on the other side. The rain was coming heavy now, angling down as the wind started to kick up. All four of them were soaked to the skin underneath their tactical vests, the rain lashing sideways in the swirling gusts.

Pointing ahead, Andrew said, "First structure is on the right, just as we come into the clearing. It looks to be a storage shed, too small for anything else. Directly across are two longer buildings, probably bunkhouses for the refugees. Next to the shed is a building with tables out in front of it, probably the kitchen. There's a small raised structure at the far end of the clearing. Probably the guard or overseer."

Above the roar of the wind, the rain and the thunder, Tony could hear the choppers. They wouldn't be of much use in this weather. He pulled a handheld VHF radio from his pocket, switched it on and turned it to the DEA chopper's frequency.

"Agent Jacobs to inbound DEA helos."

"Agent Jacobs," a voice responded immediately. "Thought you were going to start your little party without us. This is Agent in Charge McMichael. What can the Agency do for you this morning?"

"We're in two positions on the island. Two of my men have the high ground three hundred yards to the north of a clearing with five structures. The four of us are on the south end of the clearing. I don't suppose you boys have FLIR, do you?"

"Never leave home without it," came the reply. With their forward-looking infrared camera, Tony knew the DEA chopper could at least save them time and point out where all the players were.

Within minutes, as one of the helicopters held position several miles offshore, the second one climbed high overhead, circling and looking down through the pouring rain.

"Agent Jacobs, the two buildings on the west side are packed, at least ten people in each. The small structure on the east side appears empty, but the larger one is hard to tell. There's a very large heat signature inside, like a fire or heater. Someone could be near it and we can't see them. There are eight figures near the front. They appear to be sitting at tables. The building at the end has three people inside. Two look like they're wrestling and one is just sitting there watching. I see the four of you and your two men on the rock outcropping and that's it. No other heat signatures on the island. And from here, you don't look like you're putting off a lot of heat."

"Roger that, AIC McMichael," Tony said with a grin. "It's a little wet down here. If it wouldn't be too much trouble, could you have your other bird announce our arrival?"

"Stir up the anthill and see who comes out? When do you want him?"

"Two of my men will take positions outside the two bunkhouses on the west side. I feel pretty certain they're all unarmed refugees inside. The other two will move up to opposite sides of the kitchen. Our shooter has a visual on the side and back of the end building and the front of the kitchen. My guess is, everyone with a gun is eating breakfast in there. When we four are in position, have him fly over low and fast."

"Roger that, Agent Jacobs."

The four split up then, Bourke and Bender moving quickly around the west side of the perimeter, taking advantage of what cover they could find. At the same time, Tony and Linda moved around the east side of the small shed. When they got to the back of it, Tony pointed to the ground while watching the back of the kitchen. "They had Jesse in there for a while. Here's where he dug his way out. When we get to the next building, you stay on this side and move to the front corner and I'll go around to the other side."

Reaching the kitchen shack, Linda and Tony took up their positions and waited. Tony could see Bourke moving like a giant cat behind the first building. Paul knelt on the ground at the front corner. Tony would have preferred he had a machine gun or rifle, but having seen the man shoot, he knew he could cover both the door to the bunkhouse and the front door of the kitchen across the clearing more than adequately.

As soon as he saw Andrew kneel at the corner of the other bunkhouse, Tony heard the heavy beating of the chopper's blades as it approached the island from the south, getting louder and louder as the four waited.

Suddenly, the chopper soared over in a climbing turn, its blades beating hard against the air as it roared past, gaining altitude. When it disappeared into the pouring rain and the sound dissipated, Tony shouted, "This is Homeland Security! Leave your weapons inside and come out with your hands up!"

The door to the kitchen flew open and two men armed with AK-47 assault rifles ran out. One of them spotted Paul and aimed his rifle from the hip, letting loose a short burst. The bullets kicked up dirt and splintered the wood wall of the bunkhouse. Paul's 9mm Beretta jumped twice in his hand and the man went down, sprawling face-first in the wet limestone sand.

The second man spun and took aim at Paul. Before he could pull the trigger, Bourke's MP5 stitched a line from his belly to his face. He spun around like a puppet whose strings had been cut, dead before his knees touched the ground. Three more came charging out, shooting wildly. None made it more than three steps, as all four members of the team fired on them and the large boom of Hinkle's rifle mixed with the crash of thunder.

As quickly as the firefight started, it ended. Tony shouted once more, "You in the kitchen! Come out with your hands up! You are under arrest!"

One by one, the remaining gangbangers came out of the kitchen, arms raised high. Bourke's voice overwhelmed the sounds of nature as he directed them out into the middle of the clearing, hands behind their heads. When they were assembled in the middle, he ordered them to drop to their knees and lie face down on the ground.

With five of them dead and the three surviving gangsters under control, Tony moved quickly to the door and glanced inside. There was no sound or movement in the kitchen. He dashed through the door and rolled onto the floor, coming up in a kneeling stance against the side wall, his MP5 up and ready. The room was empty except two tables with chairs, a work table, a refrigerator and a stove.

At the door, Tony could hear another chopper approaching, one with a different yet familiar sound. He signaled Paul and Andrew to bring the refugees out.

Over their earwigs, the team heard their boss's voice. "Tony, this is Deuce. We'll be at the pier in two minutes. What's going on there?"

"Five tangos down, Deuce. Three more in custody." As the refugees filed out of the bunkhouses, hands raised high, he added, "About twenty refugees rescued. No sign of Jesse, but there's three people in the shack on the north end."

"Roger that. Good work, Tony. A Coast Guard cutter is en route and should be offshore in less than an hour. They'll shuttle the refugees and prisoners out to the cutter."

Tony looked toward the shack with the raised floor at the end of the clearing. There had been no gunfire or movement from there. "Donnie, you and Art come down to the main shack. I will breach and you come in behind me."

While Bourke covered the three men on the ground, Paul searched the refugees one at a time. It didn't take long. Most wore only tattered shorts.

Tony motioned Linda to follow him and they moved along the edge of the palmetto-and-scrub-oak perimeter toward where they hoped Jesse was being held. When they arrived at the corner, Tony led the way across the small covered porch, thankful for the heavy rain and thunder. He ducked under a high window and continued to the door. Art stuck his head around the corner and nodded.

Hearing voices inside, but unable to make out what they were saying over the rain and wind, Tony stepped away from the wall and lunged forward, planting his boot just above the doorknob. The door jamb splintered as the door flew open. The lower hinge was pulled loose by the impact and the door hung crookedly against the wall.

CHAPTER TWENTY-NINE

The rain was now coming in sheets, the full fury of the storm on top of the little island. So loud that it nearly drowned out the other sounds I could hear. Sounds that the two on the bed were oblivious to, completely wrapped up in an animal-like frenzy of lust. A part of my mind wouldn't let me look away, but deep down, I seemed to know and recognize the other sounds. They were coming from outside in the storm. A shrieking sound accompanied by a rhythmic beating, like African drums, it grew louder and louder until it roared overhead.

Lavolier was on his back on the bed with Horvac straddling him, riding with wild abandon. Her long dark hair was tied back and the length of it bounced with every thrust. Leaning forward and putting both hands on the wrought iron frame of the bed, she bucked even harder. She looked straight at me then, her eyes wide and wild, as dark as obsidian and full of raw animal desire. The smile on her face wasn't one of happiness. It had a rapturous and evil component.

I strained against the bindings on my wrists, ignoring the shouts and gunfire outside. All I wanted was to get to this woman. She, too, was completely oblivious to the battle that raged outside, concerned only with the battle inside her own mind and body.

Lavolier's head was back, eyes closed, the muscles and tendons of his neck straining and bulging. His hands were on Horvac's waist, guiding and pushing her back with each thrust. With his eyes closed tightly, he didn't see Horvac arch her back and straighten her body. She drew a long curved knife of some kind out of a scabbard on the bedpost, holding it with the blade down and forward.

Lifting Horvac with his hips and throwing his head back further, he missed the flash of the knife in the naked woman's hand as it cleaved the air. He was too wrapped up in his own orgasmic explosion. At first, he didn't even notice the curved blade as it cleanly severed his throat.

The wound was deep, from ear to ear and all the way to the bone. Blood shot out all over Horvac's breasts and belly as she slowly rode him down to the bed. His hands went suddenly to his throat in a feeble attempt to staunch the blood flow. He made a last gurgling sound, pink bubbles squeezing between his fingers.

Without looking down at him, her eyes focused like lasers on mine, she climbed off of the body. Lavolier was dead. The battle outside had died as well.

Horvac casually lay the knife on the table and, picking up her wet shirt from the floor, she stepped in front of me. Naked, she wiped most of the blood off her torso with the shirt. Dropping it again, she reached for Lavolier's shirt and put it on, buttoning a single button at the bottom. The rolled-up sleeves reached her forearms, and the tail of the much larger man's shirt fell almost to her knees.

Her breathing was still heavy as she knelt in front of me, placing one hand on each of my knees. Her touch was like fire, tracing a line directly from my knees to my groin.

"That was just a warm-up," she said in a sensual, almost loving voice. The sound of her words caressed my ears. "You will tell me what I want to know first. And then I will let you have me, Jesse. All of me. Do you have access to the money from the treasure?"

"Yes," I groaned hoarsely. "That and more."

Suddenly, the door flew inward with a crash, twisting on just the top hinge and wedging itself between the floor and one of the rafters. A black man rolled through after it, coming up in the corner with a machine gun pointed at Horvac.

Way back in some suppressed part of my brain I recognized him. A woman came through the demolished door frame after him, an assault rifle raised and pointed at Horvac also. She was tall, nearly as tall as me, with the broad shoulders of a professional swimmer. Her wet, dark auburn hair was plastered to her scalp and pulled back in a ponytail, and her dark eyes flashed with anger. Her jeans and denim shirt were soaked. Over that she wore body armor, with the letters FDLE over the left breast. A wide, black belt held a handgun in a holster on her hip. Her name came bubbling up through the fog in my brain. Linda.

Suddenly, my desire for Horvac shifted to this warrior woman now standing before me. Brief flashes from the past surged past the blockage in my brain. A glimpse of her standing on a beach in the moonlight, holding Neptune's trident, quickly appeared and disappeared, replaced with another image of her upturned face, the moon shining fully on it.

"Don't move!" Linda shouted at Horvac.

The nearly naked woman froze in place, splotches of Lavolier's blood smeared on her belly. I felt someone behind me, tugging at the bindings on my wrists until they parted. As I was reaching down to untie my feet, Linda looked at me and asked, "Are you alright, Jesse?"

Horvac moved as quickly as a jungle cat, lashing out with a sideways kick, knocking the rifle out of Linda's hands. She followed through with an overhand left, meant to break the taller woman's jaw, but the strike met nothing but air.

Linda rolled forward, following the lost rifle and easily dodging the blow. When she came up, she grabbed Horvac's long black hair from behind, allowing her momentum to pull the woman backward, flinging her across the room and through the broken doorway.

Horvac stumbled off the small porch, rolling out onto the wet ground. To her credit, she came up in a kneeling position with one leg straight out to the side. She looked up quickly, her hair falling down over one shoulder to the ground. The rain immediately soaked Lavolier's shirt, which clung tightly to her body.

Linda followed her through the door, back out into the rain. She slowly unbuckled her holster and dropped it as she crossed the porch. Then she stepped lightly to the ground in the pouring rain. Her head held low, she watched Horvac carefully under hooded brows.

Suddenly, the two women charged at one another, Horvac's bare feet slipping slightly on the wet ground. Linda went in low, planting her shoulder just under the other woman's ribcage. Lifting the smaller woman off her feet, Linda drove her backward into the ground.

Horvac's breath escaped her lungs with a gasp. She writhed in Linda's grasp like a wildcat, twisting and turning, trying to gain some leverage.

The two tumbled across the ground, rolling in the mud and water. I watched from the doorway, excited. Tony slipped past me and joined Art and Donnie on the porch. The sight of the two women fighting reached way deep into my brain and I liked it.

Suddenly, there was an audible crack, like lightning splintering a nearby tree, and the fight was over. The two women lay there in a heap in the pouring rain, neither moving. Horvac was on top, Linda's legs wrapped high around her narrow waist. Lavolier's shirt was twisted around Horvac's middle, exposing her body from the angel wings to her feet, the heavy rain splashing off her skin.

Horvac moved slightly, Linda's arm still wrapped behind her head, where her fingers clutched the arm opening of her body armor.

Releasing the hold, Linda grabbed Lavolier's shirt and rolled the woman's body off her. Horvac's head lolled to the side in an unnatural way. She lay face up in the mud, completely exposed, her blank, dead eyes staring at nothing.

The rain suddenly stopped as Tony stepped off the porch and extended a hand to Linda. She took it and stood up, straightening her body armor where Horvac's chin had been caught by Linda's hold, stretching and snapping her spine.

Linda glanced up at me on the porch as the sun broke out from behind the clouds. She had three bloody scratches across her cheek, the blood mixing with the rainwater and streaking her jaw and neck.

I felt something warm and sticky running down the inside of my thigh.

CHAPTER THIRTY

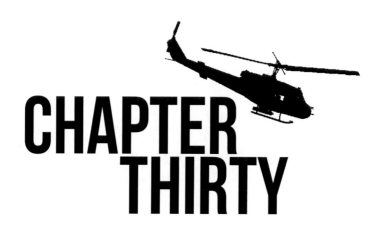

Two hours later, the effects of the drug Horvac gave me began to wear off. On his arrival, Deuce had ordered Bourke to take me into the kitchen and pour coffee into me as soon as he arrived.

The DEA choppers, along with the sheriff's helo, circled the island as the team fanned out, securing the camp first and then the rest of the island. Two more of the Zoe Pound gang were found hiding on the next small island to the north.

During that time, Kim arrived. Between Linda and Deputy Phillips, they managed to at least keep her at the makeshift pier, Linda assuring her that I was okay. Knowing the effects of the drugs, Deuce kept Linda busy and away from me as well.

After the Coast Guard took the refugees and prisoners off the island, I was deemed detoxed enough to be in mixed company.

"It was the same drug she gave you last fall?" Linda asked as we walked down the path to the pier, with Deuce.

"She said it had some kind of truth agent in it, too," I replied guardedly. "She asked if I could get the money from the treasure and I voluntarily told her I could get that and more."

"Is it worn off?"

"Yeah, I think so." Then, doing my best Schwarzenegger impression, I added, "Ask me a question I would normally lie to."

She grinned, "Are you in love with me?"

"One day at a time," I reminded her. Then with a chuckle, I added, "But, yeah, you're hot."

Reaching the pier, Kim hugged both me and Linda in turn and then both of us together. I took her shoulders and held her at arm's length. "What the hell were you thinking, coming out here?"

She started to stammer and Deputy Phillips stepped up. "It's my fault, sir. I should have stayed with her on the island."

I turned to the deputy and grinned. I'd learned that he hadn't told anyone he was joining the search and just up and did it. Most guys would have hit the road real fast. I stuck out my hand and said, "Then you have to take her back home, Deputy."

He took my hand and said, "Would it be alright with you if I called on her again?"

I just shrugged. "She's apparently beyond my control."

We left the island just after noon, Kim in the deputy's patrol boat and Linda riding with me aboard the *Revenge*. I kept the speed down to just twenty-five knots and the Cigarette quickly left us behind, roaring off with Tony at the helm and the patrol boat following behind.

"You're going awfully slow," Linda commented. She'd taken a few minutes to shower and change, and now sat in the second seat wearing shorts and a tee shirt. Shoes off, her long legs were up on the right side of the console as she leaned against my shoulder.

"I'm in no hurry," I replied.

Linda's cellphone chirped from where she'd placed it on her side of the console. She reached for it and looked at the display.

"It's a DC number," she said.

Taking it from her, I punched the button to accept the call and said, "McDermitt."

"Glad to hear your voice, Skipper," Stockwell said. "I have some information you might be interested in."

"What's that?"

"One of the people killed in the firefight at the gang's clubhouse has been identified as Elijah Beech."

"So, they were in it together?"

"No idea in what way just yet. Interrogations are ongoing, but yeah, it appears so. Got a question for you."

"Fire away," I replied.

"That First Mate job? Still available?"

"You're serious?"

"I'd want more than a buck a day, but yeah. I'm tired of the politics and the rat race."

"Okay, we can negotiate that," I said, punching in a saved location on the GPS. The plotter changed, showing the new heading. "When do you want to start?"

"I thought I already had," Travis replied.

"Good enough. Pay's eight hundred a week, plus two hundred each day we actually charter. Agreeable?"

"You have a new First Mate, Skipper."

"Great. I'm taking the rest of the day off. I want my island cleaned up and any sign of your former team gone by the time I get home tomorrow. Kim's curfew is twenty-one hundred and you'll stay on the island until I get home tomorrow." I ended the call and turned the wheel, looking at Linda.

"How did you know?" she asked.

"Know what?"

"I've been out here at night many times. How did you know where that satellite would be among all those millions of stars? And what did you use to signal it?"

"Just a matter of elimination," I replied. "Only one star in the sky doesn't move."

"The North Star?"

"Right, but it's called Polaris. I hoped the satellite would be directly overhead and with the sun coming up, I hoped it reflected light. So I watched for a few minutes and saw one star that wasn't moving. It had to be a satellite in geosynchronized orbit."

"Geosynchronous, Jesse."

I glanced over at her and grinned. "Whatever. I'm a shooter, not a rocket scientist." Pulling the bore sight from my pocket, I handed it to her. "It's a laser bore sight, for adjusting a rifle's sights."

"Pretty ingenious," she remarked. "Um, where are we going?"

"You ever been up Shark River?"

EPILOGUE

The charter with the Vets from up the coast in Palm Bay went very well the day after Linda and I returned to civilization. Some of the guys looked much too young, though many had been in the military for years. They were a tight-knit bunch and told me about how their organization, along with help from the city and other donors, bought and remodeled homes for other injured Vets. A couple of the guys had already been handed keys and were living in theirs, but they all helped in the work, along with dozens of other volunteers and the Space Coast Paratroopers Association.

Before hitting the Gulf Stream, we went out to G Marker and retrieved Peter Simpson's camera equipment, which we'd left behind after the attack. On the way out to the Stream, Kim looked over the images from the camera's card on the laptop. When she brought it up to the bridge to show me, I was amazed. Annette and Mitzi looked like surreal apparitions, floating through the air in some shots and like ghostly mermaids in others.

We'd had a great day of fishing in the Gulf Stream. I'd put Kim on the bridge and enjoyed talking with these young warriors as we fished. She'd brought Marty Phillips along, since it was his day off. Travis and I helped these young Vets, who we started referring to as "the kids," catch quite a few mahi and dozens of other fish. Some had limitations and it gave us both a huge charge to see how they quickly figured out how to overcome whatever physical limitation they had and conquer the denizens of the deep.

On Saturday, Eve arrived and Kim was waiting at the dock in her own skiff. I decided that my late wife's boat was doing nothing but collecting dust, so I'd handed Kim the keys. Eve's husband was unable to make it. He'd had a case come up suddenly involving a family who had lost a son in a random act of violence. The family was unable to hire a lawyer, so Nick and his dad took the case pro bono. They were suing the estate of Jean-Claude Lavolier.

My grandson, Alfredo Jesiah Maggio, is a handsome little man. His hair's dark brown and he has blue eyes. He barely fussed the whole time they were here. That evening, Linda and I took *Cazador* out for a cruise around the backcountry with both my daughters and grandson. He didn't make a sound the whole trip.

At sunset, we pulled up on the sand at Cape Sable and waded ashore. It seemed like a lifetime ago that the Tolivers had been murdered here. This place had always been such a quiet and tranquil place for me as a kid and I wanted it to return to being that for my kids. Eve let me take little Jesse out into the water. I walked out a couple of hundred yards, until the water was to my waist and the last of the sun was about to disappear. Just as it happened, there was a momentary green flash and I dunked my grandson under the sea, raising him back up to see King Neptune falling toward the far horizon.

"You have to be born down in the Keys to be a Conch," I'd whispered to him. "But you can be born a waterman anywhere and at any time in your life."

The following day, Eve and the baby headed back to Miami. She promised to come down again and said she really wanted me to meet her husband. I told her I was really looking forward to it.

The next morning, there was a funeral service for Annette D'Francisco up in Key Largo. Travis and I both attended. Peter Simpson and Tom Schweitzer were both there, as well as Mitzi, who introduced me to Annette's parents. I'd heard the D'Francisco name many times. They were a Conch family in the Upper Keys and Annette had been their youngest. Mister D'Francisco was an old friend of Vince O'Hare, who was there also.

The two men had pulled me and Travis aside after the funeral. Standing under an Australian pine tree, Mister D'Francisco took out a small box and presented it to me.

"Mitzi and Annette were real tight, Captain. She told us how you dove in and tried to save my daughter. Her momma and I appreciate that."

I'd opened the little box. It held two gold earrings. Knowing the significance, I handed one to Travis, who had been working as First Mate that day. Taking the other, I unfastened the ring and pushed the rigid clasp through my left earlobe. Without asking a question, Travis did the same, wincing slightly.

He did ask later, when we were running outside, off of Long Key. "Why am I suddenly wearing an earring?"

I'd turned to the man and asked, "You didn't know? You just did it anyway?"

"You did," he'd replied. "Figured it'd be rude if I didn't."

I then looked out over the horizon toward Cuba and beyond. "In the years of early exploration, sailors rarely strayed far from the coast. Few could swim and most were devout Christians. Their biggest fear wasn't drowning, but having their body wash ashore and not receive a Christian burial. They took to wearing a gold ring in their ear, to pay whoever found their body to have that done. We were the two responsible for that girl's well-being."

The following day, Travis had to go back to being Director Stockwell, but I could tell by the look on his face during the ride to Marathon, that he was hooked and would return. His job's waiting for him, at least until Kim heads back up north and I have to find someone full-time.

Things were back to normal in the Content Keys and all around the backcountry. Carl and I continued work on the boat. We hope to launch it in the spring.

A couple of weeks later, I heard through the Coconut Telegraph that O'Hare had been arrested. I'd called the Sheriff and arranged bail for him. It turned out that Vince had gotten into an argument with a guy in a bar who had then pulled a Ka Bar knife on him. The old man had called him out on his stories about being a Marine. The Battle of the Bulge hero tossed the guy all over the bar and took his knife away from him.

I realized I'd been getting a little soft lately, so I'm spending more and more time exercising. Swimming had always been my favorite way to stay in shape and I'd been neglecting my three-times-a-week routine of swimming three miles. For the last few weeks, Linda has left work early on Friday, meeting me at the *Anchor* and going on a three-mile run along the beach. Already, I've lost an inch around the middle.

Kim's still seeing Marty. I had Rusty print him a copy of the Rules for Dating a Marine's Daughter.

THE END

If you enjoyed reading this book and would like to hear about future new releases and special deals, feel free to subscribe to the newsletter on my website. Your information will never be shared in any way and I usually limit myself to sending only two emails per month with updates and book recommendations.

www.waynestinnett.com

Jesse McDermitt Series
Fallen Out
Fallen Palm
Fallen Hunter
Fallen Pride
Fallen Mangrove
Fallen King
Fallen Honor
Fallen Tide (November, 2015)

Charity Styles Series
Merciless Charity
Ruthless Charity (Winter, 2016)
Heartless Charity (Fall, 2016)

AFTERWORD

Homes for Warriors and Space Coast Paratroopers Association are real organizations. They are registered 501c3 nonprofit corporations that buy and remodel dilapidated homes in Brevard County, Florida, where I grew up. These homes are then turned over to deserving Veterans, mortgage free. I donate all of the royalties produced through the sale of *Fallen Pride* to help in their funding. If you'd like to make a donation, go to the website, www.spacecoastparatroopers.com.

RULES FOR DATING A MARINE'S DAUGHTER

RULE ONE:

If you pull into my driveway and honk you'd better be delivering a package, because you're sure not picking anything up.

RULE TWO:

You do not touch my daughter in front of me. You may glance at her, so long as you do not peer at anything below her neck. If you cannot keep your eyes or hands off of my daughter's body, I will remove them.

RULE THREE:

I am aware that it is considered fashionable for boys of your age to wear their trousers so loosely that they appear to be falling off their hips. Please don't take this as an insult, but you and all of your friends are complete idiots. Still, I want to be fair and open-minded about this issue, so I propose this compromise: you may come to the door with your underwear showing and your pants ten sizes too big, and I will not object. However, in order to ensure that your clothes do not, in fact, come off during the course of your date with my daughter, I will take my air-powered nail gun and fasten your trousers securely in place to your waist.

RULE FOUR:

I'm sure you've been told that in today's world, sex without utilizing a *barrier method* of some kind can kill you. Let me elaborate: when it comes to sex, I am the barrier, and I will kill you.

RULE FIVE:

It is usually understood that in order for us to get to know each other, we should talk about sports, politics, and other issues of the day. Please do not do this. The only information I require from you is an indication of when you expect to have my daughter safely back at my house, and the only word I need from you on this subject is "early."

RULE SIX:

I have no doubt you are a popular fellow, with many opportunities to date other girls. This is fine with me as long as it is okay with my daughter. Otherwise, once you have gone out with my little girl, you will continue to date no one but her until she is finished with you. If you make her cry, I will make you cry.

RULE SEVEN:

As you stand in my front hallway, waiting for my daughter to appear, and more than an hour goes by, do not sigh and fidget. If you want to be on time for the movie, you should not be dating. My daughter is putting on her makeup, a process that can take longer than painting the Sistine Chapel. Instead of just standing there, why don't you do something useful, like changing the oil in my truck?

RULE EIGHT:

The following places are not appropriate for a date with my daughter: Places where there are beds, sofas, or anything softer than a wooden stool. Places where there are no parents, policemen, or nuns within eyesight. Places where there is darkness. Places where there is dancing, holding hands, or happiness. Places where the ambient temperature is warm enough to induce my daughter to wear shorts, tank tops, midriff tee shirts, or anything other than overalls, a sweater, and a goose down parka — zipped up to her throat. Movies with a strong romantic or sexual theme are to be avoided; movies which feature chainsaws are okay. Hockey games are okay. Old folks' homes are better.

RULE NINE:

Do not lie to me. On issues relating to my daughter, I am the all-knowing, merciless god of your universe. If I ask you where you are going and with whom, you have one chance to tell me the truth, the whole truth and nothing but the truth. I have guns, lots of them. I also have a shovel, and five acres behind the house. Do not trifle with me.

RULE TEN:

Be afraid. Be very afraid. It takes very little for me to mistake the sound of your car in the driveway for a chopper coming in over the desert. When my PTS starts acting up, the voices in my head frequently tell me to clean the guns as I wait for you to bring my daughter home. As soon as you pull into the driveway you should exit your car with both hands in plain sight. Speak the perimeter password, announce in a clear voice that you have brought my daughter home safely and early, then return to your car. There is no need for you to come inside. The camouflaged face at the corner of the house is mine.

Made in United States
North Haven, CT
19 December 2024

62912850R00189